Death of a Ghost

X

Death of a Ghost

SUSAN KELLY

First published in Great Britain in 2004 by
Allison & Busby Limited
Bon Marche Centre
241-251 Ferndale Road
Brixton, London SW9 8BJ
http://www.allisonandbusby.com

A catalogue record for this book is available from the British Library

ISBN 0 7490 8395 6

Printed and bound by
Creative Print + Design, Ebbw Vale

SUSAN KELLY is the author of twelve previous crime novels. She lives in west London with her solicitor husband and their cat, and spends much of her time walking along the river Thames, which allows her to work out the details of her intricate plots. This is the fifth book in the popular Gregory Summers series.

Also available in the Gregory Summers series

1

As Leanne shivered in her fleece-lined anorak the thought crossed her mind, not for the first time, that November was no time for wagging off school. Spring, summer, fine, count her in, but in the worst month of the English autumn, with its fogs and drizzles, and the evenings closing mercilessly in like a cohort of the enemy before you'd even had your tea?

Not that Leanne expressed it thus; she didn't know what a cohort was. What she thought was: this is no fun; is this fun?

The classroom might be boring but it was warm, pressed up against the old-fashioned radiator that made her clothes steam when she arrived all wet from the walk in.

She suppressed the thought with guilty speed, and would never voice it to her companion, who wore nothing but jeans and a t-shirt, defiant to the elements. Murphy was her new best friend, encountered and instantly loved just two months earlier, when they had both arrived for their first term at the John of Gaunt secondary school in Hungerford, lonely and uncertain, and Murphy had marched over to her and said, 'Will you be my friend?'

Since that first meeting the girls had bunked off school three times and, on one heart-stopping occasion for Leanne, been shoplifting for chocolate at the newsagents in Hungerford High Street. Lee had hidden her illicit supplies and sneaked them back to the store later that day, a process which was more nerve-wracking than the original offence being, as it was, beyond explanation.

On their bicycles, they could roam for miles around the

Berkshire countryside. Lee had a shiny, red mountain bike, a present from her parents for her last birthday; Murphy, only an ancient sit-up-and-beg machine that had belonged to her auntie. Leanne, who had been brought up to 'play nicely' and to share, insisted that they swap bikes as soon as they were clear of the school grounds. It did not seem to occur to Murphy, who was an only child, that they might swap back at some point, but Leanne didn't mind since her affection for her friend knew no limit.

Today they raced east along the Kennet and Avon canal, annoying the anglers by disturbing the fish, answering cries of 'Why aren't you at school?' with a breezy 'Study day!'

Murphy mocked Lee for her slowness, forgetting, or ignoring, the fact that she had the superior bicycle. Without warning, she veered off the tow path at the Denford Gate, crashing over the cattle grid into the hamlet of Lower Denford, then lurched dangerously across the main road from Newbury to Hungerford into Upper Denford, her home territory, before flinging the mountain bike down without ceremony at the entrance to Oaken Copse.

Leanne, joining her after a more circumspect crossing of the A4, laid Murphy's bike to rest with some reverence and shifted both machines into the undergrowth where they would not be seen and stolen. Murphy was already barely visible among the trees. 'We'll go to that cottage,' she announced over her shoulder.

'The one with the old witch?' Lee asked nervously, as she scurried to catch up.

'Nah! She ain't a witch, anyway – she ain't got a cat so that proves it. The other one where there's never anybody there. We can break in easy, make a camp. I got biscuits I nicked from my Nan.'

Leanne wasn't happy with the idea of breaking and entering. On the other hand, the disused cottage had to be warmer than the woods, though a lot less warm than that enticing school radiator, its iron ridges thick with generations of cream gloss paint. She fell into step behind Murphy, as was her habit, and they walked the hundred yards to the clearing where the nameless cottage stood.

No name and no address, since the squat building lay at the end of a dirt track some two miles outside Hungerford and if that track had a name then it was a well-kept secret. It was not as derelict as its disuse suggested, however, since the walls were sturdy enough, the windows intact and the black-tiled roof maintained against the storm.

'Bugger!' Murphy exclaimed as she erupted into the clearing. She stopped so suddenly that Leanne banged into the back of her but her friend didn't seem to mind. 'Somebody's here. There's a car.'

A Ford Capri stood facing the cottage a few yards from the front door. Murphy read its number plate and realised with a sneer that it must be all of fifteen years old, older than she was. Even Grandpa O'Grady didn't drive a car that old and he was, by her calculations, over fifty. It had originally been white but had not been cleaned in a long time; rust was visible along the edges of the doors and on the undersides. The wheels were thick with mud.

'Let's go,' Leanne said urgently.

Murphy's voice fell to a whisper. 'No, let's look. If someone's been staying here then there might be something worth nicking for once.'

'But ...'

'And they might've gone out.'

'Without the car?'

Murphy snorted contempt. 'Probably wouldn't start. You stay here if you like. I'm gonna look.'

She moved forward as silently as a Red Indian maiden in a story. She was short for her age and had to stand on tiptoe to see in the nearest window, her plump hands with their nibbled nails clinging to the sill.

Her eyes widened to penetrate the gloom of the interior, then widened further.

'Come and look,' she shouted with no attempt at stealth.

Leanne stepped gingerly forward, her feet slithering on the papier maché of mud and dead leaves. The trees had shed early this year after the phenomenal heatwave of August and the ground was well rotted.

'What?' she asked.

'Look.'

Lee, who was taller than her friend, peered in at the window. As her eyes adjusted, she could see a shape slumped on the floor in front of the grate where two bars of an electric fire gleamed in the shadows.

Strange place to fall asleep, her mind said hopefully.

'What ...?' she began, but Murphy had moved round to the front of the house where she was trying the door. 'Murph!'

'It's not locked. Come on.'

Leanne followed her reluctantly. Already, she had a bad feeling about this. Her feet moved forward automatically in obedience to her friend while her brain begged her to run hard in the other direction.

If she took her mountain bike and raced the two miles back to school, she'd be pressed up safe against that radiator a good two hours before her mum came to collect her, to take her home to the central heating of their own modern house in Hungerford, to a hot meal and the welcoming glow of the television.

Murphy walked into the cottage as if her name was on the deeds. There was no hallway, just the living room

14

with a set of plain wooden stairs vanishing into the gloom of the upper storey. The windows were small and the room was dark even in full daylight.

Leanne advanced as far as the front door, unwilling to cross the threshold. Murphy clicked on the light – a bare overhead bulb – and surveyed the scene with satisfaction.

'Oh my God! Oh my God!' Leanne squealed, unable to take her eyes from the immobile form, which was female, clad in a terracotta dress that fell about her plump body like a medieval robe. A patterned scarf, predominating the same reddish colour, was tied round her neck, uncomfortably tight, or so it seemed to the child's eyes.

You'd hardly be able to breathe with it that tight.

The part of her mind that still hoped said that the woman's feet must be cold, lying bare like that. Why didn't she put on the slippers that lay heaped one on the other not a yard away, so inviting with their fluffy tartan lining?

Murphy walked carelessly over to the recumbent mass on the hearthrug. She bent and poked it in the belly with her finger, the digit sinking in the softness. It made no objection to this impertinence.

'Oy, missus,' she said, but there was no answer.

'She's dead.' Lee stammered. 'Is she dead? She's never dead?'

'Yeah.' Murphy turned round, her face alight with glee. 'She's only been murdered. Look.'

Lee kept her distance, clinging to the door frame, her fingers stark white from the pressure. For a second the world went dark before her eyes but she gulped in air and managed to stay on her feet. Nothing would induce her to approach that cold nightmare.

'Oh my God!'

'This is bloody *brilliant*,' Murphy said.

2

As the crow flew, it was not far from Rochester in Kent to Newbury in Berkshire, perhaps a hundred miles, say two hours' drive.

Unfortunately, the massive conurbation of London sprawled in the way, which, since he was not a crow, gave Gregory Summers two choices: he could go up the A2 and through the middle of town, braving the traffic jams, arranging to pay the congestion charge recently imposed in the capital or – with more paperwork – be exempted; or he could skirt round the city on the M25 orbital motorway, adding the best part of fifty miles to his journey and with no guarantee that there wouldn't be tailbacks there too.

Or, of course, he could summon up a police helicopter, which would have him home in half an hour.

Sadly, the last option was fantasy.

Either way it was going to be a half day's drive that Friday, one he had made the previous Friday, taking the reverse trip on the last two Mondays. His great consolation was that he wouldn't be needed in Kent next week; his work there was done.

It was customary when a police force got bogged down on a serious case to call in a senior officer from another force to oversee the investigation, bring a fresh eye to the evidence collected. When, after eleven weeks, there had been no significant breakthrough in the hunt for the man who was murdering and sexually assaulting pensioners in their own homes in Rochester, Greg had drawn the short straw and, with things unusually quiet at home in Newbury, had found no excuse not to go.

When carrying out such oversight exercises, you never knew what sort of welcome to expect from the local Senior Investigating Officer. Outright hostility was not uncommon, nor was its thinly-disguised younger sibling. It was rare for the SIO to accept the newcomer as a useful chance to review evidence and procedures and not a slur on his competence.

So he had introduced himself warily to his Kentish counterpart, Superintendent Alan Ashton, ten days earlier, the two men shaking hands, sizing each other up, exchanging banalities. Ashton was about ten years older than Greg – pushing up against the enforced retirement age for their rank of sixty – and, he judged, from a similar upper-working-class background: grammar-school boy from the days when they still had grammar schools.

'Glad to have you aboard,' Ashton had said finally, when the getting-to-know-you was over. 'We need all the help we can get. Murdering and raping old ladies. What sort of a sick bastard does that?'

'You mean raping and murdering surely,' Greg said, 'in that order.'

Ashton looked at him with weary sadness. 'I wish I did, mate. I wish I did.'

The worst scenario was that the overseeing officer got no further with the case than the locals and slunk back to his lair hearing imaginary jeers and catcalls echoing behind him. Greg was optimistic, however, partly because his clear-up rate was good and partly because his very presence would spur the local CID to prove themselves to the interloper, show the powers-that-were that they'd have had the crime cracked if they'd only had a bit more patience.

And, ten days on, they had a local schoolmaster remanded in custody and facing a number of life sentences which the judge would probably determine should mean life with no chance of parole; a mixture of hard work, determination on the part both of police officers and an outraged public and that very necessary stroke of luck which usually featured in such investigations.

Greg was carrying a caseful of kudos back to Berkshire, along with the overnight bag that had served him a full five days. He was also carrying nasty memories of the crime-scene photos, of the pathologist's reports; above all, of Simon Emerson, the quiet-voiced man who spoke in the interview room of hatred for the abusive grandmother who had raised him and whose death three months earlier had precipitated his killing spree.

Personally, Greg thought he belonged in Broadmoor, not in prison, but he knew how reluctant juries were these days to entertain pleas of insanity, wanting to use the temporary power placed in their hands to exact a full measure of vengeance for the community.

Ashton saw him off. 'Good working with you, Greg.'

'Same here, Alan. See you again some time.'

'Doubtful, mate. By next spring, I'll have hung up my truncheon and picked up my golf clubs full time.'

'Lucky you,' Greg said dutifully, since he would rather have his teeth drilled without anaesthetic than play golf.

'Drive carefully now.'

'I will.'

He was physically and mentally exhausted, looking forward to a quiet weekend at home with Angelica. He switched off his mobile so he wouldn't be disturbed and was out of Rochester and heading up the main road to London by two o'clock, crossing the bridge over the river Medway which curved beneath him in its wide sweep.

Rochester was a pretty little town – or rather city, one of the smallest in England – with its ruined castle and its improbably large cathedral; the Kent countryside was attractive in its late autumn reds and yellows, but he didn't want to see any of it again for a very long time.

Despite the fact that it was early even for the Friday rush out of London, there were traffic jams on the M25 and Greg found himself travelling no more than twenty yards at a time as he approached the turn-off to the M4 and home, frustratingly visible less than two miles ahead of him but half an hour away in the swamp of vans and lorries, cars and broken-down coaches.

On the M4, traffic was moving once he got past Heathrow airport and he was turning off at junction thirteen for Newbury forty minutes later. He debated internally whether he should call in at the police station, but it was not a hard decision to make and he swung his car onto the ring road, waving merrily at the solid rectangular building opposite – his home from home for the best part of thirty years – as he headed for the A4 to Kintbury and his real home.

He stopped at the village shop to pick up a bottle of Côtes du Rhone in case there was a wine shortage in the house. It was getting dark and fireworks were going off in a number of neighbouring gardens, their multi-coloured tails making him smile with memories of childhood: of potatoes baked black in the bonfire, of sausages bursting their indefinable innards over the plate, of parkin heavy with treacle.

Guy Fawkes Day had been last Wednesday but many people preferred to wait for the weekend before celebrating the hanging, drawing and quartering of a group of Renaissance terrorists.

He didn't know what Angie had done about supper but he was hoping for something home-cooked as he'd been living on takeaways and pub food in Kent. He'd also drunk an unaccustomed amount of beer in that hop county, feeling it swilling acidly around in his stomach as he lay down to sleep each night on the hotel's too-soft bed in his too-hot room, waking without appetite to the full English breakfast of streaky bacon, a pale egg and mushy tomatoes.

His heart lifted to see Angie's Renault parked in the drive. He pulled in behind it, climbed out of the car and wrestled the front door open. It was inclined to stick in damp weather and he had to kick it, leaving a dirty shoe mark on the maroon paint. He tutted at himself, since the paintwork was new, freshly applied less than two months ago after an age of procrastination.

He entered the hall, calling, 'I'm home.' He felt like a character in an American sitcom and wondered if he should add, 'Honey.'

'Hello, darling.' Angie came out of the study to his left and gave him a kiss which was welcoming rather than passionate. 'Barbara's been ringing every half hour since –' She glanced at her watch '– three o'clock. Seems your mobile was switched off. Said to ring her the moment you got in.'

'Fine!'

He looked sadly at the bottle of wine, which he would not get to drink for several days, and handed it to her for safe-keeping.

Greg had no difficulty in following Barbara's directions to the cottage, given that the glade in which it sat was spotlit like a film set. Besides, he knew Oaken Copse well from his boyhood; he had played here often with his mates.

He made his way carefully along the narrow dirt track and drew up alongside a posse of other cars: some marked police vehicles, the mortuary van, the Scenes-of-Crime wagon and the compact blue hatchback which belonged to Detective Sergeant Barbara Carey.

As he got out, he could still hear the distant banging of adulterated gunpowder, see the occasional splatter of colour across the sky, between the branches of trees denuded by oncoming winter.

He was nodded through by the uniformed constable whose job it was to keep nosy parkers at bay, ducking under the blue and white incident tape as the man noted his arrival on a clipboard. That way they would have a record of who had been at the scene should any stray fingerprints or DNA need accounting for.

He went to join his sergeant. He could see her some yards away, a woman of medium size, the right side of thirty. She was standing by an ancient Ford Capri talking to the senior SOC Officer, Martha Childs, whose face looked very young in her pristine white hood. He gathered that Martha had not yet gained access to the crime scene, since there was a restlessness about her which betrayed her enthusiasm to start work as she stood passing her gloves from one hand to the other.

'Bit of a hovel,' he remarked.

'Welcome home, sir.' Barbara grinned. She was also wearing the shiny white overalls that would ensure that she didn't contaminate the scene, though her hood was down to reveal short dark curls framing a pale face that was both attractive and sensible. 'Straight back in the deep end. I hear you did great things in Kent.'

'Oh, yes. I was magnificent.'

'I don't think it *is* a hovel,' Martha said quietly. 'I think it's in disguise.'

Greg blinked at this uncharacteristic whimsy. 'Sorry, Martha?'

She explained. 'If you take a close look at the structure, you'll see that it's perfectly sound – good roof, new windows and door, brickwork in decent repair. This ...' She waved her hand vaguely, her rubber gloves slapping the night, '... air of seediness is deliberately cultivated, like a duchess dressed as a bag lady.'

Greg glanced at Barbara, who shrugged. He said, 'You're very observant.'

She blushed slightly. 'Isn't that exactly what you pay me for, Gregory?'

'But why would someone want to make a perfectly good house look run down?' Barbara wanted to know.

'Maybe they're not here very much,' Greg suggested, 'and they figured it'd be less of a target for vandals and squatters if it looked ... squalid.'

Martha nodded thoughtfully. 'That would be my guess.' She indicated the ground on the far side of the Capri. 'By the way, we found the recent marks of a second car.'

'Really?' He saw now that a barrier had been set up around the spot.

'Radial tyres,' Martha said, 'bit worn – only just legal, in fact. We've taken measurements and prints. If you find a suspect, we can maybe match them.' She pulled on her gloves at last, flexing her hands to achieve a tight fit, beaming as if she meant to give him an intimate examination.

Greg turned and saw that two ambulancemen were coming out of the cottage with the body on a stretcher. As he watched, its left arm came loose in a red sleeve and flopped down, the hand bagged in plastic to preserve evidence. One of the men scooped it back on without breaking stride.

'Oh dear, I'm too late to take a look at the corpse in situ,' he said without conviction.

'I'm sure if you hurry they'll let you examine her in the mortuary van,' Barbara said, not deceived.

'... I'll survive.'

Martha said eagerly, 'My turn now.'

'Not quite.' Greg laid a detaining hand on her arm. 'I'd like a few minutes in there myself, to get the feel of the place before it's covered in fingerprint powder.' He fetched his own overalls from the boot of his car, feeling in them, as always, like an extra from a science fiction movie. 'Babs, can you catch me up? It's like I've come into the cinema half an hour after the film started.'

Martha paced up and down impatiently as the two CID officers went in at the open front door of the cottage. Barbara, as first officer on the scene after the uniformed pair who had answered the emergency call, had created a sterile pathway from the door to the staircase, a polythene sheet on which they could safely walk without contaminating evidence.

Greg stood for a moment taking in the atmosphere. If the place was in disguise then it was a good disguise since the interior was as unwelcoming as the outside.

Their usual pathologist, Dr Aidan Chubb, was packing his equipment, and glanced up to nod a greeting to Greg. 'I certified death at sixteen-twenty hours,' he announced.

'The body was lying in front of the electric fire,' Barbara said, pointing, her voice muffled behind her face mask. Greg saw that the chimney had been blocked up, the fireplace hidden with hardboard, to allow the insertion of the ugly appliance. 'Both bars were on –' she added.

'That'll make time-of-death harder to establish,' Dr Chubb interrupted, in case Greg might not know this after thirty years on the force.

'Cause?' Greg asked.

'Not much doubt about that. She was strangled with a

scarf – red and white patterned thing, nylon, very strong. Still round her neck.' Dr Chubb clicked his case shut and added, 'I'm off to do the post. Who wants to come?' He made it sound like an invitation to a party.

Greg said, 'Get Nick to do it, will you?' to Barbara.

'He did it last time,' she pointed out.

'Well, he'll be used to it then.'

Barbara followed the doctor out to convey to DC George Nicolaides the good news that he could spend the next couple of hours watching a corpse being surgically dissected and eviscerated. The pathologist was whistling a tune which Greg struggled to recognise; he ran it through his own mind silently and finally got it: *Lady in Red*.

Perfect.

He spread a handkerchief on the second-to-bottom step of the stairs and sat carefully down to examine the house, letting his eyes linger on the detail as if he were playing Kim's Game and would be examined on it shortly.

The bare plaster of the walls was whitewashed and could do with a good scrub down. He could see spiders webs in the corners of the ceiling – elaborate enough for generations of the creatures to have made their homes there – while dust motes danced in the strong lights.

Two armchairs stood to one side of the grate, a two-seater sofa to the other. The floor was bare wood, once polished but now much scratched, with a knitted hearthrug, green and brown circles, curiously depressing. It had been rucked up, presumably where the dead woman had struggled with her killer as her breath departed.

At least with strangulation there was no blood; it was a tidy sort of murder.

A bottle of Scotch lay on its side a few inches from the rug, the cap missing, the last trickles of amber liquid sticky on the floorboard. Greg could see from the label that it was a supermarket own brand, ten quid a bottle: bought by a boozer, not a connoisseur. He looked around for a glass and finally spotted it under one of the armchairs. Perhaps she'd been refilling her glass as the killer struck.

The alcoves on either side of the fireplace were filled with shelves but they were largely empty. He could see a pile of magazines on one and a portable radio on another, its flex stretched tight to plug into a power-point that looked so modern as to be out of place. If the building had been recently rewired then Martha's observation was right: the cottage was only disguised as a shack.

Now that he came to think about it the place had been more or less derelict when he was a child; somebody had taken it in hand over the past thirty-five years.

He would not examine anything in the house till Martha and her team had done their work. For now, his eyes must do the work that his hands fidgeted for.

Through a brick archway to his left he could make out a basic kitchen with black and white squared linoleum on the floor. A new-looking microwave oven stood on the work surface. Under one window there was a table, big enough to seat four as was evidenced by the four wooden chairs arranged round it. A glass bowl in the middle held two fat red apples, like something Snow White might have accepted in innocence from her stepmother.

Barbara returned, the vibration of her step on bare boards making the whisky bottle roll a half turn and back again, disgorging the last mouthful.

'You may be right,' she said. 'He didn't complain at all, just grunted and went off with Aidan.'

'Getting inured to it,' Greg said. 'Wish I could.'

'Nick's not exactly the sensitive type.' She paused then sang under her breath. 'Lady in re-e-ed ...'

'So, fill me in. Who found the body and when?'

'Two eleven-year-old girls stumbled on it early this afternoon,' Barbara said, 'skiving off from the John of Gaunt school in Hungerford. Leanne Bright and Madonna Murphy. The Brights live in Hungerford and the Murphys in Upper Denford.'

'Dear God!' Greg said. 'What sort of person calls their daughter Madonna?'

Barbara grinned. 'She only answers to Murphy. Lee was a bit upset by the whole business but Murphy was having a whale of a time. She might have done the murder herself, just for the excitement.'

'Don't! Where are they now?'

'Their mums took them home after they'd made their statements. Mrs Murphy's the down-trodden type who's nervous of any authority, but Mrs Bright was bristling with indignation at her little girl being mixed up in anything so sordid and talking about her needing counselling. I don't think either of them'll be keen on another visit from the constabulary tonight.'

'No, okay. I'll review the interview tapes, if necessary.'

'It was Leanne who cycled to fetch help while Murphy stayed with the body.'

'Have we got an ID on the corpse?'

'Nothing definite yet. I couldn't find a handbag or purse, which might suggest robbery as the motive, a burglary gone wrong when she came home and caught them at it.'

Could there be anything worth stealing here, Greg wondered? Maybe, if it was truly a duchess in rags. But surely any burglar would have heard the Capri returning and made off into the trees. Aloud, he said, 'Or somebody might have taken it to conceal her identity, or at least delay identification. What about that car outside?'

'It's registered to a Gillian Lestrange. She lives on the western outskirts of London – Isleworth, maybe an hour's drive from here.'

'Have you ...?'

'I rang the nearest station and they're sending someone round, see if there's anyone in or if any of the neighbours know where she is.'

'Neighbours? In London? Fat chance. Probably say they've never heard of her. What about this place? What's it called?'

'Ivy Cottage, officially, though there's no name plate. There's no one listed as living here on the electoral register but the Town Hall says the Council Tax is paid by a woman called Adele Finnegan. She lives in another cottage, less than a quarter of a mile away, on the edge of Upper Denford.'

'So what was this, a spare?'

Barbara shrugged. 'Have to ask her.'

'Then let's go and do that. You've been busy, Babs. Well done.' He got up. 'Now we'd better let Martha and her people loose in here before she explodes.'

3

'Mrs Finnegan?'

The woman who opened the door to their knock came into the category of Little Old Lady. She must be eighty, Greg thought, squinting as the light streaming from the room behind her rendered her little more than a silhouette in the autumn night.

He held up his warrant card, introducing himself and Barbara. She gave him a searching look for a moment, then sighed. 'It's this business about Vinnie and the Official Secrets Act, I suppose. If you've come to arrest her, she's not here. I haven't seen her in days.'

Puzzled, Greg said, 'It's nothing to do with Vinnie, whoever ... she may be.' All the Vinnies he'd met had been men; most of them had been gangsters.

'Then you'd better come in.'

She stood aside and motioned them to precede her into the hall, ushering them before her into a sitting room. This was a very different cottage from the crime scene – bigger, for one thing, the furniture old but comfortable with the cushions, ornaments and pictures which make a house a home. A central-heating radiator filled the room with warmth. It was called Honeysuckle Cottage – brighter and sweeter than ivy.

In the better light, the outline was filled in and he saw that she was of medium height and slender build, her wholly white hair cropped short about eldritch features and eyes of a blue undimmed by her years. She wore corduroy trousers and a navy Guernsey, her socked feet in slippers.

She indicated that they should sit but remained

standing herself, leaning against the mantelpiece. As Greg began to speak, she picked up a packet of *Disque Bleu*, took one out and lit it with an ancient Bic lighter.

'You own Ivy Cottage, I believe,' Greg said.

'Ivy –?' She inhaled smoke and let it out through her nostrils in two white streams, the scent summoning up for Greg the memory of a brief flirtation with Existentialism at the age of fifteen; not that he'd had any idea what that meant but anything French had been cool back then, sexy. 'Of course! I haven't heard it called that for years. We call it simply The Cottage.'

'But you do own it.'

'Technically, yes, in that my name is on the deeds and listed at the Land Registry. In reality, it belongs to Vinnie.'

Again the mysterious Vinnie, who was apparently in danger of arrest. He said, 'You've not noticed activity in the copse tonight, in the clearing?'

She glanced at the window although the curtain was snugly drawn. 'I heard some comings and goings and saw an unusual amount of light in the distance. I thought someone had lit a bonfire in there for a fireworks party. Or a rave. Bit dangerous in a wood that dense. I considered going to take a look but ... well. At my age once you get comfy for the night, it takes all the devils in hell to shift you.'

'Do you know a woman called Gillian Lestrange?'

'Certainly. She's Vinnie's ghost.'

'I beg your pardon!' Greg said.

Mrs Finnegan grinned. 'She's ghosting Vinnie's memoirs, autobiography – whatever you want to call it.'

'Can we just sort out who Vinnie is?' Barbara asked.

'My niece, Lavinia Latham. My brother Patrick's girl.'

'And you thought we'd come to arrest her?' Greg queried.

She shrugged. 'She said they'd try to put pressure on her, maybe even on me.' Before Greg could ask for further elucidation, she added, 'Since you're not here to arrest Vinnie, can I ask exactly why you *are* here?'

Normally, Greg would have suggested that someone sit down before breaking this sort of news to them, especially an elderly woman, but Adele Finnegan seemed so self-contained that it didn't occur to him.

He said, 'I'm afraid I have bad news about Miss Lestrange. We found a dead body at Ivy Cottage this afternoon which we believe to be hers.'

'Good grief!' Adele spoke with surprise but without shock. She stubbed her cigarette out on the stone fire surround and tossed the stub into the empty grate. A horrible thought flickered visibly across her face and she took an urgent step towards Greg. 'You *believe* it to be hers? So it might be someone else? It might even be Vinnie?'

'We haven't had a formal identification by next of kin,' Greg explained, 'or any sort of identification, come to that, but our working hypothesis is that it's Miss Lestrange.'

'Hang on.' Mrs Finnegan went through a stripped wooden door, beyond which Greg could see a modern kitchen, and returned with a hardback book. She removed the dust jacket and held it out for their inspection. 'Is this her?'

Greg, who had not seen the body, took the jacket and passed it to Barbara. She took one glance at the photograph and said, 'That's the dead woman, all right.'

'Oh, thank God!' Mrs Finnegan said.

Greg took the jacket back from his sergeant and looked with curiosity at the picture. He saw a heavyset woman of about thirty, made plain by strong features, with a tangle of hair falling loose over broad shoulders, as if it had never seen a comb. Dark hair, although the photo was black and white so it was hard to say if it was brown or black or even dark auburn.

Black eyes stared out at him from behind large glasses with a look that he found sardonic, even sarcastic.

A brief note said that Gillian Lestrange lived alone in London, with none of the more personal detail he usually noticed on novels. He turned the jacket over to examine the front. The book was a romance called *Playing to Win*. The blurb said that it was a love story set against the background of professional tennis. The illustration was of a rather stereotyped pair of handsome lovers: blond, tanned and fit in tennis whites with lots of flashing teeth.

'Terrible sentimental tripe,' Mrs Finnegan observed, 'and not good on detail when it comes to the international tennis circuit. I think she made most of her living from the ghost writing rather than with her own fiction. Poor Gilly, but, still, thank God it isn't Vinnie. Dead how?'

'She was strangled.'

'So it was definitely murder?'

'It was indeed.'

Barbara half rose and said perhaps she might make them all some tea, but Adele Finnegan crossed to the oak sideboard, saying, 'You can help yourself to all the tea you want, young woman, but me, I need a proper drink.' She pulled out a bottle of whisky as Barbara sank back into her chair. 'Can I get anyone else one?' They declined and she poured herself a good four fingers' worth into a tumbler.

'Damn,' she said quietly and drained half the glass.

Greg noticed that it was a single malt; Mrs Finnegan, unlike her tenant, was a connoisseur; either that or a rich drunk. 'How well did you know Miss Lestrange?' he asked.

'Hardly at all. Vinnie came to see me six weeks ago and

mentioned that she would be using the cottage this winter, somewhere quiet to work on her memoirs, somewhere they wouldn't find her in a hurry –'

'But who are these "They"?' Greg butted in, feeling as if he was swimming in mud.

This mysterious, dangerous *They*.

Mrs Finnegan answered brusquely, as if the question were foolish. 'Military Intelligence, of course. Two weeks later she turned up with the Lestrange girl and introduced us. I gave them supper. She didn't have a great deal to say for herself but apparently she's experienced in that sort of work, done a lot of "celebrity" biographies. She gave me that book and I thanked her, although it's not my sort of thing at all.'

'I think you'd better tell us a little more about Vinnie,' Greg suggested, 'about Military Intelligence and why someone might come to arrest her.'

'Okay.' She took another sip of her whisky, now visibly depleted, and sat down. 'Then I shall begin at the beginning. The Lathams are a military family. Daddy was a full colonel in the Royal Antrims and Patrick rose to the rank of lieutenant-colonel in the same regiment before being shot by a sniper in Belfast twenty years ago. Vinnie wanted to be a soldier from the moment she could talk, real tomboy.'

Hence the boyish shortening of her name, Greg thought. Lavinia sounded more like a debutante – very much the colonel's daughter.

'She went to Sandhurst at eighteen, straight after her A levels, and was a captain by the time she was twenty-five. She's always had a flair for languages – Patrick and I are half French and bilingual so perhaps it's in the genes. She did French, Arabic and Russian at A level and taught herself Mandarin Chinese for fun.'

'And that was why she was approached by MI5,' Greg said, impressed. 'Or was it six?'

'Five. That and her exemplary record. She jumped at the chance and spent several happy years as a spook. She used to come and see me whenever she was in England since we were always great friends.'

'It didn't worry you, the dangerous nature of the work she was doing?'

Mrs Finnegan snorted. 'Part of why she went into spying was because of my war record; she was always fascinated by it, made me tell her every detail over and over right from her earliest girlhood.'

'Your ...?'

Once again the old woman spoke as if Greg ought already to know this if he wasn't exceptionally slow on the uptake. 'I was parachuted into occupied France in '41, worked for three years with the Resistance as a wireless operator. As I said before – bilingual.'

Oblivious to the stunned silence that greeted this statement she returned to the sideboard, refilled her glass and lit another Gauloise.

'Wow!' Barbara said at last.

Adele Finnegan glanced at her and smiled. 'That's what Vinnie said the first time I told her about it. I lived in constant fear for three years, Sergeant, fear of capture, torture and death. I even had a suicide pill so that, if the worst came to the worst, I could avoid betraying my colleagues. I was nineteen when I went out there and possessed of an innocence you probably can't imagine in a girl that age these days.'

'Perhaps that's what protected you,' Greg suggested.

'How sentimental of you, Mr Summers. But there are times when I look back and think that those were the best years of my life. I felt so ... alive.'

'Only with hindsight, perhaps,' he suggested.

'Yes, you're right, of course. Now that I know that I wasn't captured, tortured and murdered then it just seems like an incredible adventure. And Vinnie was the same: she says that it's only by risking your life that you can live it to the full. Still, you are police officers, so I daresay you're not afraid of a little danger either. But enough about me. You want to know about Vinnie.'

'Courage clearly runs in the family,' Greg murmured.

'Thank you. Okay. 1989. The Berlin wall came down and MI5 were left twiddling their thumbs. The good years were over. They decided to take over an anti-terrorist role from the police, from Special Branch.'

'I remember,' Greg said. 'There was a lot of bad feeling.' There was always bad feeling between the civilian police force and the military who were inclined to act as if they were above the law.

'In those days the terrorist threat meant the IRA,' Mrs Finnegan said. She paused as a thought struck her. 'How simple that seems now – a few people blown up, at worst, a building or two damaged – when today we're threatened with mass gassing in our cities, dirty nuclear bombs, or a deadly plague. You can almost call it the good old days. How glad I am to be no longer young.'

Greg knew what she meant. The world had changed in the new millennium, suddenly and starkly. It was no longer clear to him, not only if he and the people he cared about would be alive next month, but whether the civilisation in which he had grown up and which he had assumed to be perennial could survive the blinkered forces of evil that cared nothing for human life, not even their own.

'Vinnie wasn't keen,' Mrs Finnegan went on. 'She'd seen her father murdered by the IRA and that wasn't a war she wanted to fight. My father's family were Ulstermen, you see.' She sipped her whisky, showing no sign that it was having any effect, unless it was the inconsequentiality of her next remark.

'I married a charming, feckless Irishman but he died young. Half French and half Irish. You'd be hard pushed to find a drop of English blood in me and yet I feel wholly English. Isn't that odd?'

When neither police officer answered, assuming the question to be rhetorical, as perhaps it was, she went on. 'So she left and set up as a freelance –'

'What does a freelance spy do?' Greg asked incredulously.

'Oh, industrial counter-espionage was a large part of it. That always sounded a bit dull, admittedly, but once she got back a kidnapped child without paying the ransom and without the police ever knowing about it. Stuff like that.'

'In England?' Barbara asked, startled.

'No, that was in the States. She does a lot of work there. None of the stupid rules about guns, for one thing.' She gestured at them. 'You're police officers and even you aren't allowed guns.'

'Ah, but we do have a mission statement,' Greg said. 'I would very much like to speak to Lavinia.'

Her eyes twinkled. 'I'm sure you would, Superintendent, but does she want to speak to you?'

'Do you know where your niece is, Mrs Finnegan?'

'If she gets in touch, I'll be sure to pass on your message.'

As they drove away, Barbara said, 'What an amazing story.'

'Her or the niece?'

'Both.'

'Of course there's another possibility,' Greg said.

'Hmm?'

'The old lady's a total fantasist.'

Barbara laughed. 'Do you believe she doesn't know how to get hold of Lavinia?'

'Not for a moment. We'll give her a day or two to make contact, otherwise we'll get a warrant to check her phone calls for the last few weeks.'

Barbara drove on in silence for a while, then asked, 'Do you agree with what she said – that life is only worth living if you're prepared to risk it?'

'Sometimes,' he said.

They'd been back at headquarters only minutes when Barbara's contact in the Isleworth police rang to say that there was no sign of life at Gillian Lestrange's flat in Amhurst Gardens and that, as Greg had predicted, none of her neighbours admitted to knowing her beyond the ritual exchange of 'Good mornings', let alone to having a key.

'We haven't got a key either,' Barbara explained. 'Her personal possessions were missing. But at least we're pretty certain we have the right person now. Hang on ...' Greg was signalling that he had something to say and she covered the handset with her hand. 'Yes, sir?'

'Whoever took her bag may try to gain entry to the flat. Ask them to keep an eye on the place overnight until we can get someone up there tomorrow.'

Barbara conveyed this message and the local policeman agreed without enthusiasm to spare the manpower for this task. She thanked him and they hung up.

Greg glanced at his watch and was surprised to find it was gone nine. He also realised that he hadn't eaten since his lunchtime sandwich.

'Let's grab something to eat at the curry house,' he said. 'SOCO will be at the cottage half the night so the best thing we can do at the moment is think about how we're going to get in touch with Gillian Lestrange's next of kin.'

'At least it's an unusual name,' Barbara said, picking up her coat, 'and, now you come to mention it, I'm starving.'

They exited via the front door of the station, leaving word where they could be found if anyone needed them.

'Publisher,' Greg said, through a mouthful of chicken balti twenty minutes later. 'Did you make a note of who published that romantic novel of hers?'

Barbara nodded as she chewed lamb tikka marsala, took a long swig of water, and said, 'Firm called Perkins, Lovell in Bayswater.'

'Okay. Somebody there may know something about her – where she comes from, if she has family – but that'll have to wait till tomorrow too.'

'Job for Andy,' Barbara said, referring to DC Andy Whittaker, currently supervising SOCO at the crime scene.

'What about the flat in Isleworth? Can we delegate that? I really need you back at Ivy Cottage tomorrow morning once forensic has finished.'

'Job for Nick,' Barbara said. 'Talk of the devil.'

Constable George Nicolaides had just come in the door of the curry house, a stocky man of Mediterranean appearance, in his early thirties, badly in need of a shave. He made straight for their table and sat down next to Barbara. A diligent waiter made a move towards them but Greg stopped him with a fierce look and he backed nervously away as Nicolaides began to speak in a low voice.

'No surprises at the PM, guv. Strangulation by that

scarf. Dr Chubb's sent some samples to the lab so it'll take a while to find out if she'd been drugged beforehand but the Doc reckons with the leverage you could get on a long, thin scarf like that, you wouldn't need all that much strength, just so long as you took her unawares.'

Greg downed the last mouthful of balti. 'No sexual assault? She wasn't pregnant or anything?'

'Like I said, no surprises ... unless you count some intimate piercings.'

'I'll read about those in the autopsy report,' Greg said quickly. 'No skin under her nails?'

'She bit her nails down to the quick,' Nicolaides said with distaste, 'so no such luck. Anyway, Dr Chubb reckons she was wearing the scarf and the murderer grabbed the ends from behind and choked her before she knew what was happening. Oh! No surprises, except that one of Dr Chubb's assistants realised that her specs were plain glass.'

'Indeed? That's odd. They didn't look much like a fashion statement.' Perhaps the cottage had not been the only thing in disguise. 'Any hope of a time?'

The young man shook his head. 'Probably late last night is the best the doc can offer. Say, between nine p.m. and three a.m., give or take. Shame about that electric fire.'

'We're assuming it was on and the killer simply left it,' Barbara said, 'but could it have been turned on deliberately to obscure time of death?'

'Interesting thought,' Greg said. 'So we'd be looking at a perpetrator with some knowledge of rigor mortis.'

'Like a former soldier, maybe,' Barbara said. 'Or a spy.'

'Am I missing something here?' Nicolaides asked. Barbara explained. He thought about it. 'So you think this Latham woman might have killed her own ghost writer? Why?'

'Maybe she found out more than she was meant to,' Barbara said.

'She'd have had the fire on, anyway, though,' Nicolaides pointed out pragmatically, 'cold night in November. No need for the killer to switch it on.'

He grinned happily, having caught Barbara out in being too clever by half. She made a face at him. He did not seem to resent her authority as much as when he'd first joined Newbury CID at the start of the year, but he didn't object to scoring a few free points.

'Time of death wouldn't help much in any case,' Greg said, 'what with the clearing being so isolated. It's not like we've got a load of neighbours for house-to-house. It's something of a fluke that the body was discovered so quickly when you come to think about it. She could easily have been lying there for days.'

He looked up and signalled to the waiter who approached a little tentatively in case he got glared at again. 'You've earned a drink after a few hours in the mortuary, Nick. Lager?'

'Please, guv.'

'Pint of your best lager. Do you want anything to eat?'

'No thanks. Somehow ... where I've just been always takes away my appetite. Funny that.' He laughed. 'Haven't eaten offal in years.' He took a packet of cigarettes out of his jacket pocket and raised one to his lips.

'Don't mind if I eat while you smoke, do you?' Barbara said tartly.

'Sorry, Sarge. Takes ages to get the stench of death out of my nostrils.'

'I attended a post mortem once,' Greg mused, 'years ago, where the body had lain in a shallow grave for eight months. It had been a mild, wet winter n'all.'

'HELLO!' Barbara said. 'People still eating here.'

'Sorry, Babs.'

She grimaced and pushed away her plate with a few mouthfuls untasted. Nicolaides looked as if he'd scored another point and lit his cigarette.

The waiter deposited a pint glass in front of the constable who downed half of it in one gulp. Greg said, 'Got a job for you up in London first thing tomorrow, Nick, take the dead woman's flat apart.'

George Nicolaides was London-Greek by birth and knew the capital better than anyone else at Newbury police station, so he nodded philosophically at this new task. Anyway, he liked being away from the station, on his own, free of supervision.

Plus, no one would be able to check his overtime claims too closely.

4

By Saturday morning, Martha Childs and her crew were done with Ivy Cottage and Greg and Barbara were free to make their own search. If this seemed like a duplication of work, it wasn't: the SOC team were scientists; CID artists. Or that was the way Greg saw it.

He began by turning over the pile of magazines he had noticed on the bookshelves the night before. They were all the same title – *Today's Author* – issued monthly, each in a garish yellow cover. He counted a baker's dozen of them, dating back just over a year with the most recent a double issue for November and December.

He sat down on one of the armchairs with the magazines in his lap in chronological order and began to work his way through them. He didn't know what he was looking for, but he would know it when he saw it.

He was gratified to find it in the third issue. The centre pages carried an article by Gillian Lestrange entitled *Life of a Ghost*. More like death of a ghost, he thought.

He examined the photograph of the dead woman at the head of the page. It wasn't the same one as Mrs Finnegan had shown him the night before – this one was in colour, for one thing – but she looked very similar: plump cheeks, ruddy, free of make-up; corkscrew hair, which he now saw to be chestnut brown; and those hard black eyes behind the huge specs.

He could hear Martha Child's voice in his head saying 'It's in disguise.' She had been talking about Ivy Cottage, but the same remark could apply to Gillian Lestrange. Why would someone wear plain glass spectacles, unless there was something in their face they wanted to hide?

He sat staring at her features for several minutes, but there was nothing familiar about them: he had seen her on no wanted poster, no news bulletin, not to his knowledge.

Subsequent magazines carried further articles by Gillian, all on the subject of ghost-writing: how to find assignments; what research you needed to do; what division of the spoils you might expect. And what was a ghost-writer, after all, he concluded, but a professional author disguised as the celebrity whose 'autobiography' it was?

Barbara, who had been clattering around upstairs, joined him at that moment. 'Nothing resembling paperwork,' she said. 'No notes about the book she was going to write on Lavinia Latham.'

'I expect they were on her computer.'

'I don't see one of those either.'

Greg put down his magazine and considered. 'If she was working away from home for a while, I'd expect her to have a laptop.'

'If she did, then the killer took it, along with her handbag, purse, whatever. Which suggests that stopping the writing of this book was the motive.'

'Is it possible,' Greg asked slowly, 'that Military Intelligence mind so much about this book that they'll stop at nothing to prevent it being published, or even written?'

Barbara shrugged. 'What are injunctions for?'

'It didn't stop *Spycatcher* being published abroad in the late eighties,' Greg reminded her. 'I even remember someone at the station – Sergeant Niall O'Brien; he was before your time – bringing a copy in from Dublin. Several people had a read and a good laugh. And in this age of the internet, all information is in the public domain before you can say *website*. It may be that the only way to stop this book being published is to make sure it's never written.'

'Then surely Lavinia Latham would be the prime target,' Barbara said. 'I don't know much about it but I assume that ghost-writers are ten a penny.'

'But she's clearly not easy to find. And if they weren't sure how much work Gillian had done – how much Lavinia had told her – then it might be necessary to clear her out of the way too.'

'Are we even sure that Gillian was the intended target?' Barbara asked. 'What if someone tracked Lavinia to this cottage and assumed the woman living here was her?'

'Sloppy,' Greg objected. 'Unbelievably sloppy for an outfit that actually calls itself *Intelligence*.'

Barbara grinned. 'I thought you subscribed to the cock-up theory of history, sir.'

'I do.'

Greg would like to believe that his masters were competent enough to carry out the elaborate conspiracies of which the paranoid suspected them; alas, he knew better.

It occurred to him that Vinnie might have acquired other enemies in more than ten years freelancing: kidnappers, industrial spies. He voiced this thought to Babs who nodded acknowledgement.

'Have to ask her when we find her,' she said.

'*If* we find her. Besides.' He held up the magazine article and pointed to the photo. 'Do you really think this woman could be mistaken for a highly-trained soldier?'

'You have a point,' Barbara conceded, taking the pages. 'I don't see her scoring well on the assault course.'

A thought struck Greg. 'I suppose there's no chance that those two kids helped themselves to her laptop? Did you ask them if they'd seen one?'

'... No.'

'Then let's do that now. And we should ask Mrs Finnegan if she has a photo of her niece.'

But when they called on the old woman on their way to Murphy's house, there was no answer to their knock, no sign of occupation. A single bottle of milk stood on the doorstep like a big sign saying Gone Away.

'So, let me run over this again,' Greg said. 'What did you do when you found the body?'

'Made sure she was dead, of course,' Murphy said condescendingly. 'I seen it on the telly loads of times. *Silent Witness*, that's my favourite – lots of gory murders and one where a whole load of people got burned to a crisp in a cinema when all the film went up.'

'Yes, I think I saw that,' Greg said with a shudder.

He smiled at the ghoulish child, who looked younger than her years but clearly had the mind of a jaded fifty-year-old, much like himself. Her short-cropped hair stood up endearingly, like a ginger lavatory brush, and he both liked her and felt sorry for her, without being certain why.

'Then I stayed with the deceased while Lee went to the nearest call box to get the police. I ain't got a mobile, see. I told my mum I need a mobile. Maybe she'll believe me now.' She looked assessingly at Greg and decided he was powerful. 'You could tell her I need one. She'd listen to you.'

Murphy was sitting well back on the threadbare sofa, her short legs not reaching the floor. The house was small and poor – a two-up-two-down terrace on the edge of Denford, not far from Honeysuckle Cottage – and the child was clearly the boss.

On Greg and Barbara's arrival, she had attempted to send her down-trodden mother away, but Greg had explained that she must have a responsible adult present.

46

Murphy had raised her eyes briefly to the heavens and told the woman to sit down and keep quiet.

'Can't afford one,' Mrs Murphy muttered defiantly and her daughter shot her a hard look, as if she might be concealing a fortune under the floorboards. There was no sign that she had, or had ever had, a father and Greg wondered idly if the child was, in fact, human.

'Rotten luck when you can't afford something, isn't it?' he said kindly.

'Huh!' Murphy said.

'I mean, there must have been things at the cottage that were tempting.'

Murphy's eyes narrowed and he saw the intelligence in them aimed at him like skewers; she understood in an instant what he was implying. 'Place was a dump,' she said casually. 'Nothing there worth nicking.'

'Madonna!' her mother protested, crossing herself. 'You been brought up better.' Greg inferred that the child was named after the Virgin Mary and not the pop singer.

Barbara realised with shock that Mrs Murphy was only a couple of years older than herself, maybe thirty-one. If this was what marrying young and playing happy families did to a woman who ought to be in her prime, then she, Barbara, was more than ever glad that she had taken a different route.

'You had a good look round while you were waiting for Leanne to come back then?' Greg said. Murphy considered this in silence. 'If you knew there was nothing worth stealing,' he added.

'I didn't take anything. All right, so I had a look round. That's how I know there was nothing worth taking. Tha's not a crime.'

'You didn't see a portable computer?' Barbara asked.

'A laptop? No way I'd have missed one of them.'

Greg looked at her sternly. 'Madonna – sorry, Murphy – if, by any chance, you knew where that laptop was, it could provide vital information to help catch the killer. If, say, you had taken it away for safe keeping ...'

The child was interested, although not in the get-out-of-jail-free card he was offering her. 'So that means the murderer took it, dunnit? Must have been someone she knew, then, had to make sure there were nothing incriminating on it.'

She folded her little arms over her non-existent chest. 'Well, tha's gotta narrow it down.'

Silent Witness had a lot to answer for, Greg thought. The little girl's reasoning was sound, however, except that she didn't know about Vinnie Latham and the complications she brought to the scenario.

He could ask to search the house – Mrs Murphy looked like the type who could be bluffed into agreeing without a search warrant – but if Murphy had the laptop she would have hidden it well. On the whole, he was inclined to believe her.

For the moment.

Murphy escorted them out in a surprising access of good manners; or perhaps she was afraid they might steal something. 'Lee's mum won't let her play with me no more,' she remarked dolefully as she held the front door for them.

'That's a shame,' Barbara said.

The child screwed up her face, recalling Mrs Bright's harsh words. 'I'm a bad influence.' A single tear formed in the corner of her eye and was gone as she willed it away. 'Lee's bin having nightmares where the murderer's still in the cottage but tha's daft 'cause she'd bin dead for hours.'

Greg reached out a hand to ruffle her hair then withdrew it hastily; she might have lice.

When he was safely back in the car, he began to laugh. Soon, Barbara joined in.

'We should give her all the facts,' he said, wiping his eyes, 'see if she can solve the murder for us. Take the day off.'

The woman who answered the phone at Perkins, Lovell, publishers had a suspicious nature.

'How do I know you are with the police?' she asked, her voice a little shrill. 'We get a lot of people ringing up demanding information about our authors – weirdos and stalkers.'

Andy Whittaker was at a loss for a moment. He hadn't encountered precisely this degree of paranoia before; usually people were oddly accepting that you were who you claimed to be. He was a tall, handsome, fair man in his late twenties, with an open and honest face which people trusted instinctively, but that wasn't much use on the phone. He didn't want to have to take a trip up to London just to show her his warrant card or, worse, ask Nick to do it while he was up there.

Why should the Greek have all the fun?

Finally, he suggested that she ring Newbury police station and ask to be put through to CID. He stressed that it was a matter of great importance. She hung up without comment and he made himself a cup of coffee while he waited to see if she was indeed going to call back or whether he had been dismissed as a crank.

He was on the point of giving up hope and pondering what to do next, when the phone rang.

'Detective Constable Whittaker,' he said, in his most formal manner, then spoiled it by backing off the receiver for one of his enormous and unheralded sneezes.

'Hello?' the woman squawked. 'Are you there?'

'Yes! DC Whittaker here.'

'Maeve Enderby at Perkins, Lovell.'

So curiosity had won the day. 'Thank you for calling back, Miss Enderby.'

'We can't be too careful.'

Andy was not a great reader – the odd Dick Francis, maybe, at least up until the moment when his horse-mad wife had run off with a racing trainer – so he was prepared to be open minded about the fact that he'd never heard of Perkins, Lovell. Even so, he suspected that they were not in the premier league of British publishing and that their authors were probably safe from the attentions of stalkers.

He said, 'I quite understand. You publish Gillian Lestrange?'

'Her fiction. Not the celebrity biographies.' Miss Enderby's voice developed a distinct sneer at the word *celebrity*. 'Is Gilly in some sort of trouble?'

'I'm afraid I have bad news, madam. Miss Lestrange's body was found in a cottage in Berkshire yesterday.'

'Body? As in dead?'

'I'm afraid so.'

'Oh. Well, I didn't know her very well. Met her twice, I think. We've only published the one book and it didn't sell very well. Don't know what help I can be.'

'I was hoping you might know something about her family background.'

'Not a thing,' Miss Enderby said very quickly, as if anxious to distance herself. 'And if it was drugs –'

'Perhaps I didn't make myself clear,' Andy interrupted. 'Miss Lestrange has been murdered.' The line went quiet and he thought for a moment they'd been disconnected. 'Miss Enderby?'

'I'm still here.' Her voice had gone quiet, suddenly

compliant. Perhaps she was relieved to have her conviction that her authors were subject to the attentions of violent stalkers vindicated. 'Let me check my files. She must have filled in an author's biography for me at some point.' Andy heard a rustling of paper. 'Berkshire, you say? She lived in West London. I can give you her home address.'

'Would that be ...?' Andy read off the address in Isleworth.

'Yes. That's right.' Miss Enderby sounded disappointed. 'Curiously, I don't seem to have any personal detail at all.'

'Not where she was born, husband, children?'

'Nothing. Not where she comes from, no date of birth. Even when authors are coy about their ages they usually give some indication and Gilly wasn't more than about thirty so I don't see why she would need to conceal it. Come to think of it, I never heard her mention a husband – either ex or extant –' she giggled at her little play on words. 'Nor children.'

'Did she have any friends who might know more?'

'Well, I would hardly know that.'

'I meant anyone at the publishing house – another author, perhaps.'

'Not that I know of. It isn't a social club and Gilly kept herself to herself. Will it be in the papers – the nationals, I mean? On television?'

'I should think so,' Andy said, puzzled.

'Might reissue the paperback then,' she said cheerily. 'There's no such thing as bad publicity. Can you make sure to mention she was a writer to any reporters you deal with?'

'Thank you for your help,' Andy said, once he had recovered from her cold-bloodedness. 'Goodbye.'

He went to hang up the phone but the woman asked, 'How was she killed?' He pretended he hadn't heard and laid the receiver gently back in its cradle.

It was odd, he thought, how often people involved in murder cases, either as killer or victim, turned out to have 'kept themselves to themselves', at least according to anyone who wanted to distance themselves from the crime.

5

Barbara's car was swinging on to the roundabout on Newbury's inner ring road, preparing to pull in at the police station, when Greg's mobile rang, making a chirruping noise like a constipated sparrow. He'd been experimenting with ring tones to find one he liked; this wasn't it. He answered and gave his name.

A male voice said, 'Deepak Gupta here, Superintendent.'

'Deep. Hi.' Gupta was one of the scientists – the forensic experts – who played such a large part in any investigation these days.

'Are you sitting down?'

'I'm in the car.'

'You're not driving it, are you?'

'Sergeant Carey is driving.' Greg added, with a note of impatience, 'What is it?'

'I ran your latest victim's fingerprints through the system a few minutes ago. Just routine, except that I got a match. Not under Lestrange, though.'

Barbara brought the car to a halt in the car park, switched off the engine and sat looking expectant, picking up what she could from one end of the conversation.

'Well, she was a writer,' Greg said, unbuckling his seatbelt. 'I suppose it might have been a pseudonym. Does sound kind of phoney, now I come to think about it. And if she had form –'

Deepak interrupted and he sounded happy. 'Nuh-huh. That's not it at all. Her prints show up in connection with a case a good fifteen years back, in Kent, but as victim, not perp. Under the name of Gillian Lester.'

'Gillian Les –' Greg was so stunned that he disconnected without another word. 'Bugger!'

Barbara was squirming in her seat. 'What, guv? What?'

'I hear the sound of a can of worms being opened,' Greg said slowly.

'Our can? Our worms?'

'Fortunately not.' He rebuckled his seatbelt. Now he knew why Gillian Lestrange was in disguise. 'Do you remember the Gillian Lester case?' She thought about it and shook her head. 'No, it would have been before your time. Come on.'

'Where?'

'Forensics. I need to see this for myself.'

Deepak Gupta seemed unsurprised at the superintendent's personal visit. He didn't even turn round when Greg and Barbara erupted into the room, but stayed sitting in his white lab coat before his computer screen, a short, dapper man in his early thirties.

'Didn't your mother tell you it's rude to hang up on someone like that?' he remarked.

'Sorry. I was shocked.'

'Tell me about it. And – let me guess – now you want to see for yourself.' He shifted over to let Greg sit at the computer screen and pointed with his neat brown hands at two sets of prints ranged one above the other.

'They took some good dabs from the girl's bedroom all those years ago, glass of water, thumb and three fingers of right hand, nice and clear. Those are at the bottom. This, meanwhile ...' he indicated the upper set of prints, 'came fresh from your corpse yesterday evening.'

Greg had never been much good at matching prints. It was an exact science, which was why people like Deep trained for a couple of years to do it. Lately, they had computer matching to cut down on the donkey work. He said, 'Talk me through it, Deep, there's a good bloke. How many points, that sort of thing.'

'Enough for me to stand up in a court of law and insist it's a match,' the young scientist said. 'It's not as if they're partials. We have a couple of million prints on the database and this was the only serious hit. Her markings are predominantly arched, which is lucky, as it's the least common type.' He pointed. 'Do you see that tented arch on the index finger?'

'Yes,' Greg said doubtfully.

Deepak laughed. 'You'll have to take my word for it then.'

'This is very important, Deep. If you're not a hundred percent certain then we could all end up looking like idiots.'

The younger man looked quietly confident. 'I'm certain and I asked Pat to verify. You know we don't even claim to have a match until two experts agree.'

'Let's get to my office,' Greg said to Barbara. 'I need to look up the details of the Lester case. Then we're probably going to have to talk to the Home Office about this. Deep, not a word to anyone.'

Gupta folded his arms across his chest, still looking very pleased with himself. 'May I be reincarnated next as a cockroach if I utter a single word,' he said solemnly.

'Uh ... yeah,' Greg said.

'Here it is.'

Greg ran his finger across his own computer screen twenty minutes later. 'Abduction and murder of Gillian Lester, fifteen years ago. It was a front-page story at the time.'

'I'm all ears.' Barbara leaned forward on her chair like

an eager terrier and Greg could almost believe that her ears were indeed cocked.

'Gillian Lester was a fifteen-year-old girl living in the village of Shorne in Kent, not far from Gravesend. She disappeared one day on her way to school. When there was no trace of her after a couple of weeks' nationwide search the Senior Investigating Officer declared it a murder hunt and arrested the stepfather.'

Barbara said, 'Hah!'

It was a natural reaction, a police officer's reaction, Greg thought. All over the country decent, honest men were bringing up other blokes' children to the best of their ability; but the moment something went wrong, the finger of suspicion pointed firmly at them. He might easily have become a stepfather himself; there had been a couple of women after his divorce who had kids but nothing had ever come of it.

Barbara cleared her throat and Greg dragged his thoughts back to the subject in hand.

'Peter Bateman,' he said, 'worked in the Chatham dockyards, as I recall, some sort of menial work. He was the last person to see Gillian alive, by his own admission, and had had a blazing row with her at breakfast that morning, also by his own admission. She was going through the typical fifteen-year-old-girl stuff – unsuitable boyfriends, skirts too short, staying out late –'

'"You can't tell me what to do 'cause you're not my real father",' Barbara supplied.

'Exactly. Despite the absence of a body or forensic evidence, Bateman was charged and convicted. He's been in prison ever since. He got life, naturally, and the judge gave him a tariff of twenty years.'

'Where is he?' Barbara asked.

Greg pressed some more buttons, waiting impatiently

as screens unfolded before him with excruciating slowness. 'Parkhurst, at the moment.'

It was a prison on the Isle of Wight, off the south coast of England, with both maximum- and medium-security inmates: categories A and B.

Barbara thought about it. 'If they were planning on letting him out after twenty years, I'd expect him to be in an open prison by now, or at least a category C.'

'I don't think they are – were.'

'Let me guess: he's always denied any involvement.'

'I daresay the Kent police still trek over to the Isle of Wight once a year to ask him where he buried the body.'

It was the hopeless paradox for an innocent man in the British prison system: a lifer could not be considered for parole until he confessed his crime and showed remorse.

'And now it seems he was telling the truth,' Greg concluded.

'Poor bastard,' Barbara said evenly.

'Poor bastard indeed.'

He flicked back to his original screen, the details of the long-dead case, and scrolled down. He came across a photograph of the missing girl, a slight creature, looking younger than her years, with fine brown hair that stopped below her ears. He stared at it, perplexed, doubts flooding his brain. Could it possibly be the same person? Could a woman change so much in fifteen years?

'It's nothing like her,' he ventured.

Barbara was also examining the picture. 'She's put on a lot of weight – easily done in fifteen years – and I'd guess she perms her hair now but ...' Her finger reached out to touch the screen. 'Look at her eyes, sir. They're so distinctive. That's why she wore fake glasses.'

Greg looked; those same sardonic eyes stared back at him, though without the filter of spectacles, and he had no more doubts. Dark eyes, windows to a soul black enough to allow her stepfather to spend fifteen years in prison for nothing.

How bad did a stepfather have to be to deserve that?

'I've just remembered something I read in a magazine once,' Barbara remarked. 'About how girls who are victims of incest may pile on the pounds, in the subconscious hope that it'll make them less sexually attractive to men, less likely to be ... prey.'

'What magazine was that?' Greg asked. '*Cosmopolitan*?'

'*Psychology Today*.'

'Really?'

'No, it was *Cosmo* but it was written by a psychologist.'

'And you think Gillian got fat as a form of self-protection?'

'I'm groping for motive here, sir, for what she did to her family. If she was being abused by the stepfather ...'

'But then she'd have got fat while she was living with them, surely,' Greg objected, 'not after she left.'

'Maybe it was an instinctive defence against anything similar happening in the future.'

'Maybe,' Greg said doubtfully. He began to read the details of the case. 'Blimey! The SIO was DCI Alan Ashton of Gravesend CID.'

'Friend of yours?'

'In a manner of speaking. He's the superintendent at Rochester now, my counterpart on the Simon Emerson case. He's due to retire next spring.'

Barbara whistled. 'Not exactly going out covered in glory, by the sound of it. So what now?'

'Like I say, we need to refer this to the Home Office. They'll have to arrange an immediate release for Bateman. I'll speak to the Chief Super at home and get that underway. Meanwhile, can you get the prison system to dig up a current address for Mrs Bateman? We'll have to ask her to identify the body, if she can after all these years.'

'Poor woman,' Barbara said. 'She thought her daughter was dead all this time only to learn out of the blue ...'

Greg finished the thought for her. 'That she is.'

DC Nicolaides drove past the West Middlesex hospital in Isleworth, west London, and realised that he'd missed his turning. He swore rather more vigorously than the minor inconvenience justified, turned left into a new housing estate, did a U-turn and came out heading back the way he had come. A café called Get Stuffed made him smile appreciation. Maybe he'd get his lunch there as it looked like a good old-fashioned greasy spoon.

This time he found Amhurst Gardens and made for the only thing that resembled a block of flats: a square, red-brick edifice, so hideous that it must have been designed by someone who hated beauty, even humanity.

Even Nicolaides, who had little aesthetic sensibility, thought it ugly, depressing.

Six flats, he deduced, two on each floor. Number four would be on the first storey. He squeezed his car into the solitary vacant space some twenty yards along the road and got out. An old woman in a housecoat appeared at her front door to rail at him in heavily accented English for parking outside her house. Nick grinned, secure in the knowledge that he was back in London, gave her a cheery wave, which couldn't be proved in a court of law to be a V-sign, and walked back up the road.

The street door was on the latch; he pushed it open and made his way up the stairs.

At the top, on his right, stood a policeman in a constable's uniform, leaning against the door of the flat, his arms folded across his chest, a picture of boredom. He straightened as Nicolaides stopped in front of him, his face wary, since the detective, in his jeans and black leather jacket, his stout black boots, was the sort of copper who could easily pass for one of the opposition.

'DC George Nicolaides.' He flourished his warrant card. 'From Newbury. Call me Nick.'

The man relaxed. 'Derek. PC Jones. Jonesy.'

'Okay, Jonesy. Any trouble overnight?'

'Not a dicky bird.'

'No sign of a spare key, I suppose?'

'I had a nose around,' Jones said. 'Above the door, checked the stairwell. Not many places to hide a key.'

'And none of the neighbours have one?'

'Claim they scarcely know the woman.'

'Then I guess we're going in the hard way. The owner won't be complaining.' Nicolaides assessed the door and found it flimsy. There were two locks, a mortice and a latch, but close scrutiny suggested that only the latch was engaged. 'Not exactly Fort Knox,' he commented, 'specially when people leave the street door unlocked. Perhaps they like making work for busy policemen.'

He took a short run and shouldered the door, hearing the lock splinter immediately. A second push sent it flying in ahead of him.

'You're a Londoner, yeah?' Jones said, following him in.

'Finsbury. Don't touch anything, Jonesy.'

'I know!'

Nicolaides debated whether to send the man away, but he'd spent enough years on the beat himself to know how welcome a skive could be. Not to mention anything vaguely interesting. Like somebody once said: ninety-nine percent boredom and one percent abject terror; that was the formula.

The door opened straight into the sitting room and he

surveyed the scene for a moment. The place smelled airless, as if the dead woman had been away for days, if not weeks, which tied in with her being out in Hungerford all that time.

The lounge was neat but characterless, neutral, with cream walls, a beige carpet and a brown three-piece suite which was slightly too large for the space, creating no natural pathway to the two closed doors in the opposite wall which he took to be bedroom and kitchen.

He could see no ornaments or family photographs. It was as if the owner had no personality or, if she had, no interest in putting it on display. A thin layer of dust covered every flat surface.

'What we looking for?' Jones asked.

'Diaries – real or computerised – files, papers, answering machine ...' Nick pulled a pair of latex gloves out of his pocket and began to walk slowly round the room, getting a sense of the place.

'Been out in the sticks long?' Jones ventured.

'Not long, no. Few months.'

'What took you out there?'

'House prices.' He had recently taken a deep breath and applied for a mortgage on a two-bedroomed terrace house near the town centre, manageable garden, some scope for improvement and an easy walk to work each day.

'Tell me about it,' Jones said. 'I still live with my mum and dad in Whitton, and my girl lives with her parents in Hounslow. Doesn't do much for my sex life, I can tell you.' Jones stood awkwardly on the door mat, shuffling his feet. 'You'd think there'd be post,' he commented, 'if she's been away long enough for this dust to settle.'

Nick glanced down at the naked mat beneath the constable's feet. 'You would at that.'

'Odd bill, like. Been in CID long?'

'Five years.'

'Sometimes think I might give it a go myself. That's odd.'

'What is?'

'No phone in this room.'

'Probably in the bedroom. Or the kitchen.'

Jones stepped forward. 'Only there's a phone socket there, look, and a place in the dust on top of this bookshelf where –'

'DON'T TOUCH!' Nicolaides bellowed.

'No need to shout. I'm not an idiot. I was just pointing.'

'Sorry.' Nicolaides grabbed him by the arm and dragged him out of the front door. 'You'll make a good detective, Jonesy. Give it a go. Why not?'

He removed his gloves and took out his mobile phone, pressing the speed dial for the superintendent.

'It's Nick, sir. I'm in Isleworth. Looks like the killer's been here before me.'

'That was Nick,' Greg told Barbara. 'It looks as if the killer paid his visit to the dead woman's flat before we even found the body.'

'Need to get SOCO up there,' Barbara said briskly.

'Get them on their way, will you, while I talk to the locals again about trespassing on their ground.'

Barbara returned. 'Martha Childs went off duty forty minutes ago and was on her way back to Old Basing but they've got her on her mobile and they'll be setting off as soon as she arrives – within the hour, they said.'

'Wasn't there someone else who could cover?' He knew that Martha had young children and found it hard to do unscheduled overtime.

'The other Senior SOCO is off sick. Martha rallied round.'

'Okay. Nick's starting house-to-house with the neighbours – see if anyone saw a stranger in the building Thursday night or early Friday.'

'So is the flat wrecked, like a burglary?'

'No, odd thing. Nick says it's really neat, just that the phone is missing, so we're assuming it was a combined telephone and answering machine and the killer wasn't going to leave us her messages. No post either. Presumably anything in the way of personal papers will be gone too.'

'This points at Lavinia Latham,' Barbara said flatly.

'How so?'

'She'd know how to search a place with the minimum of disruption. And if Gillian had found out something about her that was dangerous to her then she'd need to find any notes she'd left at home.'

'What sort of something?'

'Criminal activity. Something MI5 can't brush under the carpet. Murder. Treason. It's possible, sir.'

'It's certainly possible,' Greg conceded. 'I'm going round to the Chief Super's house. I think there's some news that can only be delivered in person. See if you can find that current address for Mrs Bateman, Babs, but don't do anything about it till you hear from me. Also, see if you can find a contact at MI5 to ask about Lavinia Latham.'

'Unlikely they'll talk to anyone as junior as me.' Barbara was as enthusiastic about spooks as he was.

'Still, if you can get a name and number, then I'll try them when I get back.'

6

Chief Superintendent James Barkiss lived in a modern detached house in one of the pleasanter suburbs of Newbury. It was a little nicer than Greg's house – more rooms, larger plot – as befitted his more senior rank, his three years advantage in age, and the fact that he had raised four children there, all now more or less grown-up although the two youngest still lived at home.

It also had a name – 'Tall Trees', for no obvious reason – and boasted a two-car garage which, like Greg's own, was seldom actually used for garaging cars. He pulled into the drive and parked in a vacant space between the Chief's car and a white Citroen which belonged to Mrs CS Barkiss.

The Citroen owner emerged from the front door as he got out of his car, carrying two plastic bags crammed with newspapers which were no doubt intended for the recycling bin at the municipal tip. She did not look surprised to see him, but twenty-eight years of marriage to a policeman had probably placed her beyond surprise.

'Hello, Edna,' he said.

'Gregory. How nice.' She put the bags down and kissed him on the cheek, her hand firm on his sleeve. He had not realised that they were on social kissing terms but then half the women of his acquaintance lunged at him in greeting these days. 'I haven't seen you for a while, not since that party last winter.' She scrutinised his face. 'I've been wanting to tell you how sorry I am about Elise Weissman.'

That explained the kiss, he thought. She was concerned about his ill-fated friendship with Elise. He'd always liked and respected Edna and now he felt a surge of affection for this plain and sensible woman with her dowdy clothes and unpainted face.

He said, 'It was a shock but I'm over it.'

'You must come to Sunday lunch one day. And bring young Angelica. Such a lovely name.'

He smiled at her, grateful for her acknowledgement of the most important relationship in his life.

She picked up her newspapers and slung them in the boot of her car to join several bags that were already there. Following his gaze, she said, 'Jim hoards papers but every few weeks I get all stern and have a purge. He's in the study. Just go on in. Will he have to go out?'

'Doubtful. Few phone calls should do it.'

'Good, as James junior is due in an hour, bringing the new girlfriend for inspection.' She grinned. 'He doesn't usually bring them home, so she must be special. I'm deciding whether to put on my mother-in-law-from-hell act.' Greg laughed. She shut the boot and got into the driving seat. 'Don't forget about Sunday lunch.'

'I'd – we'd – like that.'

'Then I shall telephone Angie.'

As she backed efficiently out of the drive, he went in at the front door which she'd left open and made his way to the study which was to his right. The door was closed so he knocked and waited for Barkiss's reply before entering.

The Chief Superintendent sat at his desk in an open-neck shirt and a pair of old corduroys. Despite Edna's purge, there was a pile of newspapers on the chair beside him and he was engaged in cutting something out of a colour supplement.

'Who said you could snog my wife, Summers?' he growled.

'Well, you had to find out about us some time, Jim.'

Barkiss laughed and put down his scissors. 'Sit down and tell me the bad news.' He listened without interruption to Greg's story, then sat in silence for a moment, thinking. Finally, he said, 'Has someone else verified the prints?'

'Pat Armstrong confirmed the match.'

'She's good, is Pat.'

'And then there's the similarity of the names – Gillian Lester, Gillian Lestrange. That's a bit too much of a coincidence for me.'

'Did they get DNA from the kid when she went missing?'

'There was no mention of it on the case files. Alan Ashton down in Rochester would be the best person to ask about that since he was SIO.'

'Same bloke you've been working with this past fortnight?' Greg nodded. 'Bad luck,' Barkiss said.

'In some ways. Good in others. Mutual respect.'

'You haven't spoken to him?'

'Not yet. I didn't want to start shouting something as big as this from the rooftops. Apart from you and me, only Barbara, Gupta and Pat know what's going on and they're sworn to secrecy. Barbara's trying to track down the girl's mother, but discreetly.'

'Good.' Barkiss removed an address book from the desk drawer and turned it open, leafing a few pages till he found the entry he wanted. He reached for the phone. 'My gut instinct is that the Home Office will want cast-iron certainty before they go public on this. We're going to be talking to people who are heavily in denial, as the therapists say.'

As it was Saturday, Barkiss was able to get through only to someone quite lowly at the Home Office in Queen Anne's Gate, what they called a babysitter. It took less than ten minutes, however, for somebody to call him back. It appeared that the permanent under-secretary who was on call that day was at his country cottage near Salisbury for the weekend and could be in Newbury in an hour.

Barkiss explained that if Mr Xavier Browne went straight to the police station in Newbury, his head of CID would be there to greet him. Mr Browne demurred, suggesting that neutral ground might be preferable at this stage but was promised the utmost discretion.

Greg raised his eyebrows at this. 'At the gossip factory?' he asked when Barkiss hung up.

'Just sneak him in the back way.'

Normally Barkiss would have said a gruff 'Keep me informed' as he showed Greg out, but this time his words were 'Do let me know what happens' from which Greg inferred that the Chief Super was as intrigued by the case as he was and as eager to find out how the Home Office intended to play it.

Barbara found a contact number for Thames House, MI5's headquarters on the south bank of the river in London. She had seen the building once on a trip to the capital, looming in concrete and green glass over Vauxhall Bridge; with its odd crenellations and buttresses, it looked as if it had been designed by a lunatic.

Everyone had been surprised when MI5 moved in there that they had been so open about their new address, but this was part of the new user-friendly security services.

Apparently.

Two years later the IRA had fired a mortar at the building from the Thames embankment, only to find it impervious even to that weapon.

She dialled and, as a man's voice answered immediately,

saying, 'Thames House,' realised that she hadn't worked out what to say. She felt towards Military Intelligence in the same way a civilian feels towards the police – vaguely guilty as if they'll find something to pin on you. Anything.

'This is Detective Sergeant Barbara Carey of Newbury CID,' she said in her most professional voice. 'I need to speak to someone concerning one of your former operatives – a woman called Lavinia Latham.'

She couldn't tell if the name meant anything to the man at the other end of the line. He said simply, 'In what context?'

'As the owner of a cottage near Newbury where a murder has taken place.'

There was a brief silence as he digested this. Then he said, 'Is she a suspect?'

'It's too early to say.'

'Give me your number,' he said, 'and somebody will call you back.'

She gave him her office number and her mobile. Before she could ask anything more, even his name, he hung up. She listened to the dialling tone for a moment then called the prison service to locate Maureen Bateman.

Xavier Browne was younger than Greg had expected – late thirties – which suggested a high-flier, a fast-track *wunderkind*. Greg had been waiting for him in front of the station, looking out for someone middle-aged, stout and florid from large amounts of port at his London club, but he had no doubts about the identity of the expensively-dressed man who drew up in a sporty jaguar as if he was expecting valet parking.

Greg, having checked his credentials and pocketed his business card, offered him Barkiss's parking place, then steered him quickly upstairs to his own office. He had never met anyone whose name began with an X before: Xavier, rhymed with Saviour.

'We won't be disturbed here,' he said, 'not at the weekend. Can I get you anything? Coffee?'

'Thank you, no.' Browne sat down, placing an immaculate briefcase on the desk in front of him, and his expression was grave. 'I am deeply disturbed by your story, Superintendent Summers, and can only hope there's been some mistake.'

Greg took his own seat behind the desk and spread his hands. 'I wish I could help you, Mr Browne, but there seems very little doubt.'

He explained about the fingerprint match.

'Fingerprints are old hat, surely,' Browne said impatiently.

'They still have their uses.'

'DNA testing's made all that obsolete,' the man asserted.

'Both are useful weapons. The fact remains that the match between the dead woman's prints and those of Gillian Lester cannot be easily explained away.'

Browne gave him a hard look, as if he blamed Greg personally for this debacle and his ruined weekend in the country. 'I'm going to need rather more than that, Superintendent, before I start releasing prisoners and shouting about miscarriages of justice. I don't even understand why this missing schoolgirl's prints were still in the system fifteen years after we got a conviction.'

It was a good point; Greg was inclined to put it down to poor housekeeping. From one point of view, it was bad luck for the Establishment.

'My sergeant tells me that she's found an up-to-date address and phone number for Mrs Maureen Bateman,' he said. 'She still lives in Kent.'

'Lester's mother? So what?'

'As next of kin, we'd have to ask her to make a formal identification under any circumstances.'

'Hold on a minute! Asking her to do an ID is tantamount to admitting that we believe the body to be her daughter's.'

'Well, yes, but what alternative do we have?'

'Fifteen years this woman's believed her daughter to be dead and you're just going to ring her up and ask her to come and look at a recent corpse?'

Greg was touched by the civil servant's sudden concern for Mrs Bateman's sensibilities, or he would have been if he'd believed a word of it.

He said, 'Actually, we would ask Kent police to pay a personal visit and arrange transport for her.'

'Which means telling more people your suspicions.' Greg shrugged agreement. 'Or maybe you've already blabbed to the Kent police.'

'I've said nothing to Kent as yet,' Greg said coldly, 'and I'm not in the habit of *blabbing*. Obviously it will be traumatic for Mrs Bateman but I can see no way round it.'

'And,' Browne said triumphantly, 'how can you be sure she'll tell the truth? That woman's been a thorn in our sides all these years, demanding that the case be reopened on practically a yearly basis, trying to get the press and the BBC to take up her cause. Tell her you've got proof her husband didn't kill the kid and she'll swear a ... a *Chinaman* is her missing daughter to get him released.'

Greg said nothing for a moment, letting the man's indignation subside. The same thought had crossed his mind but he had some faith in his knowledge of human nature and his ability to gauge Mrs Bateman's reaction to the body. He said, 'I see no option but to involve her, given the absence of DNA from the original investigation.'

'Why didn't they take DNA samples?' Browne demanded. 'If they could get the missing girl's fingerprints then I'd have thought they could have turned up a DNA sample – a hair or toe nail clippings.'

'I'm sure they could have done,' Greg said, 'but this was fifteen years ago and such tests were by no means routine then. If you have any doubts about Mrs Bateman's credibility as a witness then we can ask her for a DNA sample and compare it with the dead woman's. The mitochondrial DNA should give a conclusive answer.'

'Mitochondrial DNA.' Browne nodded wisely. 'Absolutely.'

Greg was not taken in by this, being personally familiar with the middle-aged male mind for which ignorance was never strength. 'It's DNA that passes unchanged from mother to daughter, from generation to generation,' he explained kindly. 'It'll confirm their relationship –'

'Or not.'

'Or not,' Greg agreed.

'Then I insist that we do that in any case, as a basic precaution.'

'Fine, but it'll take some days to get the results and Mrs Bateman will have gone to the newspapers by that time.'

'Can't we get her DNA without her knowledge?'

'No we bloody can't!'

The two men glared at each other for a moment then, 'How many people know about this?' Browne demanded.

'Me, the Chief Super, my sergeant, and two experts from the forensic labs who checked the fingerprints.'

'So it's been contained.'

They sat in silence for a moment, their eyes locked, as Greg wondered if Browne would dare try to bury the scandal. He believed him capable of it, of offering the sop that Bateman would be transferred to an open prison and quietly recommended for parole in a few months, left to live out the rest of his days among people who believed he was that most vicious of killers: the one who murdered inside the family.

It would be simple enough: the deceased would remain Gillian Lestrange, a woman with no relatives and, apparently, no friends. There would be no public outcry, no loss of confidence in the police, no compensation for Bateman, no blot on Ashton's record.

Yet the key to a crime was so often to be found in the victim's past and if Gillian's history were swept under the carpet, then her killer might never be brought to justice.

He was mildly interested to know what the civil servant would offer, or what he would threaten. They said that every man had his price and Greg wasn't sure what his was, only that it was more than Queen Anne's Gate could afford. He was confident also that Barkiss couldn't be bought off, nor Barbara. They had, each of them, enough imagination to envisage what fifteen years behind bars was like for a crime you didn't commit.

Browne, perhaps reading this in Greg's face, perhaps knowing that it was a hopeless case, sighed. 'Get the Bateman woman over here.'

Greg realised that he'd been holding his breath and let it out with as little noise as possible. 'I shall have to talk to the Kent Police then, so am I free to tell them the full facts?' Browne nodded wearily.

'Are you sure you don't want that coffee?' Greg asked, with sympathy.

Xavier Browne got up without bothering to answer. 'I need to talk to the Home Secretary,' he said. 'In private. I'll be in my car. Call me when you have some news.'

He left.

Greg braced himself mentally to make the phone call to Alan Ashton. He tried to put himself in his colleague's place, imagining the dismay and disbelief he would feel in the circumstances; but he liked to think that he, Greg, would never have allowed himself to get into those circumstances, would never have turned a missing person case into a murder investigation on such flimsy grounds.

He hadn't got round to deleting Ashton's mobile number from his own handset and when Alan answered with, 'What can I do for you, Greg?' knew that the reverse was also true.

'Sorry to disturb you on a Saturday,' he said, putting off the evil moment.

'Did you leave something behind that can't wait till Monday? Only I'm at the twelfth hole and I'm two under par. Got twenty quid riding on it too.'

Ignoring this gibberish, Greg said, 'It is important, I'm afraid, Alan.'

Something in the sombreness of his voice made Ashton say, 'Hold on,' and Greg heard him distantly instructing his golfing partners to play on without him. 'Okay.' His voice was loud again.

'You should probably sit down.'

'On a golf course?' His voice was tetchy. 'Get to the point, mate.'

'I have you listed as SIO on the Gillian Lester case back in the late eighties.'

'... Oh yeah, poor little Gilly. Christ! Don't tell me her body's turned up on your patch after all these years.'

In a manner of speaking, yes, Greg thought. Aloud, he said, 'What made you so certain that Gillian was murdered, if I may ask?'

'You know how it is – stepfather hostile to the kid, constant rows, maybe abuse. Last person to see her alive. It was a no-brainer.'

That sounded about right, Greg thought. 'There was evidence of sexual abuse?'

'Well ... no, but it happens.'

Ashton, Greg knew, had been married to the same woman for thirty years and didn't have much patience for people whose marriages didn't last the course, who involved themselves in the messy and convoluted business that was normal family life in the 21st century.

He had been cagey about his own situation, as a result, admitting only to a live-in girlfriend.

'Look, Greg, what is this?' Ashton was saying. 'Have you got her body, or not?'

'I'm very much afraid that we have. It looks as though Gillian Lester was murdered here in Berkshire some time Thursday night.'

There was a thud and the line went dead. Greg inferred that shock had made Ashton drop his phone. He dialled again but could get no connection. Ten minutes later his cell phone made a noise like a bunch of kids jeering in the school playground and it was Alan.

'I'm back at the club house,' he said, his voice hollow. 'Tell me the details.'

Greg explained as succinctly as he could. 'I need Mrs Bateman here as next-of-kin to do a formal ID,' he concluded. 'She still lives in your area.' He read out the address which was in Chatham. 'Do you know it?'

'Yeah, high-rise council flats, bit rough. Families won't go there these days but her being a single woman ... The local council moved her after the trial, there being a fair bit of hostility towards her in Shorne. You know how it is.'

Greg knew. *She must have known.* That was what the

gossips always said, and yet it was extraordinary what people who shared a house and a bed didn't know.

He said, 'Can you get someone over there soonest?'

'I can't face her.' Ashton's voice was tragic. 'I gave her a hard time while I had her husband in custody and I can't look the bloody woman in the eye, Greg.'

'Pull yourself together,' Greg snapped. He felt sympathy for Ashton but not as much as he felt for the Batemans. 'I'm not saying you have to go in person, just that I want Mrs Bateman here, preferably tonight.'

'What shall we tell her?'

'As little as possible. If necessary, let her think that we've found Gillian's body from fifteen years ago. I don't want her talking to the media until she's made the identification.'

'I'll get right on it.'

'Call me when she's on her way. Oh, and, Alan, were any DNA samples taken from Gillian's belongings at the time of her disappearance?'

'Hardly seemed necessary,' Ashton said.

'Well, it would be saving us a lot of bother now.'

Ashton seized the lifeline with gratitude. 'So that means you're not absolutely sure it's her.'

'Sure enough,' Greg said, and disconnected.

Ashton rang again forty minutes later to say that Mrs Bateman wasn't at home and was not expected back until the next day.

'Downstairs neighbour says she's gone to visit the old man on the Isle of Wight,' the Kent superintendent reported glumly. 'Monthly trip.'

'That's bad timing,' Greg said, since she might well have her husband home in a day or two.

'Yeah. It's a long journey and she always stays overnight.'

Sometimes it seemed as if the prison system went out of its way to make life hard for wives and loved ones; seldom was a prisoner held near his home town.

'Then it'll have to be tomorrow,' Greg said and disconnected. He rang Xavier Browne to convey the news and the civil servant said that he would return to Wiltshire and be back in the morning. Greg decided that he might as well go home too.

'Who's the geezer with the flash car parked in the Chief Super's space?' Sergeant Dickie Barnes called to Greg as he went out through the back door.

'I didn't see anybody,' Greg said, leaving the sergeant scratching his head.

As he got into his own car, he examined the business card Browne had given him more closely. F Xavier Browne. Hah! So he was just a Francis after all.

'So you're back at last.'

Tim Childs' voice was as cold as the ice in his gin and tonic. He stood in the doorway from the hall to the sitting room, leaning against the frame, no smile of welcome on his face. To his wife he looked like a stranger.

'I did ring –' she began.

'Yes, you rang. Told me again how much more important your job is than mine because I'm just a man in a suit who sits in an office all day.'

'I didn't say that.' Martha was more puzzled than angry. She eased off her coat and hung it in the hall cupboard. 'I would never say that.'

'You don't need to. You make it clear every time you dump the kids on my mother and swan off on another "important case".'

'Joyce loves having the kids.'

'For a few hours, yes, but she doesn't like being taken

77

advantage of. As if it wasn't bad enough you being out half the night –'

'You were here.' Martha felt anger growing inside her, and in her anger was hot, not cold as it was in Tim, a mutual incomprehension, the gulf between rage and sarcasm. 'They're your kids too, Tim. You could have picked them up and given them a bit of your time for once.'

He went on as if she hadn't interrupted. 'You ring her this morning at the very last minute and tell her you can't collect them because you've got to go to London, although why someone who works for the Thames Valley police would need to go to London at all ... She had plans. She had a bridge four fixed up.'

'She should have said.'

'She didn't want to "let you down".' His fingers mimicked the quotation marks and the remains of his gin slopped onto his foot.

'And where were you this afternoon?' Martha asked. 'You don't work Saturdays, Mr Nine-to-five, and yet, somehow, just lately, you're never here evenings, weekends.'

'Oh, now we're getting to the crux, aren't we?' He smiled as if she had walked into a trap set for her and it was not a pleasant smile. She knew suddenly that this moment had been a long time coming and wondered how she hadn't seen it, she who was, as Gregory Summers had remarked only yesterday, so observant.

'Are we? You tell me.'

'All right.' He flung his empty glass down on the hall table. 'You asked for it. Yes, I have been seeing someone, as it happens, a stewardess, Mandy.'

'Oh please!' She felt hysteria rise in her voice. 'Of all the sad clichés. A *stewardess*, called *Mandy*.'

'She doesn't make me feel like a waste of space.' He

pushed past her, dragging his own coat from the cupboard, not entirely steady on his feet. 'So why don't we just put an end to this farce now.' He picked up his keys from the hook by the door. 'I'll call.'

'Tim!' She was furious with herself for stumbling into his trap, for allowing him to manufacture this argument so that he could walk out on her.

Upstairs, the youngest child, a girl of three, began to wail. 'Mummy! I saw the big, bad bear again.'

'Now look what you did,' he snapped. 'You woke Claudia with your shouting.'

She hesitated. 'Tim? Are you even fit to drive?'

'Mummy!'

As he went out of the door without answering her, she stood immobile in the hall, one foot turned towards the front door to follow him, one towards the staircase and her frightened child.

It was no contest. She let him go and bounded up the stairs two at a time.

7

Greg took a copy of *Today's Author* home with him, the March edition in which Gillian began writing about being a ghost. He wasn't sure why he wanted to read it, just that it might give him some insight into the sort of person she was. After all, she must have known that her stepfather had been tried and imprisoned for murdering her; all she had to do was come forward and tell everyone she was alive, but she hadn't uttered a word.

However much she hated Peter Bateman, it took a heart of ice to condemn him in that way. He would have liked to ask Gillian about it but she was beyond his questioning now and these words, set down in print in a magazine, by definition ephemeral, were all she had left him. Or perhaps he should read that novel. What was it called? *Playing to Win*?

He had never met a novelist and assumed that you could tell what they were like from their work.

There was no sign of Angie and he eventually found a note on the dining table telling him, without explanation, that she would be late home and that he should not wait up. He poured himself a glass of lager from the fridge, cobbled together a cheese and pickle sandwich and settled at the breakfast bar with the magazine flat in front of him, leafing through it from the beginning.

Today's Author was clearly aimed at amateurs, people who had not been published, an apparently massive target audience. He'd often seen advertisements in his newspaper that said 'Do you want to be a writer?' and wondered what would happen if he were to answer them in the affirmative. The magazine carried extravagant claims from vanity publishers, along with poetry competitions whose clumsy outpourings of emotion made him smile or, once, wince.

Finally, he settled to Gillian's article. She recounted how she had been approached by an agent five years earlier to write the life story of a pop singer called Latisha who had been famous by the age of nineteen, a multimillionaire, only to see everything drift away in an endless party of drugs and promiscuity before finding God and being saved by the man who later became her husband, an evangelical preacher named Samuel Sykes.

Which made him think inevitably of Bill Sykes and the doomed Nancy.

He deduced that the autobiography was an attempt to restore not only her fortunes but also her career. The fact that Latisha had been only twenty-five at the time of writing seemed bizarre – even comical – to Greg who, at almost twice that age, could not imagine how he would fill so much as a chapter with his life story.

He leaned back for a moment, teetering dangerously on his stool, munching wholemeal bread and ripe cheddar with the tang of best Branston, contemplating his life.

Everything came into his mind in a simultaneous jumble, past and present – five, fifteen or forty years ago. He struggled to place them in chronological order.

He remembered an ordinary childhood in the Berkshire countryside, the much-loved only child of older parents, scenes apparently bathed in perpetual sunlight. He had joined the police straight after failing two of his three A levels (which had put paid to any hope of university) and found, almost to his surprise, that he was good at it and that regular promotions came his way.

In his mind's eye, he saw an early marriage and early divorce, with the birth of Frederick coming somewhere between those termini. Then followed years devoted to his work – lonely years, as he now realised.

Later, Fred had come to live with him, bringing his new wife, Angelica, only to die of leukaemia at the painfully young age of twenty-two. Leaving him and Angie alone to comfort each other, to form an unlikely couple whose chances of survival seemed sometimes so remote.

Come to think of it, there was probably a whole book there after all. If only he could see the final sentence.

Gregory Philip Summers died peacefully in Kintbury at the age of ninety-nine surrounded by his children, grandchildren and great-grandchildren, all weeping hysterically. His beloved wife Angelica mourned him for the rest of her life.

Yes, that would do nicely. Why ninety-nine? Save all the bother of a hundredth birthday party and a telegram from the Queen – or King, as it would be by then.

Children? Grandchildren? Why not? Why shouldn't he and Angie have children one day, soon? Just because he would be seventy by the time they were old enough to vote.

Things had changed since Angie had started her university course the previous year, a mature student in the psychology department at Reading. Now she was surrounded by people her own age and younger while he, Gregory, must seem like something from another world. She was frequently out in the evenings without explanation, like tonight, but why should she explain herself to him?

She had a new tutor for her second year: Dr Burnside. Since the beginning of October all he'd heard was 'Dr Burnside says this' and 'Dr Burnside says that.'

Greg thought of him as Dr Sideburns, thus reducing him to the manageable proportions of absurd facial hair.

The phone rang. There was a handset above the

breakfast bar and he answered it before the second ring, forgetting that he had a mouthful of cheese and pickle. He hurried to clear his mouth but music began to boom down the receiver.

There must be an angel playing with my heart.

'Hello?' he said. 'Hello?' The line went dead. Puzzled, he replaced the handset. He pulled his thoughts back with difficulty to the pages in front of him and washed the last of his sandwich down with beer.

It had been hard work, Gillian warned, not because of Latisha, who was no trouble, but because of the control freak, Sykes. There had been times when she'd wanted to give up but that would have meant repaying the advance she had been given. He thought there was a barbed undertone to her words – a sneering, superior attitude – but was he inventing that dislike of her because of the callous way she had treated Bateman?

When he reached the end of the article, he felt that he had learned nothing about Gillian, although a few things about Latisha. He looked at the photograph once more, studying the face, trying to read her character.

The pathologist had turned in his full report now and it seemed that she'd been drinking heavily shortly before her death, which tied in with the depleted whisky bottle rolling on the floor. That would have made her easier to kill, slowing her reactions both physically and mentally.

She was the second murder victim to die on his patch that year with an excess of alcohol in the blood. He thought that it would be interesting to know what proportion of people died drunk. Did it help? Ease the passage? Would the ninety-nine-year-old Gregory Philip Summers be demanding a final libation from all those children and grandchildren, and would they roll their eyes heavenwards as they handed him the glass?

Was it a regular thing in Gillian's case or part of the extraordinary scenario that led to her death? A drink problem might be a sign of a troubled mind, like her obesity, her piercings or the ragged nails.

Guilt? Or was it possible that her stepfather had earned the cruel and unusual punishment she had meted out to him?

Nobody took any notice of the woman standing alone on the first passenger ferry of the day, looking forward across the Solent towards Southampton, oblivious to the biting winds from the dawn sea.

The boat was not crowded that morning; it was Sunday so there were no commuters and it was early for day trippers. A couple with four children displayed remarkable patience as the youngsters ran and shrieked about the deck, playing and fighting, but the woman seemed not to hear them.

She was barely middle-aged but held herself like an old person, with little elasticity in her bearing, let alone spring in her step. She clutched a shabby overnight bag between her ankles as if it held diamonds, although an opportunistic thief would have been disappointed to find only a change of underwear and her toiletries.

Maureen Bateman had been making this journey for seven years, since Pete had been moved to Parkhurst from Wormwood Scrubs. To get from Chatham to Southampton she had to change trains twice; then a shuttle bus to the docks, the high-speed ferry to West Cowes and another bus to the prison; alighting at that tell-tale stop with other defiant wives as the driver looked after them with contempt, snorting as he snapped the doors shut behind them in an unspoken 'good riddance'.

On a normal day it took four to five hours; on a bad day

– such as when the trains were subject to a speed limit following the latest derailment or overheated tracks in summer – it might be six.

It was bad enough during the mild months; in winter it was intolerable. In another six weeks, at the solstice, the early ferry would be speeding towards the lights of a Southampton still having its Sunday-morning lie-in in darkness.

And then came Christmas. For the first few years of Pete's incarceration she'd volunteered at a shelter for the homeless in Rochester, cooking and serving a full turkey dinner, washing up far into the evening. That had passed the time, although she'd never been able to convince herself that the down-and-outs were worse off than she.

Recently, she had no longer had the strength or the will for this diversion and had spent the day curled up on the sofa in her dressing gown, eating baked beans out of the tin.

There was no question of coming back from The Island, as the locals called it, the same day. She stayed in a B&B in Newport, the cheapest she could find. The landlady knew that she was a prisoner's wife, the stand-by-your-man spouse of a murderer, and treated her with only the most perfunctory courtesy, allocating the narrowest, coldest room and refusing to provide breakfast before eight a.m. on a Sunday which meant that she must go without or miss this, the first ferry at seven-thirty.

After a year of this monthly pilgrimage, she'd put her name down for a transfer to a council house in Newport, rapidly amending that request to anywhere on the Isle of Wight; but so far no Island council tenant had wanted to move to Kent or, if they did, not to a high-rise in Chatham. She'd turned down a flat on the Paulsgrove estate in Portsmouth because the place had a terrible reputation.

With all these years of practice she hadn't conquered her seasickness, even in so mild and sheltered a channel of water. The queasiness would not fully abate till she got back to the flat she had learned, oh so slowly, to call home.

At first there had been hope, she thought, as seagulls squawked above her, boisterous as children. She had been certain in the early years that an appeal would succeed, that the nonsense of Pete's conviction would become as plain to others as it was to her.

She had written letters by the hundred and letter writing did not come easily to her, each one costing her hours of thought and labour. She wrote to Ludovic Kennedy who interested himself in miscarriages of justice. He had been kind but not optimistic. In desperation she wrote to the Prime Minister – Margaret Thatcher in that long-gone era – and finally to the Queen. Both women answered only via intermediaries and in form letters: British Justice was the best in the world and there was a process she must follow without intervention from her betters.

As the tannoy announced that they would be docking in Southampton in two minutes, Maureen turned away from the view, picked up her garish nylon bag and made her way slowly to the exit.

All hope was gone now. She could not pretend, even to Pete, even to herself, that it had not.

Maureen Bateman was deposited in Greg's office shortly after two o'clock on Sunday afternoon by a pair of uniformed constables from Kent who promptly decamped to the canteen. Xavier Browne was already there and Mrs Bateman, having been persuaded into a seat, sat looking from one to the other in a defeated way as nobody spoke.

She was in her early fifties, Greg knew, and looked every day of it, her face lined from years of worry, her hair more grey than brown, the same fine brown hair that the teenage Gillian had had. Her eyes were infinitely sad, and hazel, meaning that her daughter's cold cruel eyes came from somewhere else in the genetic melting pot.

She looked pale, he thought, almost nauseous, as if she sensed already the painful reason behind this summons.

Her clothes were shabby and ill-made, perhaps charity-shop finds: a checked skirt that hung too long on her slight figure, a brown jersey with a cowl neckline which emphasised the stark ridges of her flesh, a Macintosh which must double as a winter overcoat, tan lace-up shoes.

Peter Bateman had not been a high-earner and this past decade and a half he had earned nothing but two or three pounds a week to spend on tobacco and phone cards.

Browne cleared his throat to say something but Maureen Bateman finally found her voice.

'I don't know why I'm here. I set off from the Isle of Wight at seven o'clock this morning and they came for me the moment I got off the train in Chatham. They told me I had to come to Berkshire, that it was about Gilly. They wouldn't tell me anything more. I don't understand. I haven't even had any dinner.'

'I am so sorry!' Greg reached for the telephone. 'I should have thought. I'll have some sandwiches sent up from the canteen. What would you like?'

She stared at him as he sat awaiting her answer. She was not used to policemen being *nice* to her, not after the first few days of Gilly's disappearance. She waved the offer away, the seasickness still deep within her, the complaint mechanical. 'Have you found her body after all these years? Is that it? Why the secrecy?'

'We *have* found a body,' Greg said, replacing his receiver, 'which we believe to be that of your daughter.'

Mrs Bateman let out a gasp, though whether of dismay or relief Greg could not tell. If she truly believed in her husband's innocence then she might have allowed herself to hope all these years that Gillian was still alive. Now came confirmation of her death, if not in the way anyone had expected, and with that came closure.

'The thing is,' Greg continued, 'that the woman who ... we believe to be Gillian ... was strangled here, in Newbury, on Thursday night.'

'What! I don't understand.' Mrs Bateman tried to rise to her feet but fell back. She seemed unable to speak for a moment and Browne hastened to pour her a glass of water.

'I know what a shock this must be, Mrs Bateman,' Greg said. 'It appears that your daughter has been alive and well all this time, only to meet with death by violence ... now.'

Maureen Bateman found her voice. 'It can't be her. It can't be. I won't believe it.' Greg and Browne exchanged helpless glances. 'If she was alive then she'd have got in touch,' she went on, 'let me know that she was all right, that Pete was ...'

'I should like you to take a look at the body,' Greg said gently. 'I know it's an awful thing to have to do, but you are Gillian Lester's next of kin and the person best able to confirm her identity.'

'Yes,' she said weakly. 'I will look.'

'It's not her.' Mrs Bateman shook her head vehemently as soon as the mortuary attendant pulled down the sheet. 'I knew it couldn't be. It's nothing like her.' Her voice took on a note of hysteria. 'I don't know what you think you're playing at. Haven't I been through enough?'

'You haven't really looked,' Greg said gently. 'It's been a

long time and people change so much between the ages of fifteen and thirty. She was a child and now she's a woman. Please. Look again. Look more carefully.'

The attendant shifted uncomfortably. He had been present at plenty such viewings but had never felt like a voyeur before. Browne, meanwhile, was looking more hopeful.

Greg pulled the sheet a little further away from her face, being careful not to expose the dead woman's pudgy body and the depredations of the post-mortem, but displaying her shoulders and arms.

'If it is Gillian then she's gained a lot of weight,' he explained, 'and her hair is permed and dyed, and much longer, of course. Please concentrate on the face. Or perhaps she had some distinguishing markings?'

Mrs Bateman hesitated, then stretched out her hand and ran her fingers very slowly along the cold, dead wrist of Gillian's left arm. Greg saw three large brown moles there, in a row leading away from the hand. The odd thing was that they were joined together by a line of blue biro; a childish affectation, he thought, but perhaps Gillian Lester had never grown up because her childhood had been stolen from her.

'She always did that,' Mrs Bateman whispered. 'Sometimes I made her scrub it off but she would always draw it again.'

'Orion's Belt,' Greg murmured.

'That's what she used to say.' She turned big, sad eyes on him. 'She liked to say things me and her dad – Pete, I mean – didn't understand, make fun of us because we had no education.' She turned back to the body, bending over it, the better to examine the features. 'That's her chin – her stubborn chin.' She brushed the chestnut hair back with her hand and shuddered at the coarse feel of it. '... And one ear bigger than the other, not much, just a little.'

'Mrs Bateman, do you recognise this woman as your daughter, Gillian Frances Lester?' Greg asked formally.

'... Yes. It's her.' She turned away and Greg signalled to the attendant to put the body away before following her. She staggered out into the hall and collapsed on the nearest bench. Greg groped for his handkerchief and gave it to her as she unleashed a torrent of tears.

'I'm sorry,' he said, crouched down beside her. 'I can't make out what you're saying.'

'Pete,' she sobbed incoherently. 'Pete! They'll have ... to let ... him out ... now.' Greg glanced up at Browne, who sighed, took out his mobile phone and walked off along the corridor and out of sight.

When Maureen had calmed down Greg had some more questions for her. He found a quiet office they could use and produced plastic mugs of tea from a vending machine in the staff room. He assumed that Browne would track them down if he wanted to.

'It will help me if you can tell me about Gillian,' he said. 'If I'm to find her killer, then I need to get to know her.'

'But I *don't* know her,' Mrs Bateman said. 'I don't know the woman she's been all these years.'

'Please.'

She made a helpless gesture. 'Ask your questions. I'll do what I can.'

'How old was Gillian when you and her father split up?'

'Split up? You mean as in divorce? Oh, no. Frank died.'

'I'm sorry. I didn't realise.'

'An accident at the dockyard. She was eight.'

'The yard in Chatham?' She nodded. 'Doesn't – didn't – Mr Bateman work there too?'

'They were friends, best mates, since way back, since school. Pete was best man at our wedding. He did what he could for Gilly and me after Frank died and we became close. Eventually. I think it came as a surprise to us both. We married four years later.'

'How did Gillian feel about that?'

'Angry.' Mrs Bateman sounded resigned. 'We'd been alone, the two of us, all that time, and suddenly Pete was there, not just a family friend any more but my husband. She accused him of using her father's death to ... *insinuate* himself into our family. That was her word. She liked to use long words that nobody else knew.'

'She was twelve then? It's a difficult age.'

'She'd been daddy's princess, wrapped Frank round her little finger. Nothing too good for her.' She took a deep breath. 'I couldn't have any more children, you see, she was the only one. Pete was stricter with her than Frank.'

'And she resented that.'

'Like all teenagers, she wanted her own way on everything.'

'When you say strict ...'

'He was firm with her. He'd say no and mean it. We weren't well off – ordinary, working people – and she was always "I want this, I want that, the other kids at school have got one." You know how they are at that age.'

Greg nodded.

'Pete thought the world of Gilly because she was Frank's daughter and he thought the world of Frank. He was her godfather. He'd known her since she was a day old but she treated him like a no-account stranger.

'They made a great thing in court about a terrific row Pete and Gilly had the morning she went missing. Do you know what that row was about? She wouldn't eat any breakfast because she reckoned she was on a diet – skinny little thing that she was – and he said she must. That was all, nothing sinister, normal teenage-girl stuff.'

But the motive for a row often bore no resemblance to its viciousness, Greg knew.

'She was a bright girl,' Mrs Bateman went on, 'doing really well at school. They wanted her to stay on to do A levels, go to university even. It would have been a struggle for us financially, but we wanted her to have the chances we never had. Pete was specially keen on her getting the best education she could.'

He said, 'Did Peter's discipline take a physical form?'

'No!' Her face reddened. 'I went through all this when she disappeared, specially after they arrested Pete. Making out that he used to knock her about, that there was something ... *unnatural* about their relationship. I won't listen to all that again.'

She stood up, her fists clenching.

'It's not unheard of,' Greg said, rising with her, 'for a man to marry a widow with young children –'

'You're sick,' she said contemptuously. 'All of you bloody policemen, social workers, reporters. I pity you.'

'I'm trying to understand, Mrs Bateman, why Gillian did what she did, why she put you and your husband through so much. Because at the moment I'm struggling with it.'

'Pete! What am I doing sitting here when I should be getting Pete out of prison?' She made for the door. 'I won't let him stay there a moment longer.'

The door opened and Xavier Browne came in, as if he'd been only waiting for his cue, colliding with her. He put up his hands to her arms to steady her and she knocked them away with scorn as if his touch were leprous. He said, 'Come with me, Mrs Bateman. We need to arrange for the release of your husband.' He threw an apologetic look at Greg. 'I'll take over from here, Superintendent.'

Greg drained his tea. 'As you wish.' He felt in his pocket and handed the woman a business card. 'Give me a ring if you think of anything that might help my investigation, Mrs Bateman. I still have your daughter's killer to find.'

She took the card, hesitating in the doorway. 'Do you know what she's been doing all these years? Where she's been?'

'Not really,' Greg said. 'She was living in Isleworth at the time of her death, in west London.'

'Then what was she doing out here in Berkshire?'

'She was a writer,' Greg said, 'and she was working on her next book.'

'A *writer*. What sort of writer?'

'She did a little fiction, I think, but mostly ghost-writing the lives of celebrities – pop singers, soap stars.'

'How odd,' she said. Seeing Greg's quizzical look, she explained. 'I took up writing to pass the time while Pete was in prison. I've not had anything published but I found it ... soothing, to jot down my thoughts and feelings, stories, even poetry on occasion.'

'Perhaps the talent runs in the family,' Greg said.

'They do say it can be therapeutic,' Browne offered.

'Yes.' Maureen stiffened, remembering his presence. 'Let's go.'

8

Greg let himself out of the back door of the police station into the car park at twenty past ten on Monday morning. He had a dentist's appointment of long standing and knew that using the Lester investigation as an excuse to cancel would be mere cowardice.

It would take less than an hour and he would be morally and dentally a better man for it. He had just brushed his teeth in the senior officers' rest room and could taste the minty freshness on his tongue as he walked.

Heading for his designated parking space, he was at once aware of a woman moving purposefully towards him. She was tall – a good five foot ten in stockinged feet, he calculated, and she was wearing boots with two-inch heels – and very lean. Her clothes were inconspicuous: a pair of khaki combat trousers and a plain black rollneck sweater, topped with a full-length camel coat, unfastened despite the continuing bitterness of the wind that morning.

She intercepted him before he could use the remote control device to open the doors of his Rover, her voice quiet but penetrating.

'Are you the SIO on the Lestrange case?'

'Yes,' he said, pocketing the car key, since the dentist's leather chair of pain had receded as a possibility. 'Detective Superintendent Gregory Summers. And you, I take it, are Lavinia Latham.'

There was no possibility, he saw, that anyone but a blind man could have mistaken Gillian for Lavinia.

She said, 'I need to talk to you.'

'Not half as much as I need to talk to you.'

'Not here.'

Before he knew what was happening, her hand was in the small of his back and she was propelling him towards the roundabout. He had met the arrogance of 'spooks' before but she took his breath away. He protested.

'Hold on!'

'Not here,' she repeated. 'They're looking for me.'

'I can guarantee your safety.'

'Yeah, right! I will answer any question you put to me to the best of my ability, but not in the police station and not on the record.'

He glanced round for help but the car park was curiously empty. He sized her up, wondering if he could arrest her and take her in by force on his own. He doubted it. She looked as if she could leap tall buildings at a single bound.

She knew what he was thinking. 'I would put you in hospital.'

'I believe you.'

'Look, I don't want to play hard ball, Superintendent. I haven't come to get into a fight with you. We're on the same side because I want to help you find Gilly's killer, but we have to do it my way.'

Intrigued, he gave in and allowed himself to be taken across the roundabout, through the threading passages of the underpasses. She led him into the nearest pub, deserted at this time of the morning, and to the bar.

'Mineral water,' she told the uninterested barmaid, handing her a five pound note.

'With or without?'

'With.'

'Without,' said Greg, who hated fizzy water.

Served, they took their seats in a quiet corner of the saloon and examined each other without disguise. He knew that she was in her mid forties and could see it in the dry lines around her eyes, the odd grey hair among the blonde. Her skin was smooth and free of make-up, lightly tanned. Her body was that of an athlete, twenty years younger than her chronological age.

He was used to making snap judgments about people, used also to revising them later when the evidence could not be ignored. Just now, he thought that he liked her, but she had been trained, he knew, to conceal the body language – the little mannerisms and tricks of speech – that betrayed her true nature. He said, 'You do know there's a warrant out for your arrest?'

'Well, duh!'

'Just thought I'd mention it. To be frank, Miss Latham, I'm not interested in your quarrels with Military Intelligence –'

'Call me Vinnie. Never cared for Lavinia – too girly. Never quite forgiven the parents for sticking me with that. People tried to call me Lav at school – but not more than once.'

'I just want to find out who murdered Gillian Lester.'

'Lestrange,' she corrected him.

'Actually, her name was Lester.'

There was no point in keeping her identity secret any longer; Peter Bateman's release would be all over the news bulletins tonight and front page in the papers tomorrow. He smiled, remembering Andy's report of his conversation with Gillian's editor; the woman would be in seventh heaven.

Maybe she'd killed her for the publicity.

'I suppose these writer types all use pseudonyms,' Vinnie said. '... Gillian Lester? Why does that name ring a bell?' He explained. She let out a low whistle. 'That's a police force with egg on its face.'

'Not mine, thankfully. Did she talk to you about her background at all?'

Vinnie thought about it. 'Not much, idle conversation. Grew up in the South East –'

'Kent.'

'Left home at seventeen because her parents didn't approve of her boyfriend.'

'The parents didn't know she *had* a boyfriend and she was fifteen when she disappeared.'

Vinnie filed this information away without comment then went on with her story. 'They hung around together for three or four years then split up, amicably enough, and she headed to London to seek her fortune.' She shrugged. 'It all sounded perfectly plausible – not to mention commonplace – but then she was a writer. They make stuff up. Even biographers.'

'Yes,' Greg agreed. 'There may not be a word of truth in anything she told you.'

She sipped her water, examining his face above the rim of her glass. 'You look honest.'

'Thank you.'

'But so do the best con men. What do you want to know?'

'When did you see Gillian last?' Greg began.

'Sunday afternoon, about five. But I spoke to her on the phone on Tuesday morning, just to make sure she had everything she needed at the cottage, though I told her to ask Aunt Adele if there was anything.'

'And where have you been since?'

'Edinburgh.'

'Can you prove that?'

'I could but I won't unless it's absolutely necessary.'

'I suppose Ivy Cottage is a good hideout for someone who wants to stay under cover, miles from anywhere.'

'Actually, in my position it's more sensible to have a flat in a big anonymous block in the centre of town, but call me an old softy. I grew up round here.'

'Yes, that's the first thing that struck me about you – how soft you look.' She laughed. He went on. 'There's no one listed on the electoral register as living at Ivy Cottage.'

'Politics.' She was dismissive, contemptuous. 'What difference does it make who lives at 10 Downing Street? I'd have to be crazy to put my name on any kind of public register with the enemies I've made over the years. What do you call a politician up to his neck in sand?'

'I don't know.'

'Not enough sand!' Greg laughed, genuinely appreciative, as she went on. 'The cottage is my bolt hole. Or it was, until the police started crawling over the place. I suppose I shall have to find somewhere else now. I've been thinking of moving abroad for a while, but I didn't want to leave Aunt Adele. She's getting on a bit.'

'She seems pretty tough,' Greg ventured. 'She told me a bit about her war service.'

'Yes, she likes to bring that up but you didn't hear the half of it, I'll bet. Do you know they kept the women's role in Special Ops secret for years?'

'I didn't know that.' It seemed to have been around in the public arena for as long as he could remember.

'They thought it would look bad – men sending women to die for them.'

Other times, Greg thought, others ways. 'Did Gillian have a mobile phone?' he asked.

'Yes, there's no telephone at the cottage so she'd have needed one there.'

'You have the number?'

Vinnie extracted it from her own handset and Greg

wrote it down. It shouldn't take too long to find out which phone company she used and get a list of calls.

'Did she have a computer with her?' he asked.

'Sure, a laptop, top of the range. Treated it like a precious child and hardly let it out of her sight. She told me that all her life was there.' A thought struck her. 'Come to think of it, she said something about writing her own life story one day and I didn't say anything because I thought it couldn't possibly be very interesting, but now that I know that she was Gillian Lester ...'

'And what was in *your* memoirs that was making the secret services so jumpy?' Greg asked. She hesitated and he added impatiently, 'You were planning to *publish* them.'

'True. Still am once I find another ghost. All right. I'll give you a for instance. You remember the assassination of Mikel Ancic in London eighteen years ago?'

'Yes, of course. He was shot in Hyde Park in broad daylight by one of the opposing faction in his – Oh!'

'Yes. That was the official line.'

Shaken, Greg drained his water and got up. 'I have to nip to the gents.'

She rose. 'I'll come with you.'

'You'll what?'

'Do me a favour. I'm not letting you go in there and use your mobile to call for backup.'

Greg thought about this. 'How about I give you my word?'

'How about you give me your mobile?'

'Deal.' He handed it over.

'I'll be right outside the door.'

Greg peed as quietly as possible, embarrassed at this alarming woman being in earshot. He dutifully washed his hands, read too late the out-of-order sign on the hot-air hand drier, looked in vain for another means of drying them, shook them to get the worst drips off and went out.

'I've put my mobile number in your address book,' she said, returning the handset, 'under VL, and I've got yours.' She indicated the piece of paper Sellotaped to the phone on which the number was written, because that was the only way Greg could remember it.

'I have to go now but if you have any more questions, you can call me. You won't get through but leave a voice message and I'll get back to you as quickly as I can. Let's get one thing straight: I didn't kill Gilly and I don't want you wasting your time on me when you could be finding the real murderer.'

She left the pub but he darted after her and fell into step beside her. She wasn't having it all her own way. 'Did you like her?' he asked.

She glanced round. 'If we're still talking, then we're walking.' She led him through the town for a few minutes, then turned along the canal towpath towards Hungerford before speaking again.

'I hardly knew her but, yes, I liked her. She looked soft but she wasn't, not mentally. For someone so different from me, there was a surprising empathy and I was glad she was ghosting for me.'

They stopped by the lock and a swan gave them a suspicious look.

'We talked about children,' Vinnie said. 'I've never had any and it's probably too late now. With the sort of life I've led, it was never the right time and the right place. She said an odd thing: she said she'd never wanted children because she thought she had bad genes.'

'Well, she'll never have them now,' Greg said.

'I assumed she meant unhealthy genes – a tendency to cancer or heart disease running in the family, maybe madness, or alcoholism. You know she was a closet drinker?'

'What makes you say that?'

'I could see it in her eyes. It's something you have to watch out for in my line of business. Sometimes when I'm putting an operation together I'm thinking of taking on someone who looks great on paper, then I look into their eyes and see the craving. That's a big no no.'

'Yes, I can see that.'

'But after what she did to her stepfather I find myself wondering if she meant bad as in evil. I mean, what possible reason ...? Was there abuse?'

'Not that we know of.'

'Still, stepfathers ...'

'How hard is it to get a new identity?' Greg asked.

'Easy enough, and easier still fifteen years ago, before they brought in all the money-laundering regulations. Also, the younger you are, the easier it is.'

'How so?'

'Think about it. If you're a teenager you simply get a job – washing up in a greasy spoon, stacking shelves in the supermarket – and you tell them it's your first job out of school. They get you a National Insurance number in your new name. Suddenly you're somebody else and it's official.'

'So how would you set about creating a fake identity at your age?'

'I don't know that I should tell you that. Trade secret.'

'I'm just interested.'

Vinnie grinned. 'Thinking of running away from Mrs Summers and all the little Summerses? Okay, you go to the British Consul in a small town abroad – somewhere obscure – tell him you've had your luggage stolen: passport, credit cards, cash, the lot. So you have no means of proving your identity, but you need a new passport to get home, so he gives you one.'

'Simple as that?'

'The simpler the better, don't you think? You need a bit of acting skill: poor helpless middle-aged British tourist, distraught at being robbed, bit panicky even, doesn't speak a word of the language.'

'I could manage that bit all right,' Greg said. 'One more thing: why wait till now to publish your memoirs, all these years after leaving the service?'

'I need the money. Now it's your turn to tell me something, Summers. Fair enough?'

'Depends.'

'How did she die?'

He thought about it, then saw no reason not to answer. 'She was strangled with a scarf.'

'Well, there you are then,' Vinnie said. 'I would have done it with my bare hands.'

Barbara was hanging up the phone as Greg walked into the CID room. 'Still no sign of Lavinia Latham,' she sighed, 'and still no call back from MI5.'

'I've just spoken to her.'

'What! Where? When?'

He answered her questions methodically. 'I said I spoke to her. In the pub across the road and by the canal. Just now.' He examined his hands, small for a man's. 'I suppose I could strangle a woman manually if she wasn't too strong.'

Barbara gave him a strange look. 'Are you feeling all right, guv?'

'Yes, and I wanted to stay that way. Now, where was I going when I got waylaid?'

'Dentist,' Barbara said.

'Oh, yes.' Minty freshness; should have reminded him. Greg looked at his watch and said with satisfaction, 'Too late now. Shame. Here.' He handed her the scrap of paper from his pocket. 'This is Gillian's mobile number. See what you can do with it.'

'Might as well try ringing it first off.' Barbara reached for the phone.

'What? In case the murderer answers and gives his name?'

'I live in hope ... Nothing. Dead.'

'Could have been worse,' Greg said. 'Could have been Madonna Murphy who answered.'

'By the way, according to the Land Registry, Gillian Lestrange owned that flat in Isleworth,' Barbara reported, 'and without a mortgage.'

'Wonder where she got the money,' Greg said, 'and more importantly, who inherits her estate. Any sign of a will?'

'If there was one,' Barbara said, 'then it's gone with the rest of her private papers, but not many people that age have made a will. I know I haven't. You're not really expecting to go any time soon.'

'But the thief comes in the night when you least expect him,' said Greg, who had made a will, since Angie was not, as far as the law was concerned, any more related to him than a woman he passed in the street.

'Is Nick still in Isleworth?' he asked. Barbara nodded. 'Ring him and tell him to go round the local solicitors. One of them may have a record of having drawn up a will for her, even a copy of it. Bank accounts?'

'We're still working on that.'

A few minutes later he was sitting in his office with Andy Whittaker looking at the list of phone calls made to and from the Isleworth number.

104

'We asked Telecom to go back six weeks, sir,' Andy said, 'but there aren't many calls.'

'More out than in,' Greg remarked. He ran his finger down the list of outgoing numbers. 'Same numbers crop up time and again. Have we identified them all?'

'Most.' Andy grimaced. 'Fact is that, apart from this one call to her publisher a month back, they're takeaways – Isleworth Balti House, Syon Pizza, Green Leaf Chinese.'

'Those were her friends, were they?'

'Friends and Family,' Andy said. 'Official.'

British Telecom operated a system whereby each subscriber could nominate five of their most frequently dialled numbers as Friends and Family; then you got a discount each time you called one of those numbers.

'That's rather sad,' Greg said.

'Oh, I don't know. Most people have their internet provider as their Best Friend,' Andy said. 'I know I do.'

'Although we know she was estranged from her family.'

'That's putting it mildly.' Andy pointed. 'Not sure about this mobile number. There are calls in and out for that.'

'Vinnie Latham,' Greg explained.

'The spook?'

'Mmm. Business.'

So that was all there was, seemingly, to Gillian Lester's life: work and takeaways. If only he had some idea of where she had been since leaving the protection of her mother and stepfather, what she had done, whom she had known. Then he might have some idea of who she was, of why Gillian Lestrange had died in that rundown cottage in the woods.

As it was, he had only the shadow of a woman to avenge.

9

'It's starting,' Angie called.

Greg emerged from the kitchen, groping in his mug with a spoon for the tea bag, as the drum rolls that heralded the BBC's ten o'clock news bulletin began to reverberate through the sitting room. He dumped the wet bag on a handy newspaper and sat down on the sofa as the drums faded and the modified Welsh accent of the newsreader bade him good evening. Bellini, the West Highland Terrier, jumped up to sit between him and Angie, panting in expectation as she stared at the glowing screen.

She preferred sitcoms, but the news would do.

'And our top story tonight: As the body of missing schoolgirl Gillian Lester is found in Berkshire, the Home Secretary is demanding explanations from Kent police in what has been described as the worst miscarriage of justice in twenty years. Later in the programme ...'

He went on to announce a few further headlines, paused as the drums gave a last flourish, then turned to face a different camera.

What was that in aid of, Greg wondered?

'Thames Valley police confirmed this evening that the body of a thirty-year-old woman found in an isolated cottage near Hungerford on Friday afternoon has been identified as that of Gillian Lester, a schoolgirl who went missing, believed murdered, in Kent fifteen years ago.'

The newsreader's expression was grave as the photograph of Gillian, aged fifteen, flashed up on the screen. 'Despite the fact that no body was ever found, Gillian Lester's stepfather, Peter Bateman, was convicted of her murder and has been serving a life sentence for the past fifteen years. Mr Bateman has always protested his innocence.'

'And now we know why,' Angie said.

The newsreader frowned, as if annoyed at the interruption. 'The Home Secretary today ordered the immediate release of Mr Bateman, pending the official quashing of his conviction. Our home affairs correspondent, Mary Gilbert, was outside Parkhurst prison earlier.'

The film began. Greg had seen plenty of prisons but none as grim as this one. Part shiny new brick, part discoloured concrete, the walls stood twenty feet high. Oddly, there was a car park in front of the compound, as if it were a shopping mall. It was full now and the Isle of Wight ferries would be doing good business today.

A sensible-looking woman in her forties was standing outside the gateway, her blonde hair not moving despite the breeze visible among nearby treetops. Like the newsreader, she was still sporting her Remembrance Day poppy, scarlet on her lapel. From the quality of the light he deduced that it was about five o'clock in the afternoon.

A swarm of people with cameras and microphones were waiting in the twilight. A few yards away, a black limousine stood with its engine running, its windows darkened to the limit that the law allowed, making it impossible to tell even how many people were inside.

The BBC's camera zoomed in on the car as Mary Gilbert explained its presence, a tart note in her voice. 'Mrs Maureen Bateman is waiting for her husband's release in a car supplied by the *Outlook on Sunday*. Mrs Bateman is refusing to make a statement or give interviews to other media.'

So the *Outlook* had swooped, Greg thought, in its tabloid way, scooping up Maureen Bateman and offering her a pre-emptive sum for her exclusive story. Who could blame her? For fifteen years she'd been deprived of her husband's company and his earning power, struggling on alone like a widow who was not even free to remarry.

And what was her alternative – to turn up at Parkhurst on the bus and lead her husband away by the same means?

She had believed her daughter dead, only to find in the flash of clarification that freed her husband, that she had lost her child all over again.

Clarification? That was a good one. It was as clear as mud at the moment.

A portal opened and a pale man walked uncertainly through, accompanied by a prison warder who was carrying his paltry belongings. He was tubby under his unfastened blue anorak, a swelling belly preceding him. People grew either fat or thin in prison, stuffed themselves for want of any better way to pass the time, or wasted away from despair.

The press surged against the barrier that had been erected to keep them back and voices called to the bewildered man from all sides. The warder handed Bateman his luggage and shook his hand theatrically as camera flashes went off, making the scene as bright as a summer noon. The prison officer turned to the cameras and beamed, enjoying his moment in the limelight.

Four vast men in suits got out of the limo and came forward, surrounding an alarmed-looking Bateman and shepherding him towards the car. The flashing cameras made them appear to walk jerkily, like dancers in strobe lighting in a disco. The minders wore sunglasses, an incongruous affectation in the November dusk.

'Somebody's watched *Reservoir Dogs* too many times,' Angie commented.

As the party reached the car, the back door opened and

the woman Greg had met yesterday stepped out and flung her arms round the freed man's neck. That would be the picture that graced the front page of every newspaper in the land tomorrow, Greg thought.

The press were on her like banshees, shrieking 'Mrs Bateman! Maureen!' at her and she stepped hastily back into the luxurious interior, pulling her husband in after her. The bodyguards jumped in and the car was gone in a screech of tyres and a flurry of dust.

The reporters broke away in disarray as they charged for their vehicles to give chase and the prison warder was left looking disconsolate, his moment of glory over almost before it had begun.

He'd better buy a copy of the *Outlook* next Sunday, Greg thought, find out exactly what the grieving mother had to say. They would probably extract far more from her than he ever could. He'd seen how she'd tried to smile at her homecoming husband but he feared that somewhere along the last fifteen years she had forgotten how and that thought made him deeply depressed.

'Poor woman,' Angie said, echoing his thoughts. 'What a cock up.'

'Not my cock up, thank goodness.'

'Does it matter whose fault it was?'

'Even so ...'

The next shot was of a helicopter taking off, rising from the ground in that teetering, sick-making way they had, as if it would plunge nose-first into the ground at any moment. As it soared out across the darkened waters of the Solent, the BBC reporter noted that the helicopter belonged to Boris Meacher, proprietor of the *Outlook* group.

Lord Outlook, as he was known to *Private Eye*.

The Welsh newsreader repeated that the Bateman case

was being described as the worst miscarriage of justice in a generation and went over on a video link to Bateman's solicitor who dutifully described it thus.

Greg eyed the lawyer without enthusiasm – a short, rotund man in a blue suit. Ambulance chaser, he thought dismissively, or some lackey of the *Outlook*'s. He distrusted short men: the Napoleon complex. He looked an arrogant little so-and-so, like most solicitors; calm, a little stilted with his lawyer's jargon and his clichés.

'And now the rest of the day's news. The Earl and Countess of Wessex today –'

Greg muted the sound just in time for the phone to ring. He picked up the receiver and said, 'Summers.'

'Oh, you're there.' Ashton's voice sounded unbearably tired. 'I tried your mobile but it was switched off.'

'It's getting late,' Greg said neutrally.

'Tell me about it. I've spent the last eight hours at Headquarters in meetings. The Chief Constable sat in on one of them, glaring at me every ten seconds like it was my fault.' *Whose fault was it*, Greg wondered, *if not yours?* 'And me three months from retirement,' Ashton went on. 'You couldn't have waited to find the bloody woman's body?'

'Don't shoot the messenger, Alan.'

'No. Sorry. But it's a guts-for-garters job, if ever I saw one, and I was the SIO. I shall be lucky to walk away with my pension intact.'

'You exaggerate, I think.'

'Yeah, maybe, but the Batemans are gonna be suing for a small fortune if they've got any sense. Anyway, thing is, the ACC wants me to send one of my officers to Newbury to work on this case, represent Kent. After all, you're going to be delving into where the hell Gilly's been for the past decade and a half, I take it.'

Greg was silent for a moment and Ashton continued. 'You can say no, of course, but you'd be helping me out of a jam, mate ... Don't make me beg.'

'I don't really see any problem,' Greg said slowly. 'We're a bit short-handed, as it goes, and if your man is willing to pull his weight –'

'None weightier,' Ashton said, relieved. 'I'm sending DCI Stuart Peck. He's a real high flier, my right arm.'

'I don't remember him,' Greg said in surprise.

'No, he's been on holiday the last couple of weeks. Malta. Got a flat out there. All right for these young bachelors. He worked on the Gilly Lester murd – disappearance way back as a young DC.'

'Okay. Send him over.'

'Great! He'll be on the road within the hour.'

'What? Tonight?'

'Sooner the better and there'll be no traffic. Can you find him a bed?'

Greg sighed. 'At this notice? If he doesn't want to sleep in a cell, I suppose he'd better have my spare room.'

'You're a star.'

Ashton took down Greg's address and rang off. Angie, who had heard only half the conversation, raised her eyebrows and Greg explained that they were expecting a guest. She shrugged, picked up the remote and flicked over to BBC2, bringing the sound back in the process.

Newsnight was starting and Jeremy Paxman was furrowing his brow in that quizzical way he had as he asked, 'Peter Bateman. Cock up or conspiracy? Are the police under so much pressure to make quick arrests that they seize on the nearest suspect before they're even sure that a crime has been committed?'

Greg wrested the remote from Angie and switched it

off. She laughed, got up and said, 'I'm going to put in an hour on the internet, then bed.'

'While I, apparently, shall be sitting up till the small hours.' Greg made himself another cup of tea and settled back on the sofa with a sigh. He picked up his copy of *Jude the Obscure* and opened it at the bookmark on page 136.

In the autumn he liked to do comfort reading, looking back over old friends he knew he would like, friends who would spring no nasty surprises on him. It didn't matter if he fell asleep mid-chapter, or lost his place; his old friends were very forgiving.

He was surprised when Angie called down a good-night to find that an hour and a half had passed, although Jude was no nearer to realising his educational ambitions. The phone rang immediately, presumably a call held up by her being online. He should get a second line put in. Soon. He waited for her to answer it in the bedroom but, as it continued to ring, concluded that she had either gone deaf or was shut up in the bathroom.

He lifted the receiver, wondering who was ringing after midnight. It could surely only be Ashton again.

'Hello. Alan?'

Heaven ... must be missing an angel.

He hung up. He heard Angie's voice floating from the landing above. 'Who was that at this time of night?'

'Wrong number,' he said.

10

Angie came out of the bedroom just after eight the next morning, yawning and stretching. She could hear breakfast noises from the kitchen, along with the smell of toast which brought saliva to her mouth.

She was wondering sleepily why the bathroom door was closed when it opened and a strange man came out.

'Bloody hell!' she said.

'Hello. Did I startle you?'

Thinking quickly, she decided that to dive back into the bedroom would be undignified, as would using her hands in an attempt to cover what were normally her more private regions. She concluded that the best thing was to carry on a normal conversation as if she were not naked.

'You must be DCI Peck. I'd forgotten you were coming ... well, that must be obvious.'

'Stuart Peck.' He grinned, keeping his eyes on her face like a true gentleman. 'But my friends call me Pecker.'

'Do they indeed!'

'Hold on.'

He ducked back into the bathroom and emerged with a bath sheet which Angie wrapped gratefully round herself.

'Thanks.'

'I didn't know Mr Summers had a daughter, a grown-up daughter.'

'He hasn't,' she replied, rather coldly. 'I'm *Mrs* Summers.'

'Oh God! Sorry. I thought ... I didn't think ...'

She relented. 'It's okay. There *is* a big age difference. I'm Angie.' Now that she was not at such a disadvantage she had time to scrutinise him. She saw a tall, slender man in his late thirties, with a good thatch of blond hair and blue eyes. He wasn't wearing a suit but a pair of well-pressed navy chinos and a sports jacket gave much the same effect, although his blue and white striped shirt was open at the neck. She noticed that his skin was well bronzed for such a fair man, especially in November.

'Nice tan,' she remarked.

'Just got back from Malta,' he offered. 'You been there?'

'Can't say I have.'

'I love it, got a place out there. It's like Hastings only with sun and cheap wine. Maybe you and Mr Summers'd like to borrow my flat some time this winter.'

'Maybe.'

She spoke without enthusiasm and he added, 'Twenty-two degrees in Sliema last week and the sea still warm enough for swimming.'

'Lucky you.' She stepped round him. 'I've really got to pee.' The bathroom door closed behind her.

Peck shrugged and made his way downstairs, following his nose to the kitchen.

'I'm making scrambled eggs,' Greg said, on seeing him. 'I hope that's okay.'

'Terrific.'

Two pieces of toast popped out of the toaster and Peck picked them up gingerly and placed them on the toast rack which Greg had dug out of the depths of a cupboard in an access of gentility. It was made of cheap pine and had been concocted by Frederick in the course of some woodworking class at school ten years earlier.

The superintendent took a jug out of the microwave, examined the yellow contents critically, stirred them with a fork and put them back for ten more seconds. Breakfast was always a bustle in this household, but he liked it that way.

Years ago, as a uniformed constable, he'd been called to a sudden death – natural causes, as it turned out. He and his partner, Mike Trewin, had stood shuffling their feet in the kitchen until the medical examiner had done his work upstairs and they could figure out whether to call CID or not.

The deceased had laid the table for breakfast: a plate and knife precisely aligned, marmalade, butter, sugar, bran cereal, a slice of wholemeal bread waiting in the toaster and even an egg sitting on top of the stove in a pan of water.

'Waste of bleeding time that was,' Trewin had said, indicating the preparations. Life was what happened while you were making plans, which was why Greg was never prepared for any meal in advance. That was his story and he was sticking to it.

'I met your wife,' Peck said.

'Oh ... right.' Greg was surprised that Angie should have introduced herself thus. As far as he was concerned they were together for life but she was his son's widow and, under British law, they were not allowed to marry.

He gave the scrambled eggs a final forking and turned them out onto a dish. Plates, knives and forks were found and butter and marmalade produced from the fridge. The two men sat down to eat.

A few minutes later they heard Angie come bounding down the stairs, respectable now in jeans and a sweat-shirt.

'Want some scrambled eggs, sweetheart?' Greg asked. 'There's plenty.'

'No, I'll leave you two boys to talk shop. I'll take Bellini for a quick run then I've got a ten o'clock lecture. Hey! I never knew we had a toast rack.'

Note to self: do not tell boyfriend his guest has just seen you starkers. She and Peck exchanged a brief, conspiratorial grin and she knew that he would not be talking either.

Grabbing a piece of toast in one hand and her coat from the hook by the back door in the other, she headed towards the front door yelling, 'Bellini! Walkies,' causing a hasty scampering of clawed feet on the parquet.

'Lecture?' Peck queried as the door slammed behind her.

'Angie's doing a degree in Psychology at Reading.'

She must be even younger than she looked, Peck thought, and very nicely put together, as far as he'd been able to ascertain out of the corner of his eye. Summers was – what? – pushing fifty. It was ridiculous.

'Cute,' he said.

'What?' Greg gave him a sharp look.

'... Your dog.'

'Oh, yeah. She's a darling. So, you worked on the Gillian Lester disappearance.'

'Yeah, few weeks after I got into CID. It was my first big case. And, as I lived in the next village to the Batemans, I was pretty involved, out with the search parties every day, even on my days off. We were combing the area for the best part of a fortnight before Superintendent Ashton – DCI Ashton as he was then – declared it a murder investigation.'

'Yes,' Greg said. 'Whatever possessed him to do that?'

Peck's manner grew a shade cooler. 'Mr Ashton's always been a bit of a hero of mine, sir. He looked after me in the early days, took me under his wing.'

'But without a body?'

'A) the CPS had been prepared to prosecute without a corpse for a few years by then.' Peck grabbed the thumb of his left hand with his right. 'B) –' index finger '– we had enough witnesses – neighbours, school friends of Gilly's –

to swear that she and Bateman were at each other's throats like cat and dog. C) –' middle finger '– the two of them were alone in the house before she vanished. D) –' ring finger '– we found the clothes she was last seen wearing a few days after her disappearance, wrapped in a bin bag and dumped at a landfill.'

'I didn't realise that,' Greg admitted. 'D, I mean.'

'And there's a big patch of woodland near Shorne – sort of place a body could lie undiscovered for years. Alan's been expecting the remains of Gilly Lester to be unearthed there by ramblers any time these fifteen years.'

'But why were you so certain she hadn't just run away from home?' Greg asked. 'Kids do it all the time.'

'She hadn't taken any spare clothes or, as far as we could see, any money. Her savings account at the Gravesend building society remained untouched. It was only a few quid but she'd surely have taken it.'

'And she had no boyfriend?'

'Not that anyone knew about. Okay, so she might have kept him secret from her parents but her schoolfriends were adamant there wasn't anyone too.'

'Hmm. Okay. Where was Mrs Bateman the morning Gillian disappeared?'

'She had a job cleaning an office block in Gravesend,' Peck explained, 'early start before the staff got in. Bateman prepared breakfast for himself and Gilly. They were always alone in the house from five-thirty weekday mornings.'

'I see.' There must be many poorer households with unskilled workers where similar arrangements applied, Greg thought, which did not make them sinister.

'It was – it seemed like – a no-brainer.'

Parroting his boss's phrases, Greg thought. There was no doubt that Peck was Ashton's creature, his blue-eyed boy. Literally. Who would take over as superintendent when Ashton retired? There was a good chance that the Lester fiasco had just scuppered Peck's chances, tarring the whole department with the same brush, but if he put in a good showing here in Newbury, he might yet salvage the job.

The younger man was still talking. 'Circumstantial, maybe, but it all added up okay and the jury thought so too.'

'Well.' Greg swilled down the last of his coffee. 'Let's get down to the station and introduce you to the team.'

'What I was wondering,' Peck said, getting slowly to his feet, 'was whether I could take a look at the body.'

'You knew her?'

'Like I say, I lived in the next village. I knew the Bateman family well enough to say hello to.'

'You might find it hard to believe it's the same woman,' Greg warned him.

Outside the front door, he said, 'We'd better take both cars. I'll drive slowly and you can follow me.'

'Okay.' Peck wielded a remote control and a black BMW convertible responded with a beep and a flash of its lights. Greg felt like asking if he was on the take but, as Ashton had said, being single made all the difference.

'You're right,' Peck said. 'I never would have recognised her. Gilly Lester was ... *petite*, looked younger than fifteen, just a little girl. Now you'd put her at – what? – thirty-five. Easy. Fat is so ageing.'

He glanced complacently down at his own flat stomach. Greg thought that he looked as if he worked out at the gym, had a six-pack.

'And the hair,' Peck went on. 'What is that – a bad perm?'

'But you *do* recognise her?' Greg asked.

The younger man hesitated. 'Now that I know, I suppose, yes, it is her. What a criminal waste.'

'I expect that's what Mrs Bateman's saying,' Greg said sourly, 'and her poor husband.' Life was finite and when they'd taken fifteen years of yours away, no recompense was adequate, but he could hardly blame Peck for the fiasco, no more than a humble rookie at the time.

'Are you done?' he asked more gently. Peck nodded and the two men took a pace backwards as the mortuary attendant slid the body into its icy capsule.

'Can't understand women who let themselves go like that,' Peck remarked. 'Another thing about the case,' he added, as they left the building. 'You never met Bateman. Mr Ashton did.'

'Creepy?' Greg asked.

'Loner type, nothing to say for himself, can't make eye contact. Something not quite right about him. You know?'

'Maybe he's shy,' Greg suggested.

'Yeah, right! Never had a girlfriend till his best mate died then he swoops in and scoops up the widow and kid before the bloke's cold in his grave.'

'Mrs Bateman told me they didn't marry till four years after his death,' Greg said sharply. He didn't like policemen who twisted the facts to their own advantage.

'Yeah? Maybe.'

'So he'd have been well cold by then.'

'We even went back and had a look at Lester's accident,' Peck went on, undaunted. 'Did he fall into that machinery or was he pushed type of thing.'

'And?'

'Well, it was an accident,' Peck conceded. 'Loads of witnesses and Bateman nowhere near.'

'You sound as if you still think Bateman's guilty of something,' Greg remarked, 'even now.'

'Yeah, well, mud sticks, dunnit.'

Idiot, Greg thought.

He took Stuart Peck into Newbury police station and explained his presence to the reception staff who seemed largely uninterested.

'If it's Monday, it must be a new DCI,' Sergeant Dickie Barnes said, cheerfully unfazed by the evil look Greg was giving him.

'It's *Tuesday*,' he snapped.

'Whatever.' He turned to Peck. 'Did he tell you what happened to the last one?'

Greg steered his temporary colleague away before he could answer, up the stairs to the CID room where he found Barbara in sole occupation. He did the introductions. Peck walked over to the far wall to take a look at the pictures: crime scene, post-mortem, Gillian at fifteen, Gillian at thirty. Barbara went over to explain the leads they were following up, her finger tracing the line of the arrows scrawled on the whiteboard in red and yellow marker.

Peck stood with his hands on his hips surveying the progress of the investigation so far. It didn't look much at the moment, Greg conceded mentally, but there was always a time at the start of any enquiry when that seemed to be so, when he despaired of bringing the case to a satisfactory conclusion. Sometime, preferably over the next few days, the gaps would be filled in, new lines drawn, and a picture would gradually take shape.

He spent a lot of time staring at this wall during any case, waiting for the penny to drop, for the moment of revelation when he would clap his hand to his forehead and exclaim, 'Of course. How could I have been so blind?'

'You might as well have the DCI's room,' he told his guest, indicating the office sectioned off from the rest of CID.

'Won't your DCI mind?' Peck asked, as if he had not heard the banter downstairs.

Greg and Barbara exchanged glances. 'We're between DCIs at the moment,' the superintendent said glibly, 'so make yourself at home.' Peck wandered into his new office and placed his briefcase on the bare desk.

'Where is everyone?' Greg asked his sergeant.

'Nick's gone up to Isleworth again, still hoping someone will have seen the intruder. It's close to a hospital, apparently, so he reckons people would be wandering about, even late at night. He's going to try to waylay some of the nurses who were on the late shift Thursday night.'

'That's convenient.'

'That's what I thought. What is it with men and nurses' uniforms, anyway?'

'That's unfair,' Greg protested. '... It's any sort of uniform.'

She snorted. 'And I sent Andy over to Honeysuckle Cottage to see if Mrs Finnegan's back and can let us have a photo of Lavinia Latham.'

Greg raised his eyebrows. 'Now that I've seen Vinnie and can get hold of her by telephone, I'm not sure we really need that.'

'I'd like to show it around the Denfords,' Barbara said stubbornly. 'See if anyone saw her hanging about on Thursday night.'

'Still banging that drum?' Greg asked.

'It's a theory,' Barbara said, 'and one I'm not prepared to dismiss yet. She told you she hadn't been here since the previous Saturday. If I can prove she was lying about that ...'

'You know, I think you and Vinnie Latham would get on really well,' Greg said. 'You've got a lot in common.'

'Why? Does she think I did it?'

Greg laughed. 'What about MI5?'

'I've left four messages now, but still nobody has called me back. Perhaps you should try. A superintendent might get more joy than a sergeant.'

'Well ...'

Peck came out the office, having tried the swivel chair for size, checked the contents of the filing cabinets (empty), then run out of things to do. 'Where do we start?'

'Have we got that SOC report from Isleworth?' Greg asked Barbara. 'What's the big hold-up? They went there on Saturday.'

'I just got off the phone again with Martha Childs. She's had some sort of domestic crisis. One of the kids ill, I suppose, I didn't like to enquire too closely. She was very apologetic and said she'd bring it up in the next half hour.'

'Okay,' Greg said. 'Can you send her to my office when she gets here. Meanwhile, can you fill DCI Peck in on all the details and current lines of enquiry.' As she opened her mouth to speak, he added, 'And that includes your own particular bee in the bonnet.'

He respected Barbara's instincts and was prepared to keep an open mind about Vinnie Latham.

She murmured, 'Thank you, sir,' as he left the room.

Greg met Andy Whittaker coming up the stairs.

'No sign of life at Honeysuckle Cottage, sir,' he reported. 'Her nearest neighbour says he hasn't seen her all weekend and there's a couple of pints of milk on the doorstep now, like she left in a hurry.'

'Sounds suspiciously as if she decamped after my visit Friday night,' Greg said. 'Come up to my office, Andy, and help me do a likeness of Lavinia Latham on the computer. You're much better with the software than I am.'

Half an hour later, Greg was satisfied. Even trained as

he was to observe people, he found doing computer pictures of them hard, though not as hard as the days when they'd used Photofit and it had been like doing a jigsaw where each available space had a dozen pieces that would fit while the finished picture was visible only in your memory and not on a convenient box lid.

'There,' he told Andy. 'Get copies made of that. She's tall, about six foot in her heels. No spare flesh on her.'

'I'll get right on it,' Andy said, and rose.

Greg detained him. 'Can we get that software on my computer whereby you take a photo and age someone digitally, get an idea of what a person might look like years after they were last seen?'

'You'll have to talk to Forensics about that,' Andy explained. 'It's a skilled job.'

'Okay, thanks.' The young man left and Greg took out his mobile phone, ringing the number listed as VL. He got a message, as expected.

'Miss Latham, it's Gregory Summers. Have you got your Aunt Adele? Because, if not, it looks like she's gone missing. Call me.'

He picked up the piece of paper Barbara had given him and rang the number for MI5. He left a message, emphasising his seniority and the urgency of the matter. The young woman on the end of the phone sounded less than impressed and insisted that all previous messages from Thames Valley police had been passed on as requested.

There was a knock at the door as he hung up and his secretary, Susan Habib, came in to tell him that Martha Childs had arrived. She showed the senior SOC officer in and went out, closing the door behind her.

He was so used to seeing Martha in her white SOC overalls that he hardly knew her in civvies: black tailored trousers, a red jersey and a youthful bomber jacket. He was surprised to find that she was rather an attractive young woman with her matte black hair falling to her shoulders in a heavy bob about delicate features.

He smiled and gestured her to sit. He thought she looked subdued and tired, which he put down to two long working sessions. She'd been at Ivy Cottage half of Friday night, then in Isleworth Saturday afternoon, so that no doubt accounted for the shadows under her eyes. There was nothing worse than setting off home at the end of a long shift, only to be pulled back in by an emergency. And hadn't Babs said something about a sick child?

'What have you got for me?' he asked. His mobile phone immediately rang, wishing them both a merry Christmas musically. He apologised, both for the interruption and the premature tune, and answered it.

'It's me,' Vinnie's voice said.

'Have you seen Aunt Adele?'

'She's with me for safe-keeping. Mind you, she's already going stir crazy.'

Greg leaned back in his chair and swivelled to gaze out of the window. He lowered his voice. 'You think she's in danger?'

'Don't know and can't take the risk. Until I know why Gilly died, I can't be sure that it wasn't me they were after and Aunt Adele makes a wonderful hostage, don't you think?'

'I suppose she might,' he admitted, 'but we don't seriously think the killer was after you.' Particularly if he was prepared to countenance Babs' theory that Vinnie herself was the murderer. 'Tell me, do you have any enemies apart from MI5, any sort of price on your head?'

Vinnie laughed. 'Several, I should think. If you can spend years as a freelance soldier without pissing someone off enough to want to kill you, then you're probably not doing your job properly.'

She added with a note of pride, 'I even had my own fatwah a few years ago.'

'I'm impressed. How come?'

'Fetched back a fourteen-year-old girl whose father had sent her to Pakistan for a forced marriage.'

'Who paid you to do that?' he asked, curious.

'Her mother's family.'

'Any names – of people who might want you dead?'

'Sadly, they don't send out a greetings card with "We have taken out a contract on you" engraved on it.'

He wanted to ask her how many people she'd killed in the course of her career, but it seemed ill-mannered.

'But,' he said instead, 'a killer would have to be blind to mistake Gillian for you.'

'True,' Vinnie said, 'but he might have been searching the place, looking for a clue to my whereabouts, when she came in and caught him at it and he killed her to stop her talking.'

Did she sound paranoid? he wondered. Was this calm and disciplined woman ever so slightly off her head?

'I suppose you think I sound paranoid,' Vinnie said. Greg started in his seat, his chair back bumping abruptly upright, convinced that she was reading his thoughts. 'Paranoia is a way of life in my line of work and the paranoid are the ones who survive longest. Gotta go. Can't be on air too long.'

And the line went dead. Greg slowly folded up his own phone and put it in his pocket. He might not have a lot of time for Military Intelligence but he didn't believe that they would kill an innocent bystander, or kidnap an old woman like Aunt Adele.

But maybe he was just naive.

He said, 'Sorry about that,' and turned back to Martha.

11

It occurred to Barbara quite quickly that Stuart Peck was a bit of all right: tall, fit, nice hair, good tan. She liked his clothes too: well-made but casual. No wedding ring. Normally, she wouldn't consider getting involved with a fellow officer, but Peck was with another force, so that didn't count, rather like her sporadic relationship with DI Trevor Faber of the National Crime Squad.

Though no more than averagely pretty, Barbara had no trouble attracting men and knew her own worth. She didn't come on strong but put out subtle signals and waited to draw them in. Peck was more than willing to be friendly. He suggested she call him Pecker and, when she demurred at that, offered Stuart.

'Frankly, Babs,' he said, 'I've been sent here to do damage limitation, but it's like trying to clean up an ocean with a squeegee mop. The way I see it a) Superintendent Ashton is going down hard and b) all I can do is make sure I'm not crushed when he keels over. Does that sound callous?'

'Realistic.'

'I mean, I pity the bloke, I really do, but there's no sense in both of us suffering. Am I right?'

Barbara was making sympathetic noises as Andy came in with the pictures of Lavinia Latham. She introduced the two men and they shook hands.

'So who's this?' Peck asked, picking up the topmost copy from the pile. 'Not bad ... for her age.'

'Her name's Lavinia Latham,' Barbara explained. 'She'd employed Gillian Lester to ghost her autobiography for her. That's what she was working on when she was killed. The scene of crime belongs to this woman.'

'Gilly was a writer?'

'You seem surprised.' Barbara took a copy of the picture and pinned it to the board on the enquiry wall. Defiantly, she drew a red line from it to the autopsied corpse and added a big question mark.

'I knew the Bateman family slightly,' Stuart was saying. 'A) they were very ordinary people, working class, uneducated. B) Gilly was a shy little thing. Quite bookish, I suppose, but I'd never have imagined her turning out a writer.'

'Well, presumably till three days ago, you didn't expect her to turn out as anything,' Andy said. 'Since you all thought she was dead.'

'I wouldn't have known the place had been searched,' Martha said, 'if DC Nicolaides hadn't been so sure.'

'That professional a job, eh?' Greg said.

'I mean, when he pointed out the missing telephone, I could see it all right but that's really the only proof we have that anyone was there, that and the fact that there are no personal papers of any sort.'

'And a similar gap where the computer would have stood, I gather.'

'In the bedroom, yes. Desk top empty in the middle with clutter round the edges – an in-out tray, some reference books, dictionary, thesaurus. Then there's a cork board on the wall above with pins but no papers.'

Greg thought of the message board above his own desk at home: it contained such diverse items as recipes he'd cut out of the Sunday papers full of good intentions, photos of his and Angie's recent holiday in the Italian Lakes and a cartoon that made him laugh. Assuming that Gillian's board was similarly eclectic, then the intruder had swept the contents wholesale into his bag of swag.

He said, 'You went through the books, I take it.'

'Shook out every volume in the flat. No secret messages, no hidden notes, nothing. Sorry.'

He grinned. 'I don't think I've ever found anything hidden in a book; it's something that happens in the movies. There's a theory the victim might have had a drink problem. Did you find a liquor cache?'

'No, but alcoholics don't have stores of drink – they buy a bottle as they need it and polish it off.'

'Okay.' He wasn't going to ask how she knew that, preferred not to know. 'What about the lock?'

'Trouble is that Nicolaides forced the door when he gained access, leaving the lock in splinters. I removed it completely and sent it to the lab for analysis but I couldn't see any scratches, any sign that it had been picked.'

'The theory is that Gillian's killer took her bag with her keys in it and simply let himself in.'

'I see. Well, we dusted the area but got nothing usable, just a load of the victim's prints. If you want my opinion, whoever went into the flat was in and out in a matter of minutes, was wearing gloves, maybe carrying some sort of case to pile everything he took into.'

'Any chance it was a professional burglar?'

'Only thing is that they don't usually bother to cover their tracks like that. You know the way they start with the bottom drawer so they can leave each one open as they go. It's more like the sort of search your own officers would carry out if they had to leave everything tidy behind them.'

'Or someone from the security services?'

'Well ... yes. I suppose.'

'And you told Nick your theory about the suitcase?'

'I mentioned it.' She gave him a wan smile. 'He made a sucking noise through his teeth, which I took to mean that he's made a mental note of it.'

'That sounds like Nick. Thanks, Martha.'

'I'm really sorry it's taken so long. If there had been anything important, obviously ...'

'Don't worry about it. I know what it's like to have a sick toddler on your hands.'

'Sorry?'

'Isn't one of your children ill? I thought that was why you'd been absent.'

'... Something like that.'

Greg got to his feet and made to escort her to the door. She rose slowly and for a moment he thought she was going to say something more.

'Was there anything else?' he asked.

'... No. Nothing.'

She left.

Greg went back to Forensics but the only person present was Dr Pat Armstrong, a good-natured woman of forty-six who was in a wheelchair and whom he thought of always, therefore, as being about four feet tall. He'd once been to her bungalow and been disconcerted to find all the kitchen units two feet off the floor, forcing him to stoop for everything. It had given him some idea what it was like to live in a world that was not designed for you.

'No Deep?' he asked.

'Day off,' Pat said. 'We do get them occasionally. He's got a lot to do for this wedding.'

'Whose wedding?'

'*His* wedding,' she said patiently.

'Deep's getting married? I've not been invited.'

'He hasn't asked anyone from the office as he didn't want them to feel morally obliged to stump up for the air fare to Mumbai.'

'Mumbai?'

'Bombay. Whatever. His uncle's fixed him up with some nice girl out there.'

'Oh!' Greg thought of Deepak, who'd been born in Slough, as being every bit as English as he was. It came as a shock to learn that he was about to have an arranged marriage.

'That's her on his desk. Indira.'

Greg followed Pat's nodding head and picked up a framed photo that sat in pride of place next to Deep's Arsenal mug.

'Blimey!' he said, looking at the exquisite oval face above a jewelled sari. 'She's gorgeous.' He was fond of old Deep but you had to admit that the man was no oil painting.

'Yeah, and she's a doctor, a paediatrician. I reckon Uncle Roshan did a bang-up job.'

'There's maybe something to be said for this arranged marriage lark after all,' Greg commented, returning the photograph carefully to its place. 'Will she be able to practise here?'

'Eventually, after some requalifying. Get this. Deep's trying to decide whether to ride to the wedding ceremony on a white stallion.'

'Goodness! Is that his fiancée's idea?'

'God, no! Her family think it's old-fashioned and really rather vulgar but Deep quite fancies it. The snag being that he's never been on a horse in his life, let alone a stallion.'

'Sounds like he'll end up in the Emergency Room instead of on honeymoon,' Greg commented.

'So,' Pat said, 'can I help, Superintendent?'

'I expect so.' He explained what he wanted and she nodded vigorously, swerving across to the nearest computer on her chair, propelling it with strong hands before he could offer to help. She pressed a key, sending a screensaver of swirling galaxies into oblivion.

'I enjoy doing these,' she said with a grin. 'Now where's the original?'

He showed her where to find the photo of Gillian that had been issued fifteen years ago and she moved a copy expertly into another piece of software, waiting as the picture slowly resolved and the cursor kept its hourglass shape.

She sat with her tongue protruding slightly from her mouth as an aid to concentration. Her fine red hair fell over her face and she swept it back with an exclamation of annoyance and anchored it in her shirt collar, revealing a long neck that still sported its summer freckles.

'Okay,' she said, as the hourglass dissolved into a vertical line. 'What do we want?'

'Fifteen years older for a start,' Greg said, his hand resting lightly on the back of her chair as they both gazed at the screen. He watched as fine lines appeared around Gillian's eyes and mouth, a faint coarsening of the skin on her cheeks and forehead as time and ultra violet wrought their unremitting damage.

'The main thing is that she's gained a lot of weight,' he added. 'Fifty, sixty pounds, maybe more.'

'Phew!' Pat said. 'Only she's really skinny here so that'll make a big difference to the shape of her face.'

She pressed a few keys and he saw the flesh of Gillian's face gradually swell, making her eyes smaller as they were compressed by the layers of fat. Even her nose seemed to shrink. The weight went on the way it did in real life, not overnight but pound by pound, year by year. Soon, her features were not so much shaped as shapeless.

'Tell me when to stop,' Pat said.

'Bit more. Stop.' He judged, by the folds of her neck, that

it was right. 'Now the hair; longer, a few inches below the shoulders, and a frizzy perm ... Great. Now give her some big glasses with heavy black frames.'

'Sounds like she went out of her way to uglify herself,' Pat commented. 'Why?'

'I wish I knew.'

'How's that?' she asked a moment later.

'Yeah, that's pretty much what I expected.' It wasn't identical to the author's photo on her dust jacket but the two women could easily be sisters. He showed Pat the picture of Gillian at thirty. 'What do you think?'

She took it and stared long and hard at the two versions. 'Same woman, though her own mother would be hard pushed to recognise her.'

'She was.'

Pat wheeled her chair back and looked up at him in satisfaction. 'Does that help your investigation?'

'I already knew it was the same woman.'

'Oh!' she said, mildly annoyed.

'But it's nice to have confirmation.'

'I can do you if you like.' She laughed up at him. 'Show you what you'll look like at seventy.'

'Thanks but no thanks. See you.'

'I can make you bald,' she yelled after him.

12

In the middle of the afternoon, Susan Habib, Greg's secretary, rang through to say that a Mr Palmer was calling from Thames House. He seized up the telephone. 'Summers!'

'Harry Palmer here, Superintendent, at Thames House. I gather you left a message.'

'Only about half a dozen,' Greg snapped, 'over the past three days.'

'Sorry,' Palmer lied easily. 'Only just come through to my desk. Something about Lavinia Latham? Can you tell me what your interest is?'

'I have a dead body,' Greg said crisply. 'A murder. You may have seen something about it on the news last night when a man was released from prison after fifteen years.'

'Oh!' Palmer sounded mildly interested. 'The cottage near Hungerford. What was her name?' He answered himself immediately. 'Gillian Lester. That's your case? What has it to do with Vinnie Latham?'

'She owns the house where the body was found.'

'Does she indeed? Always wondered where her bolt hole was.' Palmer was silent for a moment. 'So you'll be wanting to speak to her.'

'I have already done so.'

This surprised the MI5 man into silence again. Finally, he said, 'So you know where she is?'

'No.'

'Oh.' He was a disappointed man, but soon recovered. 'Is she a suspect in the murder case?'

'Not really. Should she be?'

'Okay, let me tell you a few things about Vinnie Latham,

Superintendent. She was a hot-head, sacked from the service for taking too many chances, not only with her own life but with other people's. She's a loose cannon – a rogue operative, if you like, practically a psycho. And now she's a mercenary, however you dress it up. You can't believe a word she says.'

'Sounds like you know her pretty well,' Greg commented.

'I was her regular partner. We worked together on numerous occasions on one of which she almost got me killed. And,' he added for good measure, 'she's been out of the job for more than twelve years. She's yesterday's news.'

'And yet a publisher thinks there's a market for her book,' Greg said, 'and you want to stop her publishing it. You have a warrant out for her arrest.'

How could you tell when a spook was lying? His lips were moving.

'Formality,' Palmer said glibly. 'She signed the Official Secrets Act and she has to abide by that. We have to get tough with her *pour encourager les autres.*'

'So you're not actively looking for her?' Greg asked innocently, since he deduced that Palmer had not asked if he knew Vinnie's whereabouts out of idle curiosity. 'So none of your people have been to the cottage near Hungerford in the last few days?'

Palmer made scoffing noises as if he found the suggestion preposterous. 'She's not worth the effort. I can assure you we're not actively pursuing her.' He giggled. 'Mind you, I'd say that even if we were.'

He hung up. Greg wondered why the name Harry Palmer sounded familiar, then recalled that it was the name of a secret agent in Len Deighton's early spy novels. Michael Caine had played him in the movies. So the man wouldn't vouchsafe his real name, not even to a senior police officer.

'Sod you,' he murmured to the purring receiver, 'and sod the horse you rode in on.'

If he had to choose who to trust out of Vinnie Latham and 'Harry Palmer', he'd put his money on Vinnie.

Psycho, indeed!

'I still think I should contact the police,' Adele was saying at that moment.

'Honestly, Auntie. I can't see that it's relevant.'

The two women were relaxing in the best suite at a country house hotel in Oxfordshire. The remains of their lunch, smoked salmon sandwiches, lay on the round table in the bay window, framed by a perfect view of the Cotswolds in their regal autumn colours of crimson and gold. They were speaking in French in case of eavesdroppers, although most of the hotel's ancillary staff seemed to struggle with English.

'A woman gets murdered in the cottage and you don't think a man snooping about is important?' Adele said.

'It was three days earlier,' Vinnie reminded her. 'You just said so. If Gilly was murdered in the small hours of Friday morning, then how can a man hanging about on Tuesday evening have anything to do with it? He was probably walking his dog.'

'Didn't see a dog,' Adele muttered stubbornly, 'and it might have been a dry run, checking the lay of the land. We did them all the time in France.'

Vinnie sighed. 'That was a very long time ago, Aunt Adele. The world has become a rougher place since then.'

'Rougher? I've seen the sort of evil you can scarcely imagine, my girl. Look, Vinnie, I was brought up to co-operate with the police. I know that things are different in

Military Intelligence but surely it could do no harm to talk to that superintendent.'

She searched her memory, unblemished by the years. 'Gregory Summers.'

'There's no guarantee he can be trusted.'

'You don't trust anyone any more,' her aunt said sadly. 'It's no way to live, child.'

The telephone rang and Vinnie snatched it up. 'Valerie Harrison ... Yes, of course it's me, Spencer. Uhuh ... You have? That's fantastic.' She grabbed a pen and sheet of paper and began to take notes. 'Brilliant! What's the address? Thanks.'

With a final flourish of her pen, she hung up. 'That was ... Where are you going?'

'To pack,' Adele said, 'then home.'

'So!' Barbara said, when Greg told her of his fruitless conversation with 'Harry Palmer'.

'So?'

'Gillian realised from her interviews with Lavinia Latham that the woman was a complete fantasist and Lavinia, forced to confront the truth about herself, snapped and killed her.'

'Bloody hell!' Stuart Peck said.

'I think DCI Peck speaks for us all,' Greg said. He looked at his watch. 'Time to call it a day. I have plans. Stuart, can I leave you in Babs's capable hands?'

She could help him find a hotel for the night, if he hadn't already fixed something up.

'No problemo,' Peck said.

'Could I have a quick word, sir?' Barbara said.

'Yes, of course.'

They went out into the corridor and she said in a low voice, 'I'm not quite clear what DCI Peck's position is here. Do I treat him like one of our own and take orders from him, or what?'

Greg shrugged. 'Act like he's our temporary DCI ... But if you have any doubts, you can always refer it to me.'

'I'm thinking of buying a cow,' Piers Hamilton said, easing the cork out of a robust Spanish red.

Greg poked his finger in his ear and wiggled it about in a pantomime way. 'There must be something wrong with my hearing. I thought you said you were buying a cow.'

'I'm a Commoner,' Piers said, as if that explained it.

'Well, I didn't think you were royalty, mate.'

'A Hungerford Commoner, you idiot. It means I have the right to graze my cow on the Common.'

'The right but not the obligation,' Greg said. 'You'd have to milk it every day, for a start.'

'Good point. Perhaps further reflection is advisable.'

Piers poured two large glasses of wine and held his up to the light to admire the colour. Two pizzas were crisping in the oven; real boys night in.

'What's on the pizzas?' Greg asked, sniffing as the aroma drifted from the adjacent kitchen.

'Pepperoni,' Piers said, in dramatic Italian-waiter mode. 'Marscapone, salami, provolone. Probably other Italian words ending in vowels.' He was a tall, fair man of thirty-one, invincibly good-natured and confident in his own beauty. He wore combat trousers very like those favoured by Vinnie Latham though with less justification; his khaki t-shirt had 'Follow Me, Men' written across the back. 'Oh, and sun-dried tomatoes.'

'Agh!'

'You don't like sun-dried tomatoes?'

'I had my appendix out when I was ten,' Greg explained,

'and the doctor gave it to me to keep, and the next time I saw it it was sitting on my plate in a fancy restaurant.'

'We'll pick yours off.' Piers sipped the wine. 'Fruity,' he said, handing Greg his. 'I thought you'd cry off this evening what with this dead body on your hands.'

'You know I can't talk about that, Piers.'

'I know.'

'But I can always spare a couple of hours for a drink and a chat with a friend.'

They sipped their wine in congenial silence for a moment. Then, 'Who's the tall, thin blond I saw lurking behind you on the local news this lunchtime?' Piers asked.

'Oh, that'd be Chief Inspector Peck. He's with the Kent police. Rochester. And I don't know that he was lurking.'

'Sounds like he has a lot to lurk about,' Piers commented, 'if Kent made this massive cock-up all those years ago.'

'Nothing to do with him – he was just a constable back then. Now the poor bastard has to help clear up the mess.'

'I thought he might bat for my side,' Piers said, ''cause he's quite tasty. Wishful thinking probably.'

'Not as far as I know although, come to think of it, I haven't actually asked him and nor am I going to. He's not married, for all the help that is.'

'Then have him washed and sent to my tent.'

Two years earlier this conversation would have made Greg uncomfortable and having a gay man as a close friend would have been unthinkable. How odd that seemed now. Why had he kept such a closed mind all those years?

'He stayed with me and Angie last night,' he said. 'Be nice to have the place to ourselves again tonight.'

* * *

'Thing about Malta,' Peck said, taking a swig of his pint, 'is a) you've got your sea and sand; b) you've got your history and stuff, and c) the natives are friendly and speak English.'

Barbara looked surreptitiously at her watch as he went on. He might be good-looking, well-dressed and single but she had rapidly concluded that Stuart Peck was a world-class bore. Thank God he'd billeted himself with the Super last night and not with her.

Even so, she resented Gregory Summers making an excuse and dumping him on her for the evening.

She noticed that he was still talking, apparently under the impression that she was still listening. 'Only to think that this time last week I was sitting on my balcony, gazing out over a glorious blue sea, with a chilled glass of the local white in my hand.'

'And now you're sitting in a pub in Newbury with a pint of Fuller's,' Barbara said. 'What an anti-climax.'

'I could maybe fly you out there for a week or two this winter if you fancied it,' Peck concluded. 'Over Christmas?'

'I think I've used up all my leave for the year, sir.'

'Shame.'

'Yeah.'

Peck guffawed suddenly, snorting beer out of his nose in an unattractive manner. 'Sorry! Just remembered, driving out along the M4 last night, what's the deal with having a town called Maidenhead? I mean. *Maidenhead.*'

Barbara smiled politely, thinking him puerile. 'Yes, it is a little odd. Mr Summers grew up in the Thames Valley so he takes it as a matter of course, can't see the joke.'

'Well, I'd better be getting back to Kintbury,' Peck said, draining the last of his beer and lumbering to his feet. 'Don't want the Super sitting up for me two nights in a row.'

143

'You're staying there again, are you?' Barbara queried. She could have sworn Gregory Summers had told her that the DCI would check into a hotel today.

There was a noise outside, as of dustbins being knocked over. Piers leaped up and headed for the stairs.

'Just a sec.'

Greg went to the window and watched with interest as Piers shooed a pair of teenage boys, neither of them older than fourteen, away from his back door.

'What are you doing in my back passage?' he snapped camply.

'Old poof,' one boy replied, kicking him on the shin.

Piers came limping back upstairs. 'Did you hear that?' he asked indignantly.

'I've heard you refer to yourself as a poof on more than one occasion,' Greg pointed out.

'*Old*, Gregory. He called me *old*.' He flopped into his armchair, rubbing his leg. 'You know it's ages since I had a proper boyfriend.'

'Not since Karl,' Greg said, 'with a K.'

Piers winced. 'Don't talk to me about Karl-with-a-K. Okay, I can get sex any time I want it –'

'Which is more than any straight man can say,' Greg pointed out.

'But it'd be nice to have someone to potter about with, go out to dinner with, try on clothes with. A *partner*.'

'Yeah, that is nice ... apart from the bit about clothes.'

Piers sighed. 'I *am* getting old. You don't know how lucky you are, Gregory, to have Angie.'

'Oh yes,' he said. 'I do.'

Angie opened the door to Stuart Peck's knock.

'Oh, hi,' she said. 'Greg isn't in yet. He's gone over to

Hungerford for a drink with his best friend, Piers Hamilton, and when those two girls get gossiping ...'

'Don't suppose you have a spare key,' he said, 'save a lot of bother.'

'Oh ... yeah, there's a spare set here somewhere.' Angie rummaged in the drawer of the hall stand and found a pair of keys, unaccountably attached to a grinning Cornish pixie, which she gave him.

'Cheers,' Peck said, pocketing them. He yawned. 'Think I'll turn in, seeing as a) it was a late one last night, and b) it's been a long day. G'night.'

'Yeah ... goodnight.'

'... Unless you're in the market for a nightcap.'

'Got an essay that's giving me trouble.'

'You can download them from the internet, you know.'

'Sorry?'

'You can find an essay on the internet and pass it off as your own.'

'Isn't that dishonest?'

'So?'

'Thanks, but I can't see the point.'

'You get a good grade.'

'That really isn't the point, Stuart.'

'Okay, Mother Teresa. Some other time.'

He gave her a big smile and bounded up the stairs two at a time. Angelica blushed, suddenly embarrassed about the morning's display of flesh. She would never be able to forget that this man had seen her naked.

She could have sworn that Stuart Peck was meant only to be staying the one night with them. Not that it was a problem; they had the space. She went back to the study and her troublesome essay.

She was still working on it when Greg got in an hour and a half later. 'Burning the midnight oil,' he said,

145

planting a kiss behind her left ear and thinking about how lucky he was.

'How was Piers?'

'Fine. Fancy showing an old man a good time?'

'Shush.'

'I have a pair of handcuffs somewhere.'

'Not so loud.'

'You're wearing a lot of clothes. I bet you're hot. I can help you with that.'

'Shhh. Have you been drinking?'

'Not really. I was driving. We could do it in the sitting room.'

'Shush!' She raised her finger to her lips, since he clearly didn't understand the concept of shushing, and glanced up the stairs. 'Are you crazy? What if Stuart came wandering down?'

'Huh?'

He was cleaning his teeth twenty minutes later when the phone rang. He glanced at his watch; again, it was late for a phone call; again, Angie showed no sign of wanting to answer it. He went into the bedroom and picked up but said nothing.

Angie babe, are you all right? he heard. *Tell the radio goodnight. All alone once more, Angie baby.*

'Not work?' Angie asked, as he hung up.

'Wrong number.' He returned to his ablutions. What next, he wondered? There were only so many songs about angels or Angies. Hadn't Mick Jagger sung one about David Bowie's wife Angie, some time in the dim and distant past when he and Greg were both young?

With the Christmas season approaching, perhaps it would be *Hark, the Herald Angels Sing.*

13

'Yeah, I moved in there 'bout six months ago. It's nothing much but it's very handy – crawl out of bed and be on the ward ten minutes later. I share with Oonagh, Irish girl. We get on all right. She's a right laugh, when I can unnerstand what she's saying.'

The young woman stopped talking long enough to slurp a mouthful of the murky coffee that the hospital canteen provided, while Nicolaides looked encouraging. After two days of hanging around Isleworth, he had hit the jackpot at last. She was Nadia (which she pronounced Nadger) Polycarpou; not only was she a nurse at the West Middlesex Hospital but she lived in the same block of flats as Gillian Lestrange, on the floor above her.

Somehow he had missed her each time during house-to-house but that was the nature of shift work. He'd spoken to the liquid-vowelled Oonagh and agreed that she was not easy to follow.

Nadger was in her mid-twenties, Nicolaides estimated, petite but rounded in the right places, with her hair dyed a honey blonde and no roots showing. He wouldn't have known she dyed it at all, had not her eyebrows been dramatically darker above brown eyes, a not-displeasing effect.

She worked on the geriatric ward and he thought she was wasted on the old timers. They should put her in the sexual dysfunction ward, save a fortune on Viagra.

If his mum could see him drinking coffee with a pretty Greek-Cypriot nurse from Green Lanes, she'd shriek with joy and start planning the wedding, probably be knitting baby clothes. Coppers often married nurses, which was crazy when you thought about it because, what with both of them working shifts twenty-four-seven, they'd be lucky ever to meet; but then maybe that was the secret of a happy marriage.

He wondered if she had a boyfriend and tried to think of a way to ask that might be germane to his enquiries.

'Can't say as I knew her, though,' Nadger went on, crumbling a ginger biscuit on her plate and conveying it to her wide pink mouth. 'Say hello to on the stairs, like. Matter of fact, we didn't get on that well. She was always moaning about me and Oonagh making too much noise up above her. I mean, we *are* on shifts – sometimes we get in at all hours and you can't always be quiet as a mouse. It's not like we was tap dancing up there.'

Nicolaides made sympathetic noises.

'Yeah, bit of a sourpuss. Oonagh reckoned it was being so fat that made her grouchy; not getting any, if you know what I mean.'

Nicolaides knew what she meant.

'So I was glad when she said she was going away to Berkshire for a coupla weeks.'

She pronounced 'Berk' to rhyme with 'work' but Nicolaides wasn't in a position to criticise, as it had been only on his first day at Newbury that his own pronunciation had been sarcastically corrected: *Bark*shire.

'I knew she was a writer, mind,' Nadger continued, "cause she asked me once about my uniform and said if she ever needed any insider info 'bout nursing for a book she'd know where to come.'

'What about her car?'

'That old wreck? I couldn't figure out why she didn't get something decent, being a writer, cause they make loads of money, don't they? You see it in the papers all the time. That Jeffrey Archer makes millions.'

'It doesn't really matter how well you knew her –' Nicolaides began.

'You do need a car round here, mind, 'cause it's miles to the nearest station and the buses are that slow –'

'What I need to know is whether you saw anybody going into her flat on Thursday night, probably in the small hours. You were on the night shift, you say?'

'Late shift,' she corrected him, licking sticky crumbs from her lips. 'But I stayed on a bit that night because one of my old gents – Mr Drewson, Albert – was on his way out and I sat and held his hand till he'd gone and he hung on like grim ...' She giggled and put her hand coyly over her mouth like a Geisha. 'Grim *death*, I was gonna say.'

'So what time did you get home?'

'It was gone two, I remember, and I was really glad I didn't have far to walk – just across a well-lit road, though I like to think Albert's ghost was seeing me right, all young and up-for-it again, hoping to watch me in me scanties.'

Her story made him uncomfortable. He was used to death – violent death – and the Super had apparently decided that he was number one choice for post-mortems, but he realised that Nadger saw far more of the grim reaper than he did and was more at ease with him, probably welcomed him to the geriatric ward and told him to park his scythe while she made him a nice cup of tea for the journey.

'So you didn't see anybody hanging about?' he asked. 'Or lights on in Gillian's flat. Or your flat mate – might she have seen something? Or any friend you might have round ... like a boyfriend, say.'

Well, that was adroit, he thought, *Not!* She must know that he'd already spoken to Oonagh who'd spent that night at her fiancé's.

'Or you need a boyfriend with a car,' she said, still on the subject on transport and the lack of it in Isleworth. She gave him an assessing look. 'You got a car?'

'Well, yeah. Hard to do my job without.'

'But is it white with a red stripe and "Police" written down the side?'

He grinned. 'Plain clothes cop. Plains clothes car. It's a Vauxhall Astra. White.'

She said, 'Mmm ...' He wasn't sure if that passed muster or not. He said, 'So ...?'

'What was the question?' He repeated it. '... Not that night,' she said slowly.

'Meaning?'

'Earlier in the week. Let me think. Tuesday night, maybe? I got in just after eleven and the bulb had gone on the landing and I was walking up and he was coming down, gave me a scare, very light on his feet. I said something like, "God, you gave me a fright" but he didn't answer and I thought "Miserable sod".'

'Which flight of stairs was this?'

She thought about it. 'From the ground to the first floor.'

'So he might have come out of number four?'

She shrugged. 'All I know is he didn't come out of ours, 'cause I said to Oonagh "Who was that miserable sod then" and she said, "Dunno what you're on about, Nadge".'

'So, what did he look like?' Nicolaides asked. She was a bit garrulous, he thought, which was fine in a witness, not so good in a girlfriend. She hadn't answered the implied question about the boyfriend but he was having second thoughts about asking her out anyway.

'Like I say, light was out, otherwise he wouldn't have startled me like that. He was just a shape in the darkness. He was tall, mind.'

'Taller than me?' He stood to let her get a good look at his physique, which was only five-foot-ten but solidly built, even muscular. Might as well put the wares in the shop window and keep his options open.

'Couple of inches taller, maybe, and thinner, bit skinny.'

She gave him the once over and licked her lips again, although there were no crumbs left. He decided that he couldn't afford to be fussy. So what if she could talk for England? After a few dates, he could just stop listening. His dad hadn't heard a word his mother had said in thirty years.

'Don't suppose he was carrying a case?' he asked, remembering Mrs Childs' theory.

'Mmm. Come to think, he had a bag of some sort, banged against me as he passed.' She put her hand up her skirt and rubbed her left thigh, making it a sensuous act. 'Gave me a bruise right on my tattoo.'

He thanked her and gave her his card with his phone number, making a note of her home telephone. Tattoo, eh? When this case was over and she was no longer a potential witness ...

Over the road, Gillian's flat was sealed off, a new lock fitted to the splintered door and with blue and white incident tape forbidding entry.

Nicolaides stood on the first landing and looked up. When Nadger said the bulb was gone she was speaking literally. It hadn't simply blown; someone had removed it.

'Hey, you!' PC Jones came sprinting up the stairs, his right hand holding the top of his baton. 'Oh, it's you,' he said, disappointed.

'All right, Jonesy?'

'I'm just keeping an eye on the place when I go by now.'

'Bulb's been removed here,' Nick said.

'Yeah, I noticed that when I was here the other night. Meant to bring one but I forgot. Block like this, no caretaker, everyone thinks it's someone else's responsibility. I mean, what does a bulb cost?'

'Could have been taken by whoever searched the flat,' Nicolaides said.

Jonesy considered this. 'Or could equally well have been nicked by someone in the flats who needed a new bulb late one night.'

He wasn't wrong, Nick thought. Probably *would* make a good detective one day. He patted him fraternally on the arm as he left. 'Keep up the good work, Jonesy.'

Outside, he stood for a moment looking at the rubbish bins by the front door. It must be collection day. Was there any chance that the intruder had shoved the pilfered bulb in the nearest bin? He lifted a lid at random and stared without enthusiasm into the muddle of take-away wrappers and microwave meals for one, the typical detritus of single people's bins, very much like his own.

He knew that he ought to rootle through but told himself that the intruder was too canny to have left fingerprints on the bulb. Apart from anything else, it would have been hot, so he'd have used gloves or a handkerchief to protect his fingers from burns.

'You're excused bin duty,' he said under his breath.

Besides, what could a tall, thin man wandering about on Tuesday have to do with the death of Gillian Lester two whole nights later?

'Not got Gregory with you today,' Sergeant Maybey asked as he held the door open for Greg on Wednesday morning.

The superintendent looked at him, perplexed. '*I'm* Gregory, you dimwit.'

The sergeant was unoffended. 'I meant DCI Peck. We've nicknamed him Gregory, after the actor. Gregory Peck,' he added, in case Greg hadn't got it yet. Dick Maybey was in charge of nicknames at Newbury police station, self appointed. It took up a lot of his time.

'You don't think that might get a bit confusing?' Greg asked mildly.

Maybey considered this. 'I see your point. Oh well, back to the drawing board on the nickname front.'

'He's with Barbara at the moment, over in Oaken Copse. I'm meeting him at the inquest in –'

The sergeant erupted. 'OH NO!'

Greg spun round to see what had elicited this reaction. Had someone come into the station carrying a bomb? A machine gun? A headless corpse? All he saw were two harmless looking people: a man in his sixties who was dramatically bald in tweeds and a raincoat; and a pleasant-looking woman of about fifty who could easily be selling raffle tickets for the Women's Institute.

'Lay visitors,' Maybey hissed.

'Ah!' Lay police station visitors arrived unannounced at least once a fortnight to make sure that offenders in the cells were being treated properly: that they knew why they were being detained, had been offered a solicitor, a meal where appropriate and a doctor if necessary.

Greg knew that Maybey had no real objection to them since he ran his custody suite by the book, but they took up valuable time. They were appointed by the council's police committee and were supposed to reflect the demography of the area but were, inevitably, largely middle-aged, middle-class and white.

The sergeant strode forward with a smile of welcome strapped to his face. 'Professor Osborne, Dr Tilbury. How nice to see you, as always. Come this way.'

Greg went up to his office, shaking his head. Hard to believe that Custody Sergeant was one of the most responsible roles in the whole station.

He considered suggesting Alphabet Boy as a nickname for Peck, but he didn't want to have to explain it.

Andy reported that he had tracked down Gillian's bank accounts and done the paperwork to make Barclays in Hounslow divulge the details. She had a current account with them containing three hundred and eighteen pounds and there was just over a thousand on deposit.

Her Barclaycard was maxed out to its credit limit of three thousand pounds and it was over a year since she'd paid off more than the monthly minimum. Like the local solicitors, the bank had no knowledge of a will.

She had no regular incomings, banking a largish cheque three or four times a year. Outgoings were the usual: household utilities, sixty pounds a week in cash for food and daily necessities. She was usually overdrawn by the time the next cheque arrived.

Presumably the credit card was the luxuries.

Hard up, Greg thought, and averagely bad at managing what she had. Averagely messy.

She had needed money, which made him think of blackmail, which brought him back reluctantly to Lavinia Latham. But who in their right mind would cross Vinnie?

Vacuuming was not Angie's favourite activity but once a fortnight she would drag the hoover from the cupboard under the stairs and do the whole house at once, get it over with. It was odd, she thought, that, however equal the relationship might be between her and Greg, she always ended up doing the hoovering.

As an essay for Dr Burnside was giving her particular

trouble, this morning seemed like a good time for displacement activity. Once in such circumstances, she had resorted to cleaning the windows.

She did the ground floor and was half way up the stairs when a sound distracted her. She switched off the hoover for a second to listen. As she'd thought, the phone was ringing. She switched the machine back on again and vacuumed with renewed vigour.

She could still hear the phone ringing, perhaps twenty times before the caller gave up. She ran the hoover round the bedroom carpet then picked up the handset by the bed and dialled 1471.

'You were called today at ten-forty-seven,' the mechanical voice said. 'The caller withheld his number.'

She hung up and wiped a patch of dust off the bedside table with her hand. Then she sat down rather suddenly on the patchwork quilt and began to cry. She didn't try to stop it but let herself weep copiously for several minutes till the fit stopped of its own accord.

She found she felt much better. She wiped her eyes on her sleeve and resumed her mindless housework.

Should she do the spare room? In a way it seemed like an intrusion, but to leave it seemed mean. Oh, who was she kidding? She wanted to nose through Stuart's things. She pushed the door open and went gingerly in.

Peck hadn't brought much with him from Kent, but what he had brought he had distributed generously about the room. His suitcase lay open on the floor, blocking the route to the window, while a pair of jeans, two shirts and an assortment of pants and socks lay across the foot of the bed.

Maybe he suffered from cold feet in the night.

She gave up all pretence of cleaning and crossed to the chest of drawers to examine the pile of objects on top: a grubby handkerchief, a set of keys, presumably to his house in Kent, aftershave, deodorant, fake tanning lotion – that explained a lot – hairbrush with a few blond hairs in it, large box of tissues.

She picked up a couple of bottles: moisturising cream *and* exfoliant. Somebody fancied himself. She tried to imagine circumstances in which Greg would use moisturiser and failed but the image of him smearing the stuff carefully over his nose and cheeks made her giggle.

She left everything undisturbed and closed the door carefully behind her. The telephone began to ring again and she took a sudden decision to clean the bathroom while she was in the swing of things.

Greg's mobile rang as he opened his office door, a few tinny bars of Mozart, apparently played on a hurdy gurdy. The display flashed the letters VL.

'Miss Latham,' he said, flopping into his chair.

'Made an arrest yet?' she asked.

'No.'

'Good. Well, not good, but I wouldn't want to have wasted my time. I have a present for you. I don't know how helpful it'll be but at least it'll fill in some background. It's called Philip Abernethy and he'll be with you around lunchtime as he's driving down from Northampton.'

'Miss Latham –'

She'd hung up. When he tried to call her back, there was nothing, not even her voice mail.

'Bloody woman,' he said.

14

Greg was surprised by the size of the crowd outside Newbury Town Hall that morning. He'd expected the country's press to be there for the inquest but had not anticipated so many members of the public filling the Market Place across from the strange building that looked as if it had been stolen from Tuscany on some commando raid.

He was on foot and slipped in unnoticed at the side door. Peck was already there, slurping coffee from a paper cup.

'You found it okay then,' Greg said.

The DCI didn't reply to this pointless question but nodded to a nearby door which had just opened.

'The bereaved,' he said grimly.

Maureen Bateman and her husband walked through the door and stood for a moment in the hallway, looking faintly bewildered. Greg got a close look at Peter Bateman for the first time and saw an exhausted – perhaps broken – man.

No doubt the *Outlook on Sunday* was putting the couple up at a luxury hotel or safe house while they told their story. It would be as far removed from a prison cell as it was possible to get, yet Bateman looked as if he hadn't eaten or slept in days.

Prisoners longed for release, Greg knew, but when their incarceration came to such an abrupt end – without the usual preliminaries of open prison, weekend visits home, a part-time job, the gradual resumption of normality – their reaction was not always as expected.

Bateman was probably lost without his routine, his

hard and narrow bed, brusque warders telling him what to do twenty-four hours a day, the bars at his window. He felt exposed, even endangered.

He thought the Batemans looked awkward together, standing slightly apart, not touching or making eye contact. Had he not known who they were, he might have taken them for strangers thrown into conjunction by circumstance.

For Maureen, it must be as if her husband had come without warning back from the dead. She was used to doing without him, to surviving, unable even to touch him on her monthly prison visits beyond a brief hug on meeting, every movement scrutinised by prison warders alert for the covert passage of drugs from hand to hand, mouth to mouth.

He found that he was expecting them to put on a show of solidarity, perhaps hold hands, at this ordeal.

Ordeal? It must be that, the murder of their daughter, and yet there could be ambivalence too, towards the girl who had put them both through hell.

The *Outlook* minders were present, four of them, still in sunglasses, their muscled shoulders too broad for their jackets. They didn't attempt to look inconspicuous, as a truly professional bodyguard would, but bounced on the balls of their feet, their eyes everywhere, their fists ready. More ornament than use, Greg concluded, there to intimidate.

Behind them was a small, fat figure in a blue suit whom he recognised from the television as the Batemans' solicitor, the man he thought of as Napoleon.

Mrs Bateman noticed Greg and turned her head deliberately away. He looked away too, not wanting to be caught staring, having no desire to intrude. He went to say something to Peck but the DCI put down his empty cup and walked towards the Bateman party. The bodyguards bristled at him but, knowing a policeman when they saw one, did not have the nerve to stop him.

'Mrs Bateman.' he spoke in a loud, confidant voice. 'It's Stuart Peck, from Lower Shorne. Don't you remember me?'

She peered doubtfully at him. 'Stuart ... Not Sally Peck's little boy?'

'Not so little these days.'

'No ...' Her manner warmed and she shook the hand he was holding out to her. 'Young Stuart. Of course I remember you. How is your mum?'

He bowed his head. 'She passed away some years ago, I'm afraid. Breast cancer.'

Maureen clapped her hand to her mouth. 'I'm so sorry, Stuart. I hadn't heard ...' She sought about for another topic of conversation. 'Didn't you used to want to join the police?'

'I did.' Peck looked her straight in the eye without shame. 'Join. Detective Chief Inspector in Rochester now.'

'Oh.' Her manner grew cold again. 'Then I don't understand what you're doing here, Mr Peck, unless it's some sort of cover up. That's it, isn't it? You're here to cover that bastard Ashton's back.'

'No way is that going to happen, Mrs Bateman ...'

'Hello, Superintendent.'

Greg glanced round at being thus hailed and saw Xavier Browne, now in his workaday office suit, grey with a darker stripe, the same expensive briefcase hunched under his right arm. 'The Home Secretary wants me to keep a watching brief,' he explained.

'Fair enough.'

'There are calls for a full public enquiry into Kent's handling of the case.'

'So I gathered from the BBC. Will there be one?' Browne shrugged ignorance: it was not his decision. 'The Home Secretary should look on the bright side,' Greg added. 'Mr Bateman was jailed under the Conservatives.'

It seemed that Peck had succeeded in placating Maureen Bateman who was introducing him to the solicitor.

'It's Superintendent Summers, isn't it?'

'Yes, sir.'

Greg turned to shake hands with the West Berkshire coroner and introduced Browne. He'd never seen Dr Derek Walpole smile, but then his job was akin to that of the undertaker in that he was always in the company of the bereaved; worse, since the undertaker dealt mostly with those who had died peacefully of illness or old age, whereas Dr Walpole was confronted daily with the angry and bewildered relatives of sudden and unexplained death.

'Quite a scrum out there,' Walpole remarked glumly. 'And in here.' He glared at the *Outlook* bodyguards and the chief minder hastily took off his sunglasses and folded them into his top pocket; his colleagues followed suit in unison, as if it was a stage routine they had rehearsed.

'Press from all over England,' the coroner went on, satisfied with the efficacy of the official scowl he had perfected over the years, 'and a good few rubberneckers.'

'High profile case,' Greg said.

'I watch TV too, Superintendent. You know I won't tolerate histrionics in my court. Any trouble and I'll have the place cleared.'

'We have extra officers outside in the Market Place,' Greg told him. 'I can bring some in, if you like.'

'No, let's get started. Those, I take it, are the mother and stepfather.' Walpole paused. 'Is he going to be all right?'

Greg and Browne followed the direction of his gaze.

Even allowing for the pallor of years of incarceration, Peter Bateman looked white enough to faint. As they watched, Peck took his arm and led him tenderly into the room where the inquest was to be held, the tabloid bodyguards hovering uselessly around them.

As they passed the three men, Bateman was explaining himself to Stuart. 'I knew she was still alive, you see. Gilly. I mean, I knew I hadn't killed her, so it stood to reason ... All these years one of the things that kept me going was the thought that little Gilly would turn up safe and well one day. But now ...'

But now all hope is gone, Greg finished for him silently.

Dr Walpole had no intention of drawing out the proceedings for the pleasure of the media. While the law required that the inquiry into a sudden death be opened as soon as possible, immediate adjournment was the norm in the case of a murder.

He took evidence of Gillian's identity and cause of death then adjourned until such time as the police had finished their enquiries. It took all of five minutes. Greg had known what to expect but the Batemans looked dazed, as if they'd been short changed.

As he followed the *Outlook* party out of the room he heard Bateman turn to his wife and say pleadingly, 'We don't have to go back to that hotel, do we, Maur?'

'Just a couple more days, Pete. It's really nice there. You said yourself how posh the bathroom is. How private.'

'I want to go *home*.' His voice was quiet but clear, determined. 'I want to go back to the house in Shorne.'

'The house in Shorne is gone,' she said, a note of irritation creeping into her voice. 'You know that. I've explained enough times. I couldn't stay there, not with everyone thinking ... *Home* is a high-rise flat on an estate in Chatham.'

'Then it'll be handy for the docks,' Peter said hopefully.

The fat solicitor turned away not, Greg could see, catching his eye, in embarrassment, but in genuine distress for the deluded man who thought he still had a job in the docks. His irrational dislike for the lawyer ebbed and a glance of sympathy flashed between them.

'The docks closed long ago.' Maureen's irritation had become exasperation. 'I've told you that too. There's no job for you there. It's a ... *theme park*.'

As in so many places in old industrial Britain – the docks, the mines, the factories – real work, making things, had given way to the service industry. Thus men whose fathers and grandfathers had mined tin in Cornwall humiliated themselves in olde-yokel costumes as they served cider and pasties to tourists.

Greg thought it unlikely that Bateman would work again. After all this time, he would not know how. Besides, Peck was right and mud stuck. Long after the details of his case had been forgotten, people would look sideways at Peter and mutter that he'd been inside.

He wondered how much the *Outlook on Sunday* was paying the couple and hoped they'd held out for a fat sum, something that would let them make a fresh start, perhaps in a new part of the country. He knew that whatever compensation Bateman received for his miscarriage of justice might be years in coming.

'Press'll be camped on your doorstep too, Peter,' the head minder chipped in, putting his sunglasses back on as if he felt naked without them, prompting a reflex response from his colleagues. 'You'd get no peace.'

'I doubt I shall get any peace anyway,' Bateman said wearily. 'Please, Maur.'

She looked helplessly at her entourage. 'One more day, Pete. Okay?'

'Oh, very well.' He subsided, used to obeying orders.

One of the bodyguards opened the back door and called to the others that it was all clear. In an instant the Batemans were shepherded out to their limo.

Only 'Napoleon' remained and he came over to Greg, his hand outstretched. 'Jonathan Atkins, Superintendent, of Atkins & Son, solicitors in Rochester.'

'Yes, I saw you on TV.'

'Oh, God! Did you? I was so scared, I must have seemed very wooden. I pretty much said what they wanted to hear.' He smiled a sweet smile. 'My grandfather, Eric Atkins, represented Mr Bateman at the time of his arrest fifteen years ago. He went to his grave insisting that Peter Bateman had suffered a terrible wrong.'

So he was no ambulance chaser, no newspaper lackey. Greg could see now that his suit came from Burton's and fit his strange shape ill. 'It seems he was right, Mr Atkins.'

'So, I inherited the Batemans' woes seven years ago. There wasn't much work involved – an attempt at an appeal in 2000 which didn't reach first base – until Maureen rang me on Sunday night and gave me the shock of my life.'

'It's been a shock to us all,' Greg said.

'I don't want to talk about the initial miscarriage of justice – I know that's nothing to do with you – but I think it's important to Peter's peace of mind – and Maureen's too, of course – that Gilly's killer be brought to justice as quickly as possible. Then perhaps they can move on.'

He felt in his pocket for a business card. 'So if there's any way in which I can help, do call me.'

'Thank you.' Greg was glad to find the Batemans' solicitor was prepared to be helpful and not hostile and regretted his earlier dislike of the man. When would he learn not to trust first impressions?

A bodyguard appeared in the doorway and said, 'You coming or what, Mr A?'

Atkins smiled an apology and left.

Help the Batemans move on, especially Peter. There was nothing Greg would like better; but at the moment he had no leads in his murder case, and no real suspects.

15

Peck announced that he was going back to Ivy Cottage to rejoin Barbara. Greg returned to the police station.

On his way in, he encountered two inexperienced young constables, Jill Christie and Emily Foster, escorting a subdued-looking teenager into the custody area.

'Well, well,' he said. 'Loyd Evans, a regular customer. What is it this time?' Evans had a string of convictions for shop-lifting, burglary and minor vandalism; since he was only sixteen the magistrates had been lenient with him so far – too lenient in Greg's view.

His hobby was setting off car alarms; he had no interest in stealing the vehicles but would bounce up and down on the bonnets until the siren shrieked into the suburban night and every householder in the street dialled 999.

'Caught him selling amphetamines outside a Fat Fighters meeting,' Emily said with a grin. 'In that church hall opposite Marks. Told the women they'd help them lose weight. Ten quid a time.'

Greg raised his eyebrows. 'Progressed to dealing drugs now, Loyd. You really are on the slippery slope, aren't you?'

'They're only breath mints, Mr Summers, swear on my mother's grave.'

'That reminds me,' Greg said to the women. 'He's only sixteen, whatever he's told you. Make sure to call his mother, Myfanwy, who is alive and well and living on state benefits.' He turned back to Loyd. 'There's no point in lying, boy, the lab will soon tell us what the pills are.'

'Breath mints, Mr S. I swear. Tic Tacs. Wouldn't touch no drugs, me. Seen what they do to people, like.'

'Let's have a look,' Greg said.

Jill produced a transparent bag containing a dozen white pills. Greg took one out, sniffed it – it smelled of peppermint – and popped it in his mouth. The constables looked impressed and slightly apprehensive, while the Custody Sergeant tutted quietly to himself and raised his eyes to the heavens at this breach of protocol.

'That's a Tic Tac,' Greg told them. 'Ten quid a pop? Book him in and charge him with fraud.'

'Aw, Mr Summers.'

He walked up to his office with a spring in his step, rather pleased with this little encounter, giving rookie cops a lesson in practical policing. Most front-line policing was done by constables barely out of nappies, a fact kept secret from the public who were fed a diet of TV cop shows where grizzled old men with twenty years service under their belts dispensed wise justice.

He stopped in the outer office where Susan Habib was jabbing ineffectually at her computer screen.

'It's frozen,' she announced. 'Again.'

'While you're waiting for it to be fixed,' Greg said, 'I'd like you to pop into town and see if you can find me a copy of a novel called *Playing to Win* by Gillian Lestrange at any of the local bookshops.'

Susan bridled. She was a plain woman of only average intelligence and with an idiosyncratic take on the art of spelling. Given these handicaps, Greg thought she might make an effort to be pleasant so that people could at least say of her 'Susan has a good personality'; instead, she cultivated a sullen disposition and was inclined to take offence where none was offered.

As now. 'I thought we'd established that it was not part of my job to run your personal errands, Mr Summers,' she said through tight lips.

'It's not a personal errand. It's work. The author is our latest murder victim.'

'Oh. Then surely a member of CID –'

'Just do it!' Greg said, sweeping into his office and slamming the door. He felt pleased at a rare victory. Half an hour later he got a call from Xavier Browne which pulled him back down to earth.

'The Home Secretary has appointed a judge to hold a public enquiry into the jailing of Peter Bateman,' he said. 'Thought I'd let you know before you heard it on the news. It's Mrs Justice Gore, but she won't start work until the Lester woman's murder has been solved. We felt it might muddy the waters.'

So, no pressure there, Greg thought, as he hung up. He rubbed his eyes; he half wished the white tablet *had* been an amphetamine. He looked at his watch. It was half past twelve, which might count as lunchtime, when his present from Vinnie Latham was due.

Philip Abernethy was a prosperous looking man in his early fifties. He arrived at one o'clock and accepted Greg's offer of lunch without unnecessary fuss. The two men adjourned to a quiet corner of the police canteen.

'I'm sorry I didn't come forward before,' Abernethy began. 'I'd heard about the murder in Hungerford on the news, of course, and the subsequent revelations of the victim's identity, but I didn't make the connection until your officer came to see me first thing this morning.'

'My officer?'

'Tall, slim woman, blonde. Lavenham?'

'Latham.'

'She was your officer?'

'She's another force,' Greg said. A force of Nature. 'What do you mean about not making the connection?'

'Well, I knew her as Gillian Liversedge, then Gillian Abernethy, of course.'

'She was your wife?' Greg said, startled.

Abernethy looked appalled at the idea. 'God, no! She was my stepmother. She married my father, Walter Abernethy.'

'Can we begin at the beginning? How long ago did you know her?'

He thought about it, ate a forkful of shepherd's pie, and said, 'Eight years – nearly nine, because it was in the spring that I first met her. My mother had died the previous autumn and my father was no housekeeper. I offered him a home with my wife and me but he wanted his independence so he employed a string of part-time women to clean and cook.'

'A string of them?'

'None of them lasted long as he was rather a demanding old man. When Gillian turned up, I assumed she'd survive no longer than the rest since she was little more than a girl – twenty, twenty-one – and seemed to have no more clue about housework than Dad did, judging by the state of the house that day and the lunch she served us.'

'But she did last,' Greg said.

'You could say that.' He gave a hollow laugh, forking up some peas and carrots. 'She seemed so young and callow.'

'That's one thing she wasn't,' Greg said. 'Callow.'

'A month later I got a letter from Dad announcing that he and this woman had been married quietly at Stamford register office the previous day. I suppose he didn't have the nerve to tell me over the phone.'

'You must have been horrified,' Greg said.

'I'll say, but what could I do? It was a *fait accompli*.'

'Was he a rich man?' Greg asked.

'Not especially. There was the family house in Stamford, of course, and he had a good pension but that would die with him. He had a few thousand in the building society but she went through that pretty quickly – expensive holidays, a new car for her, that sort of thing.'

'And your father ...?'

'Dead about a year later. Heart attack. Nothing sinister about that; he'd had a bad heart for some time and we always thought he'd go before Mum, but she didn't exactly encourage him to look after himself. He started smoking again after her arrival and there was always a bottle of whisky open when I went there to check up on him, which wasn't often as she made it clear I wasn't welcome.'

Encouraging an old man to lead an unhealthy life wasn't murder, Greg thought, not even manslaughter.

'Maybe she just wanted him to enjoy what time he had left,' he suggested.

'That was what I tried to tell myself. Anyway, he'd made a will leaving everything to her and there was nothing I could do about it, all perfectly legal. It's not as if he wasn't in his right mind and, after all, it's hardly unreasonable for a man to make provision for his widow.'

'So what became of her then?' Greg asked.

'I have no idea. She put the house on the market the moment she got probate and when I rang her a few weeks later – to ask if I might have some personal memento of my father – I got the new owners. Seems she'd used a house clearance firm to dispose of the contents.' With a note of bitterness, he concluded, 'She'd taken the money and disappeared without trace.'

She was good at disappearing, Greg thought. He said, 'You're certain we're talking about the same woman?'

'Chief Inspector Latham showed me some photos, one

of her at fifteen and one recent. Neither actually looked like the woman I knew at first glance but on closer examination I could see that they were what she had been and what she would become.'

'So what did she look like when you knew her?'

'Plump, but not exactly fat. Her hair was that same colour but shorter and not so curly.' He shivered slightly. 'It was the eyes that convinced me, those greedy, malevolent eyes.'

'You must have hated her.'

'Yes,' Abernethy said simply. 'I hated her. My parents were married for forty-five years and that was our family home, where I grew up, and it was all soured, spoiled. I'm not a callous man, Superintendent, but it sounds to me as if she finally got what she deserved.'

'As a matter of form, sir, I must ask you where you were on the night of November sixth to seventh.'

'In Frankfurt,' he said promptly. 'On business. I went to the opera with a client in the evening, then I had a breakfast meeting at my hotel in the morning.'

It was as good an alibi as Greg had heard in thirty years, except for the man who'd been in a prison cell on a drunk and disorderly the night his wife fell down the stairs and broke her neck.

'So that explains where the money for the flat in Isleworth came from,' Barbara said. She had finished taking down Abernethy's statement and he'd signed it and left. 'And it gives us some idea of what Gillian was up to during the missing years.'

'There may be more than one disgruntled stepson for all we know,' Greg said. 'Are we any nearer finding a will?'

'None of the solicitors Nick has spoken to so far have

170

heard of her. She could have used a firm in central London. It's a bit of a needle-in-a-haystack job.'

'You've tried Somerset House, on the off chance that she might have registered a will there?'

'I have and she didn't. Why would she?'

'No reason,' Greg said, since most people didn't realise that it was even possible to register a will with the Probate Office, a document that could not then be easily super-seded. 'In the absence of a will,' he mused, 'that leaves Mrs Bateman her sole heir.'

'You don't really think money was the motive for this murder?' Barbara queried.

'No. I think she was killed by somebody who hated her, and I'm starting to think that may be no short list.'

Barbara waved her copy of Abernethy's statement. 'I'll get this alibi checked out then.'

She left.

It took Susan Habib well over two hours to return from her visit to Newbury and Greg was starting to think that she'd gone home in a huff when she tapped on the door of his office to announce failure.

'Waterstones had one copy last week but sold it the day after the murder,' she reported. 'They've taken orders for two dozen more since. Smiths are also awaiting delivery. They both asked if I wanted to order a copy, but I thought I should ask you first.'

'Okay,' Greg said. 'I shall try other means.' He added, 'Thank you, Susan,' and she snorted and left.

There really was no such thing as bad publicity.

He sat at his desk mulling over the case when a horrible thought struck him. Suppose Barbara was right and Gillian Lester had found out something about Vinnie Latham that she wasn't meant to. Okay, Vinnie might have acted fast but there was someone else who was protective of

Vinnie and that woman was not lacking in courage or the will to act.

She had also been right in the vicinity of the crime at the time it was committed and Gillian would not have hesitated to let her into the cottage.

Just because he liked the old woman, that didn't mean she wasn't a killer. In fact, he knew she was a killer, only she'd done it in wartime, to Nazis, which was okay; except that it meant you could do it: you knew how to kill and live with the guilt, and that set you apart from other people.

Maybe the charming, feckless Irish husband had died young because she'd murdered him.

Outside it was a mild day, dry with a glimmer of sun. He needed to be out of the office, in his car, alone with his thoughts if he was ever to see his way through this puzzle.

He spent five minutes looking for his mobile phone, then gave up and rang the number from his desk. He heard it cooing like a dove in the outer office and Susan's surprised voice said, 'Mr Summer's phone ... Hello?'

He hung up, went out, extracted the phone from her and put it in his pocket. 'I'm going out for a bit, Susan. I'm on my mobile if anyone needs me.'

He noticed that her computer screen was still frozen.

He got in his car and drove to Upper Denford, expecting to find Honeysuckle Cottage still closed up and empty. He was surprised, therefore, when Adele Finnegan opened the door to his knock.

'You're back,' he said.

'Dearly as I love Vinnie ...' she stepped aside to let him in, following him into the sitting room, 'I'm used to blessed solitude and after three days she was driving me crazy. Did you like your present? Mr Abernethy?'

He turned to face her. 'Just what I always wanted.

Which reminds me – please tell your niece not to go impersonating a police officer.'

'I doubt if she did. She has that air of authority and people make assumptions.'

'Would you mind telling me where you were on Thursday night, Mrs Finnegan?'

'Oh, so that's the way your mind's running.' She grinned with genuine merriment, showing pre-war teeth, crooked and more yellow than white.

'Routine,' he said, 'covering all the bases.'

'And what's my motive supposed to be, just as a matter of interest?'

'To protect Vinnie.' Greg was beginning to feel foolish.

'Uhuh. From what?'

'Something Gillian found out that she wasn't supposed to.'

'Interesting. Let me tell you something about Vinnie; like most military people, she's deeply conservative. She would go to any lengths to do something she believed to be right, but nothing on earth would make her do something she knew to be wrong. The skeletons that were about to fall out of MI5's cupboard were not hidden there by her. Okay?'

'... Okay.'

'Now that we've got that cleared up,' Adele said, 'I was about to call you, since I remembered something I thought you ought to know.'

'Oh, yes?'

She gestured to him to sit and he did so. As before, she remained standing, giving herself, wittingly or unwittingly, a psychological advantage. He suspected that very little Adele Finnegan did was unwitting. She leaned against the mantelpiece as she spoke, her arms folded across her bosom.

'There was a man hanging about on Tuesday evening. It's probably irrelevant as Gilly died on Thursday, but it's unusual to find people in the copse after dark at this time of year. It's not as if he was walking a dog, even.'

'What time was this?'

'Early. Six-ish.'

'Can you describe him for me?' Greg asked.

'Alas, no. It was the dark quarter and all I could see was the shape of him. I didn't recognise him as anyone local, that I can tell you. He was tall and quite thin, though well wrapped up against the weather.'

'Would you know him again if you saw him?'

She thought about it. 'Perhaps. Probably not.'

He got up to go. 'Well let me know if you do.' He remembered something. 'Oh, yes! Could I possibly borrow that novel of Gillian's?'

'Sure.' She fetched it.

'I'll return it as soon as possible.'

'Don't worry about it. I shan't want to reread it.'

He opened the book at the front and saw that Gillian had signed it on the flyleaf. *For Adele with best wishes from Gilly.* 'Might be worth something,' he commented, 'so I shall be sure to return it.'

As she saw him out, she said, 'I think you must be Keats' watcher of the skies.'

'Pardon?'

'Gregory: it means a watcher.'

'I didn't know that.'

'Rather appropriate for a policeman, don't you think?'

'Yes,' he said, pleased. 'I do.'

It was a good job for a nosy parker, as George Formby had said of cleaning windows. If Adele Finnegan was a liar then she was a good one, giving the impression that lying was beneath her dignity. The fact that she had spent

174

three years in occupied France peddling falsehood to everyone she met did not slip his memory.

He'd sometimes had arguments late at night in the bar at courses and conferences about whether men or women made the better liars. Most con artists were men, true, but Greg maintained that mendacity came more naturally to the female of the species, although that might be nothing more than the sourness of the deceived divorcé.

He drove slowly back through Lower Denford, over the river Kennet and into Kintbury, bypassing his own road and carrying on up the hill through Inkpen onto the Berkshire Downs. After a few minutes, he pulled off the road and into the car park at Combe Gibbet, a Neolithic long barrow that marked the highest point for miles round.

It was a site popular with tourists and ramblers but he was the only person there that day. He took out his mobile and called Nicolaides.

'Tell me again what your nurse said ...'

She said she had a tattoo. Nicolaides had thought about little else since. A tattoo of what? Exactly where?

'About the man she saw on the stairs on Tuesday night,' Greg continued, oblivious to the fact that his constable's thoughts were tumescently elsewhere.

'Not a lot.' Nicolaides forced himself to get a grip on the subject. 'Tall and thin and carrying a bag.'

'Is that really the best she can do, Nick?'

'It was dark, sir. The bulb had gone on the stairs. Literally. Somebody had nicked it.'

Greg considered this. 'Did you check the bins for it?'

'... They'd been collected the morning I went there.'

'That's bad luck.'

'That's what I thought.'

'What sort of light fitting is it?'

175

'Sir?'

'Is it fixed close against the ceiling, or dangling?'

'Dangling.'

'Then he'd have held the fitting to steady it as he removed the bulb. Get SOCO to dust the ceiling rose for prints.'

'Right away.' They hung up.

Greg got out of the car. There was no shelter in this high place, no respite from a frisky wind; he turned his collar up, climbed nimbly over the stile into the long barrow and walked to the gibbet. The original gibbet was long gone, of course, but was always replaced after wind or lightning or time had destroyed it; although it had not been used since the 17th century it was part of Newbury's history and also, perhaps, a warning.

He leaned against the post, unworried by its gruesome past, accustomed to it since childhood. No ghosts walked here, or not for young Gregory Summers, son of the Berkshire downs, on his bike, in his short trousers, his knees scarred and grazed, out for the whole day with sandwiches and a freedom that children no longer enjoyed.

He was standing a thousand feet above sea level: on one side the Vale of Newbury, to the other the fertile farms of Hampshire. He looked out over the familiar and beloved landscape without seeing it, trying to clear his mind.

He would come anew to his case as if he were an officer from another force, brought in for oversight.

Gillian Lester had been fifteen at the time of her disappearance and looked younger. It was not impossible that she had run away on her own – kids did it every day and could be seen begging, or worse, on the streets of London – but it would have been much easier if she'd had someone to help her, to provide money and shelter.

She'd told Vinnie that she'd run off with a boyfriend her parents didn't approve of. The fact that the Batemans knew of no such boyfriend to approve or disapprove did not mean that he didn't exist. And if she'd run off with a man then he had a lot to answer for, not least the fact that she was below the age of consent.

And she had spoken to Vinnie of writing her own memoirs. What if it had been her – Gillian's – secrets and not those of MI5 that had led a panicking someone to murder?

A tall, thin man. That had been the description given to him by Adele Finnegan and to Nick by his tame nurse. Vague enough to cover millions of men. And both on Tuesday, not Thursday. A tall thin man: he'd heard those words from someone else's lips recently, he was sure of it, but from whom? He shook his head. One day, soon, it would all be clear to him; just not today.

He drove carefully back down the unmade track, his car flinging up loose stones on either side, skidding once. What with this and Oaken Copse maybe he should get an off-road vehicle, a four-wheel drive; but he'd feel stupid parking at the supermarket in it.

He had to stop at the end of the track to wait for a tractor to make its plodding way up the hill, a few bales of mangy-looking hay its only cargo. As he waited, he glanced back at the gibbet.

From here it was a tall, thin man, being crucified.

16

Barbara stifled a yawn. Seldom had she been at such an empty crime scene. Not that she particularly liked sifting through the detritus of the newly dead, which often included soiled underwear and spoiled food, but at least you might learn something about them that way, even if only that they were an insanitary slattern.

Clearly Vinnie Latham lived out of a suitcase and used this place only for sleeping. Even the attic was devoid of the usual old furniture and tatty suitcases full of clothes that might one day come back into fashion. The kitchen cupboards yielded up a dozen tins of beans, a can of tomato soup that was past its use-by date and some rice with what looked suspiciously like mouse droppings in it.

The fridge had been more helpful, containing provisions that Gillian had bought for her stay from Somerfield in Hungerford, ready-to-eat meals that could be shoved in the microwave and which would not keep her from her work.

Martha Childs had just gone rushing off back to Isleworth following a phone call from Nick. It was a nuisance to have two scenes of crime so far apart, especially when one of them was in another police force's jurisdiction, but it could have been worse: Gillian could have lived in East London.

Andy Whittaker was acting as exhibits officer for the case, ensuring the integrity of the chain of evidence, so that at the eventual trial he could swear on oath that none of the exhibits had been contaminated. It was a necessary but tedious task, one that every constable tried to avoid, except for Chris Clements, Andy's former partner when he'd been in uniform, who was a bit of an anorak so that cataloguing stuff – preferably Star Trek memorabilia – was his idea of fun.

Andy nudged Barbara and rolled his eyes towards the upper storey. Barbara could hear Stuart Peck, his voice quite clear through the uncarpeted floors.

'So if you fancied a couple of weeks in Malta, maybe over Christmas.'

She heard the youngest SOC officer, Janie Morrison, only two years out of school and still impressionable, say, 'Ooh, that sounds lovely, sir.'

'DCI Peck hasn't invited me to his holiday home yet,' Andy whispered.

'You're the wrong gender, my friend.'

'Hello. Is anyone there?'

Barbara went to the door. 'Mrs Finnegan? You're back.'

'So people keep telling me. I thought I'd take a walk over this way, see if you'd finished with the cottage yet.'

'It'll be a few days still,' Barbara explained. 'Did you want to use it?'

'No, just to be sure it's secure.'

'Well, it's the safest house in Berkshire at the moment,' Barbara said. 'It's swarming with police officers.'

'Good point. Well –'

'Babs! Have we –?'

DCI Peck came down the stairs at that moment, a dark shape in the gloom of the little cottage, making them all jump. Mrs Finnegan stared up at him.

'Whom have we here?' he asked. Barbara explained and he offered Mrs Finnegan his hand. 'Been hearing a lot about your niece,' he commented.

'How do you do.' She examined his face as if memorising it, continuing long enough, Barbara thought, to make a less vain man uncomfortable. 'I'll leave you to it.'

180

'I'll see you out,' Barbara said.

She was glad of some fresh air and, on the fine autumn afternoon, fell companionably into step with the old woman, not needing to slow her usual brisk pace for her as they headed back along the track towards Upper Denford.

'Who did you say that tall man was?' Mrs Finnegan demanded suddenly.

'DCI Peck. He's not one of our officers, down here on behalf of the Kent force.'

'That being where Gilly went missing all those years ago?'

'Yes.'

'So how long's he been here?'

Barbara thought about it. 'He got here late Monday night.'

'*This* Monday, after the murder?'

'Well ... yes. Obviously.'

'Obviously,' Mrs Finnegan agreed.

Greg had to empty the rubbish bins after supper that Wednesday evening, not a favourite job. If he could employ a footman to do just one task about the house, it would be this. With all the division of labour among modern couples, he reflected, somehow emptying the bins remained a strictly male function: dirty and smelly.

He trailed dutifully around kitchen, sitting room, study, bathroom, bedrooms, emptying all the waste paper baskets into his master, Xtra-strong, plastic sack. When it was full, he knotted it with a piece of string, heaved it over his shoulder like Santa's present sack, and let himself out of the back door into the garden.

As he headed for the shed, the security spotlight came on below the guttering, sensitive to his movement, and he saw something stir out of the corner of his eye. He stood stock still, then turned very slowly to find himself face to face with a fox, frozen in the unexpected beam. It was a skinny creature, little bigger than a ginger cat, its black eyes mournful in the winter darkness.

If the government had their way, fox hunting would soon be outlawed and then, no doubt, his garden would be knee deep in the animals. He would be expected to enforce the ban, too, as if he didn't have enough laws to police, and thousands of ordinary people, previously of good character, would acquire a criminal record in a concerted campaign of civil disobedience.

As if there weren't more important things to legislate against. He had occasionally followed the hunt on his bicycle as a boy. It had been the highlight of a dull winter weekend.

'Shoo,' he said and the fox, obligingly, shooed, gliding noiselessly into the rhododendron hedge. It would get slim pickings here anyway since he kept his rubbish locked safely in the shed until Friday morning when it went out on the pavement for the binmen.

He felt no animosity towards the fox, so long as it didn't attack his beloved Bellini.

Slamming the shed door shut and locking it, he turned to look back at the house, his castle. The security light had gone off now and he could see the kitchen illuminated like a beacon calling him back behind his drawbridge.

Except that he could now see the invader, the marauder, the Visigoth, Stuart Peck, standing too close to Angie, who was creased up with laughter at something he had said, her face turned to him in friendship and pleasure. As Greg watched, he put his hand on her arm to emphasise some point and she did not draw away.

He felt no animosity towards Peck, so long as he didn't

make eyes at his girlfriend, but had the bloody man moved in permanently? Hadn't he heard of hotels? Wasn't it bad enough that she had some secret admirer on the phone at all hours of the day and night with his angel-themed songs?

He hurried back into the house. 'Stuart,' he said calmly, a big smile glued to his face. 'Still with us?'

'Can't tell you how much I appreciate your hospitality, guv,' Peck said easily. 'You get so desperate stuck in some grotty hotel when you're out in the field. Well, you know.'

'Yeah.'

Bellini came into the room, made straight for Peck, headbutted his calf, then sat gazing up at him in adoration. He leaned down to scratch behind her ear and she mewed with delight.

Traitor, Greg thought. In a minute he'd be asking her if she fancied a trip to Malta.

Peck took his mobile out. 'Just dialling up a pizza. Can I get you two anything?'

'No thanks,' Greg said. 'We've eaten.'

He went into the sitting room, feeling his back bristling. Peck was like a cockerel who thought the sun came up solely to hear him crow. Greg fancied a really good sulk. He sat down in his favourite armchair, closed his eyes and breathed deeply while he counted to a hundred.

When he opened them again, Angie was standing quietly in front of him, watching him with a mixture of concern and amusement.

'Out with it,' she said, her hands on her hips.

'You and Peck are getting very pally,' he said.

'Hah! Is that all?' She lowered her voice, glancing back towards the kitchen. 'You're jealous of that creep? Do me a favour.'

Greg felt much better. 'Is he a creep?'

'Trust me, Gregory. A) he fancies himself a ladies' man which is a major turn-off; b) he's not very bright and, frankly, a bit of a bore, and c) I could never go for a man who exfoliates his skin and uses fake tanning lotion.'

He laughed at her acid imitation of Peck's conversational style, all desire to sulk fled. She perched on the edge of the chair and his arm fell naturally around her waist. It was a good time to ask her about the phone calls but, somehow, he didn't. Why spoil a tender moment?

She bent her head and whispered in his ear, her breath tickling. 'Is he staying much longer?'

'Oh, I do hope not.' He kissed her. 'Did I ever tell you the story about Frederick and the naked ladies?'

'... No.'

'He was three, nearly four, and he was staying with me for the weekend. So I asked him what he'd been doing that week and he said, "I seen lots of naked ladies, Daddy". Turned out Diane had taken him to the gym with her, into the women's changing room. God, I was envious.'

'You like looking at strange women in the buff, huh?'

'... No.' He shuddered theatrically. 'Hate that.'

'That's a good story. What made you think of it?'

'Dunno. Just popped into my head.'

'Stuart didn't say anything then?'

'About what?'

'Nothing.'

Barbara stood outside the Tally Ho in Hungerford New Town, waiting for her colleague to catch her up. She'd ducked into the pub to make sure he wasn't there ahead of her but hadn't been tempted by the noise and bustle that night and had come back outside for her vigil.

She stood jiggling from one foot to the other, trying to

keep warm, wondering why she hadn't put a heavier coat on. Maybe she'd been hasty in turning down a Christmas trip to Malta, but since accepting would surely mean getting rather more inside her than just sunshine and cheap wine, she'd stick with her decision.

A black saloon car drew up alongside her and the window came electrically down, the driver leaning across to hail her, a second man silent in the passenger seat. Assuming he wanted directions, she put her face into the opening.

'You prostitute woman?' he asked enthusiastically. The accent sounded Slavic, she thought, maybe Balkans.

'No, I not prostitute woman,' she replied, drawing back.

The man looked downcast, his moustache wilting with disappointment. 'I told in England prostitute womans stand on street corner.'

'That's often true,' Barbara agreed, 'but not in Hungerford, not on a week night.'

'Oh. Sorry. Thank you.'

'You're welcome.'

'I buy you drink-maybe-dinner?' he said hopefully. 'I speak the English good, yes?'

'You speak English *well*,' she corrected him automatically.

'You see,' he said to his passenger. 'I tell you I speak the English good.'

She showed him her warrant card. 'Now push off before I run you in for soliciting.'

The man winced and said something. She didn't recognise the language but it seemed a fair bet that he was swearing. The car drew away, accelerating loudly.

'What did he want?' Nicolaides asked, appearing out of the darkness beside her.

'Lost his way. Any joy in Upper Denford or Radley?'

She felt rather than saw him shake his head in the darkness. 'Couple of people thought she looked familiar and one man said "Isn't that old Mrs Finnegan's niece?" but nobody's seen her here in the past week. How about Lower Denford and Avington?'

'Also a big heap of nothing. Oh, well. She could get to Ivy Cottage without coming through any of the villages, but it had to be tried. Thanks for your help, Nick.'

'My pleasure, ma'am.'

'Why did you call me that?'

He shrugged. 'Everyone says you'll be an inspector in a year or two so I was just practising.'

'Who's everyone?'

'Everyone. You're studying for the exams, aren't you?'

'Yes,' Barbara admitted, 'but that's a long way from promotion and I'm not sure I even want it as it'd mean a move back to uniform.'

'Only for a year or two,' Nicolaides said. 'The old man would have that uniform off you in no time.'

'I beg your pardon!' They both giggled then Barbara added, 'Still, a year's a long time to be pushing paper and then there's the loss of overtime so you're hardly better off for all the extra responsibility. Come on. I'll buy you a pint.'

'Fine by me,' he said, heading for the lounge bar.

As they drank their beer and shared a packet of crisps, he asked, 'Is he attractive, Mr Summers?'

'Yes,' Barbara said readily, 'in a slightly-over-the-hill sort of way.'

'But Angie Summers is younger than you, isn't she?'

'A good four or five years.'

'It can't last, surely.'

'I'm not so sure, but I think that's the thing in the world the governor's most afraid of.'

Nicolaides sighed and downed half a pint of beer in a mouthful. 'I can't stop thinking about that post mortem.'

'Why this one in particular?'

He grimaced. 'Never seen a bird that fat naked before.'

'Oh, charming!'

Greg saw what Adele Finnegan meant about *Playing to Win*. If reading for pleasure, he would not have got beyond the first couple of chapters, in which the hero and heroine met during their first senior Wimbledon one impossibly hot June day, fell in love at first sight at the age of seventeen, but were separated by fate in the shape of heartless coaches, greedy parents and the fact that they had no language in common apart from broken English.

He ploughed on. By half way through he was mildly interested to know if the little Albanian girl and the strapping Swede would see love conquer all. He suspected that he knew the answer. He detected no irony in the story and found it strange, given what he had so far learned about Gillian Lester, that she had such apparent faith in the power of true love to prevail.

Was this the woman who had let her stepfather go to jail, who had married Walter Abernethy for his money?

Was this a woman who'd had her clitoris pierced? Not the clitoral hood but the clitoris itself, as the pathologist had been at pains to emphasis, pain being the operative word.

Was this the real Gillian, hidden beneath a hard carapace?

'What you reading?' Angie asked. He held the book up to show her. 'Your latest dead body?' He nodded. 'Any good?'

'No.'

'That's a shame,' she said. 'It would have been nice for her to have written a good book before she died.'

Greg hadn't thought of it that way. He put the novel down and smiled up at her. 'Do you think women make better liars than men?'

'Yes.'

'You do?'

'We're better at everything.'

On which note, she made a graceful exit.

17

Greg found a song running through his head the next morning, try as he might to expel it.

'*Just call me angel of the morning,*' he warbled, pulling on his grey wool socks. '*Angel.*'

Out of the corner of his eye, he saw Angelica flinch, but she kept her voice casual. 'Why are you singing that?'

So that was one of them. 'Dunno. Just popped into my head. Dance?' He grabbed her and began to twirl her round but she disengaged herself with a frown, said, 'Oh, grow up' and left the bedroom. He followed her.

'Nice tenor, guv,' Peck said, beaming on the landing. 'Sing with the station choir, do you?'

'Don't think there is one,' Greg muttered.

He no longer felt neutral towards Stuart Peck; in fact, he had an urgent need to slap his honey-coloured face, his fake face. He laced his fingers behind his back for restraint. He disliked the man and, he realised, distrusted him. In what giddy world had he risen to be Chief Inspector, this tall, thin man with the bogus tan?

'Do you know the Met used to have a minstrel show?' Peck said, oblivious to the imminent danger to his bland features.

'Minstrel?' Greg was baffled, envisaging lutes, men in tights, courtly love.

'Black and white minstrel. Disbanded now, of course. Political correctness.'

'I should think so!' Angie marched into the bathroom and slammed the door on them both.

'Political correctness gone mad.' Peck pulled a face, expecting Greg to join in his disapproval.

Greg looked stonily at him and twined his fingers more tightly, wishing that Angie wouldn't march about the house dressed only in her underwear while Peck was there. He made an effort and asked, 'So what are you up to this morning, Stuart?'

'Thought I'd hang out at the mobile incident room in Denford, if that's okay with you.'

'Perfect. That'll free up Babs. Send her in to the station, will you? I have a little job for her.'

'Now are you quite sure, Mrs Bateman?'

Constable Mary Chase was at her most sympathetic and, as victim liaison officer for the Medway area, her reserves of sympathy were vast.

She stood in the boxy sitting room, assessing the flat out of the corner of her eye as she waited to be offered a seat and the inevitable cup of tea. She could see that Maureen Bateman had tried to make the place nice but lacked, not so much the money to achieve that end, as any sense or understanding of style.

Items did not match. That was the fashion now, as Mary knew from the home-decoration magazines she and her boyfriend pored over for the modest terraced house they had bought six months ago. Eclectic, they called it, but Mrs Bateman's furniture was not eclectic but a mish-mash; it was old-fashioned without being charming, worn without being comfortable.

'Only I can stay as long as you want,' she added. 'I'm here for you for days, weeks, months if necessary.'

'You're very kind, Constable Chase –' Maureen Bateman said coolly.

'Mary, please.'

'– but I've seen enough of the Kent police force to last several lifetimes.'

Mary Chase looked as if she'd been slapped. Her whole body sagged, as if her denim skirt and neat red blouse with matching cardigan were the only things holding her up. 'We're all gutted about what happened, Mrs Bateman.'

'Yes. Yes.' Maureen manoeuvred her towards the door like a prize-winning sheepdog.

Young as she was, Mary didn't give in easily and she tried again. 'Let me at least make you both a cup of tea before I go.' She glanced past Maureen to where Peter was sitting at the kitchen table in his pyjamas, his head in his hands. 'I'm sure Mr Bateman could do with one.'

'We just want to be left alone,' Maureen said.

'Is there anything I can do for you, Mr Bateman?' Mary asked, bypassing his keeper.

Peter raised his head and looked at her for the first time, although it was more as if he looked *through* her. He spoke to his wife and not to her. 'Is that a social worker?'

'Er, no,' Mary said.

'It looks like a social worker.'

'She's police,' Maureen snapped. 'Family liaison. We had one when Gilly disappeared – spying on us, as it turned out. Tall man who smiled too much. Remember?'

'No. It was a long time ago. Why isn't she in uniform?'

'How should I know?'

'We aim for informality,' Mary offered. 'I'm here not as part of the murder investigation, Mr Bateman ... Peter, but to support you and your wife. And then there's the press down in the car park,' she added to Maureen. 'I can help deal with them if they become too importunate.'

The minders were gone, the story told.

'They'll get bored very quickly when they find there's nothing to see,' Maureen said.

'I can even fetch the groceries for you, so you don't have to run the gauntlet.'

'We'll manage. There are tins.'

Mary had now been manoeuvred to the front door and was forced to capitulate.

'You have my mobile number,' she said.

'Yes.' Maureen closed the door behind her and sighed. 'I suppose some people find it a help,' she remarked. Her husband made no reply. 'Do you want anything, Pete? Coffee? Elevenses?'

He didn't look at her. 'What I want is to turn the clock back fifteen years. Can you do that?'

'You know I can't. No one can.'

'Then shut up and leave me alone.'

'Are you getting dressed today?'

No reply.

It was lunchtime before Barbara arrived in Greg's office.

'Sorry for the delay,' she said. 'Some old gent on house-to-house reckoned he'd seen something nasty in the wood-shed but it turned out to be nothing. I think he was just after some company. I should send the Mormons round.'

'No real rush,' he said.

'Good to have that extra pair of hands all the same,' she remarked, 'even if it is only temporary. Stuart said you had a job for me.'

'Yeah. Which airlines fly to Malta?' Greg asked.

Barbara wrinkled up her face as she considered this. She had long reached the conclusion that it was easier simply to answer the superintendent's questions, however esoteric. 'At a guess, British Airways and Air Malta. Scheduled flights, that is. There'd be all sorts of charter flights from places like Stansted and Luton.'

'But those would be for package holidays. If you owned your own place out there, then you'd probably need to take a scheduled flight, wouldn't you?'

'I guess. I only know one person who has a flat in Malta,' the sergeant added, after a pause for thought. She was starting to see her extra hands melting away like those of a snowman at the spring thaw.

'Yes, and can you see if that person was booked on a flight out there about two and a half weeks ago.'

'... I'll get right on it. Hello, Martha.'

'Hello, Babs.'

'Bye, Martha.' She left, closing the door behind her, leaving the SOC officer smiling wearily after her.

'Sit down, Martha,' Greg said.

'It's okay. I'm not stopping. I just came to tell you about that fingerprint you were looking for.'

'The one on the ceiling rose?' Greg got up in his eagerness.

'Not quite,' she said. 'It was on the ... I don't know what you call it.' She did a mime. 'The plastic light fitting itself where you would grasp it to change the bulb.'

'Yes. Right. Of course.'

'Only thumb and two fingers but nice and clear. So that's gone straight to Mr Gupta in Forensics. I'll be getting home.'

'Thanks for your hard work, Martha,' Greg said. 'I know we've been pushing you these last few days, what with sending you up to the Smoke and all, but it really is appreciated.'

He saw tears forming in her eyes and stared at her in alarm. 'Don't cry,' he said, then cursed himself. If there was one thing guaranteed to open the floodgates on a woman's tears it was saying 'Don't cry'. Shouldn't he know that at almost fifty? What he should have said was, 'Go on, have a good cry.' That would have shut her up.

Sure enough, she burst into tears, loud ragged sobs. Greg stared in horror, certain the whole station could hear her. What had he done or said to bring this on? He thought frantically but every word he had uttered since her arrival seemed wholly innocent.

He crept nearer and patted her on the shoulder. 'There, there,' he said helplessly. 'There, there.'

She turned towards him, stumbled into his arms and began to sob against the lapel of his jacket. This did not strike him as an improvement in the situation. He looked worriedly at the door of his office. What if Susan Habib picked this moment to walk in?

How would it look?

He felt in his pocket for a handkerchief and, pushing her away gently, offered it. She grasped it and snivelled into the white cotton for a moment.

'I'm so sorry,' she said, when she could speak. 'This is embarrassing. You've always been so kind.'

'Do you want to tell me about it?' he asked, hoping that she didn't. 'Is it the sick child?'

'Huh? No, the children are fine. It's Tim.'

'Your husband?' He had a dim idea that Mr Childs worked at Heathrow airport, possibly for British Airways, in some managerial capacity.

'He's left me.' Her voice began to shake again. 'For an air hostess.'

Greg almost said something foolish like, 'Oh well, an *air hostess*' – an inappropriate response to an awkward moment, like laughter at a funeral. They were every man's fantasy, after all, something about the mixture of uniform and servility. Luckily, he stopped himself in time.

'Called *Mandy*,' she wailed.

'Stupid name,' he sympathised briskly.

She gave a little laugh through her tears. 'Yes. Isn't it?'

'Quite unsuitable for a grown woman,' he added, getting into his stride.

'She's twenty-two, apparently, so she scarcely qualifies as a grown woman.'

'Oh.'

Twenty-two-year-old stewardess? Way to go, Tim.

'I'm ...' She wiped her tears, recovering. 'I can't apologise enough, Superintendent.'

'It's all right,' he said, feeling more relaxed. 'When did this happen?'

'Saturday. He used my being out at Ivy Cottage all night and then having to dash up to London as an excuse.'

'Oh, lord!'

She shook her head. 'It was just that: an excuse. He was deliberately picking a fight so he wouldn't feel so guilty, so much in the wrong.'

She seemed calmer now and he asked, 'How are you coping – I mean, practically?'

'Tim's mum's been brilliant. She's furious with him. Look ...' She gazed helplessly at his handkerchief then put it in her jacket pocket. 'I must go. Thanks for being so ...'

Before he could stop her, she stepped up to him again and kissed him on his cheek. He gave her a big encouraging smile, intended to praise her stoicism and expedite her departure. Then, somehow, she was in his arms and they were kissing.

Proper, grown-up kissing.

With tongues.

There was a knock on the door.

'Come in,' he croaked, shoving her away from him. 'Babs! That was quick. Thanks a million, Martha.' He knew he was gabbling like a guilty man and forced himself to slow down. 'I'll let you get off now.'

Barbara gave the older woman a curious look as she passed her. It had to be pretty obvious, Greg thought, that she'd been crying; hopefully, not so obvious that she had been kissing. Barbara made no comment but, waiting till they were alone with the door shut, said, 'You were right.'

'The words every man longs to hear.' Greg mentally dusted himself down and resumed his seat. 'About what?' He felt flustered and hoped it didn't show. He wiped his lips surreptitiously with his hand. He felt as if he could still taste her and it was so long since he had kissed anyone but Angie that it tasted weird, like biting into what you thought was fish and chips and finding you'd got a curry.

Barbara sat down opposite him and announced with a note of triumph, 'Stuart Peck was booked on a British Airways flight from Gatwick to Malta on the 25th of October but *he didn't turn up*. He never checked in for that flight.'

'He didn't catch a later flight?'

'BA have no record of him travelling with them at that time and his ticket was non-transferable so he'd have had to pay again if he'd taken a different flight.'

'And Air Malta?'

'They've never heard of him. They fly from Heathrow, anyway, so it'd make no sense for him to travel with them, not based in Kent.'

'Fantastic.' Greg slammed his fist on his desk, his recent embarrassment forgotten in the excitement of this revelation. 'I knew I was right.'

'Did you?'

'No ... Only hoped I was wrong.'

'There could be all sorts of reasons why he lied about his movements,' Barbara ventured.

'Such as?'

'Shut away in a love nest with somebody else's wife?'

'Possibly.'

She rested her elbows on his desk, her pointy chin on her hands. 'Tell me what you're thinking, sir.'

'I'm thinking that Gillian Lester was awfully young to run away from home on her own, that there had to be a boyfriend in the picture, an older man.'

'Stuart?'

'Why not? He was – what? – twenty-three, lived in the next village, knew the family. And, as a constable newly drafted into CID, he was perfectly placed to monitor the investigation into her disappearance, make doubly sure she was never found.'

'Oh!' Barbara sat up straight. 'And he's doing it again now, making sure he's part of the murder enquiry.'

'Yes!' Greg said. 'I bet if I rang Ashton he'd tell me that Peck volunteered for this thankless task.'

'So does that make him our killer?' Barbara asked.

'Let's ask him, shall we?'

As Greg got to his feet his phone rang. He snatched up the receiver and snapped, 'Summers!'

'Gupta.'

'Oh, hi. Congratulations on your ... forthcoming nuptials.'

'Cheers. Can you step round to the lab?' Deep said. 'It's important.'

'I'm on my way.'

'Who's being forthcomingly nuptialled?' Barbara asked as she followed him out of the room.

'Deep Gupta.'

'No kidding!'

'Wait till you hear about the stallion.'

'Well, this is quite a week we're having, Superintendent,' Gupta said, looking as if he would like to rub his hands together in glee. 'Two sets of fingerprints, both getting a match on the computer, neither for a convicted criminal.'

'Spare me the riddles, Deep.' Greg was prepared to humour him, give him a bit of rope.

'The prints Mrs Childs brought me this afternoon belong to ...' he paused for a dramatic flourish ... 'a serving officer with the Kent police.'

'Yes,' Greg said. 'I thought they might.' He would have laughed at the disappointed look on Deep's face, had he been in any mood for mirth. 'Come on,' he said to Barbara. 'Let's get over to Denford.'

18

They had set up the mobile incident room in a lay-by on the A4, between the villages of Upper and Lower Denford. When Greg and Barbara arrived they found Andy and Nick alone.

'Where's DCI Peck?' Greg asked abruptly.

Andy glanced around as if expecting to find him hiding in a corner. 'I thought he was with you, sir.'

'And I thought he was with you.'

'He stopped by first thing,' Nicolaides offered, 'but he didn't stay long. We've pretty much got everything we're gonna get from the locals and he told us to hang on here and drove off.'

'When was this?' Greg asked.

Nick shrugged. 'Mid-morning, I guess.'

'Could he have gone back to yours?' Barbara asked.

'Angie! My God! Angie's all alone at home with a murderer.'

Nick and Andy stared at him as if he'd gone off his head. Barbara frowned and said, 'Steady on, guv. We don't –'

Greg picked up the phone then thought better of it. 'I'm going straight there. You three get back to Oaken Copse, see if there's any sign of him at the cottage.'

'Do I arrest?' Barbara asked doubtfully.

'No, he may be dangerous. He has no idea we suspect him at the moment so keep it that way. Tell him casually that he's wanted back at the station and then radio ahead so they're ready for him.'

He ran out of the room and they heard his car start and skid away, followed by some angry hooting.

Nick said, 'Would someone mind telling me what the hell is going on?'

Greg burst in at his own front door four minutes after leaving his colleagues, having driven from Denford to Kintbury in a personal record time.

He had an image of Angie trussed up, helpless and bewildered; worse, dead on the hearthrug like Gillian Lester, her dishwater blonde hair dull with blood. It made him put his foot down on the accelerator in impotent rage and take his anger out on other motorists.

It was probably a miracle that he got home in one piece.

There was no sign of Peck's car but that didn't reassure; it just meant that he'd abducted her and gone on the run.

'Angie!' he yelled as he erupted into the hall. 'Angie!'

'Yeah?' She came wandering out of the kitchen, munching noisily on an apple. 'Whassup?'

'Oh, thank God! Is Peck here?'

'Stuart? No. Haven't seen him since breakfast.' Greg sat down on the nearest chair and breathed heavily. 'Are you all right, chuck?' she asked in a stage Yorkshire accent.

'I am now.' He got up, his heart still beating with unnatural speed, and took her by the shoulders. 'Look, Angie. I have to go out again. I want you to bolt the front door behind me and put the chain on. If Peck turns up, don't let him in whatever you do.'

'Gregory, you're frightening me.'

'I haven't got time to explain but you'll be fine if you just do as I say. Don't open the door to him, not even on the chain. Make sure all the other doors and windows are locked and bolted. Call me at once on my mobile if he turns up. Do it now, right behind me. Okay?'

'... Okay.'

He took his mobile out, dialling as he walked. 'I'm

going to call Piers, see if he can come and sit with you. Don't open the door to anyone else. Maybe Barbara,' he amended.

She followed him to the front door. 'Gregory, there's something I need to talk to you about.'

He paused with his finger on the speed dial. 'Is it the phone calls?'

'How did you know?'

'Doesn't matter. It'll have to wait, darling.' He pressed a tender kiss to her forehead. 'Whatever it is, I'll deal with it, don't you worry. Piers? It's me. Need a big favour.'

Honeysuckle Cottage was a low-built oblong with a slate roof, its yellow brick weathered by a hundred and fifty years of mild English winters. A stout wooden door stood in the centre of the front elevation, the goal of a gravel path which ran straight between well-stocked flower beds, now displaying the last chrysanthemums of the year.

A clapboard porch was overgrown with the eponymous climber, but the yellow and white flowers that had filled the air with their scent all summer were long gone.

On each side of the porch stood two square windows, mullioned to the thickness of bottle glass, matching openings on the floor above. The sparsity of the distance between lower and upper windows suggested meagre headroom, a home built for some Victorian lady who struggled to reach five-foot three.

The tall, thin man had left his car in a side road and walked the two hundred yards from Upper Denford proper to the cottage at the southern edge of Oaken Copse. Passers-by, of whom there were few, would assume that his collar was turned up against the autumn night and not for disguise.

His coat was dark. He wished that men still wore hats the way they did in films from the 50s.

He had been travelling aimlessly all afternoon, his mind frantic in contrast to the automatic responses of his driving. He would have liked to take a closer look at the cottage by daylight but his car was distinctive and he stayed well away until night began to fall.

At one point, he pulled onto the motorway and began to head east at ninety miles an hour, slowing when he realised that now, of all times, he could not afford to be pulled over for speeding, when even the flash of his credentials might prove inadequate.

He'd got as far as Slough, the idea in his head that the Channel Tunnel was only two hours' drive away and, once there, the whole of continental Europe lay open to him and, beyond, even the vastnesses of Asia or Russia. Then common sense had prevailed and he'd left the M4 at the next junction, swinging all the way round the roundabout at the top and heading back the way he had come, still sticking to seventy miles per hour, his right foot twitching to demand greater acceleration.

He stepped into the hedge as a car passed him, hurrying, its headlights on full beam, not touching him. He emerged and surveyed his prey. All four downstairs windows glowed at the edges where the curtains were not quite snug, leaving the upper storey in darkness. The sight brought an involuntary smile to his lips. It was a town-dweller's dream, a cottage from the lid of a jigsaw puzzle.

He glanced casually round. His map told him that this road would be used only by locals and it was not yet quite the evening rush hour. Any cars that passed would be speeding home, the drivers indifferent to foot passengers.

He had taken enough statements to know how little eye-witnesses saw, how much less they remembered.

He picked his moment and crossed the road at an angle, his back turned to oncoming traffic, losing himself at once in the hedge that marked the front boundary of the property. He set one foot on the path and winced at the noise of the gravel, moving quickly onto the grass verge which took him silently to the door.

Aunt Adele opened the front door of Honeysuckle Cottage and squinted into the twilight, light streaming from behind her to illuminate her visitor.

'It's DCI ... Beck, is it?'

'Peck,' he corrected her.

'Peck, Beck ... I've been expecting you. You'd better come in.' She glanced behind him into the emptiness of the night. 'Is it cold? You're well wrapped up.'

She turned away without waiting for an answer and he shut the door behind him and followed her into the sitting room. She was wearing track-suit bottoms and a smock-type garment with deep pockets, gum boots sticky with new mud.

'In the garden till last light,' she explained, following his gaze. She stood facing him, her back to the fireplace, her expression grim. 'Sixty years ago I wouldn't have let you realise that I'd recognised you. I must be losing my touch.'

Sixty years ago such a slip would have cost her her life. Things were different now. Or were they? Now, as then, she was prepared for anything.

'It's not what you think,' he said.

'So have you come to explain what you were doing hanging around Oaken Copse last Tuesday night – two nights before Gilly died – when you belong to the Kent force and had no business here?'

'It's not what you think,' he repeated, moving a step closer, his face unreadable.

'Stay where you are.'

Adele reached into the right-hand pocket of her smock and, suddenly, there was a gun in her hand, a revolver, ancient but lethal.

Peck took a step back and raised his hands in automatic response to the weapon. 'What the hell do you think you're doing?' he demanded, his pale face flushing in what seemed like genuine indignation.

'A little old lady, that's all I am. Aren't I? Harmless. Helpless. I see it in people's faces as I walk down the street in Hungerford. Or, rather I don't; they don't notice me, don't see me. I am irrelevant.'

Her voice was perfectly calm, her hand steady as she aimed the gun straight at his head, her spare hand bracing the wrist. And if her words sounded slightly mad, there was nothing of that in her eyes.

'Handguns are illegal,' he said, the brusque police officer.

'So is murder.'

'Just give the gun to me.'

'I think not.'

'Mrs Finnegan –' Peck took a step forward again.

'You thought you could come here tonight and intimidate me, maybe kill me the way you did Gilly –'

'Now, hold on. I haven't killed anybody.'

'– well, guess again.'

'We both know you're not going to use that gun,' he said. He had done the Bramshill courses – hostage, siege – and struggled to recall it now that he was tested. 'What is it? Your father's old service revolver from World War Two?'

'It's *my* old service revolver from World War Two, sonny.'

204

He laughed. 'In the ATS, were we?'

'Something like that.'

'It'd probably blow your hand off after all these years.' He advanced another cautious step. 'So let's just be sensible about this, shall we?'

'I clean and oil it once a month. It's in full working order, I can assure you. Of course, it's not an automatic. The bullets are slower to come into the chamber, but that isn't a problem as one shot is all I need.'

'Give me the gun, Mrs Finnegan.'

'Don't come any nearer. This is your last warning. Stop right where you are and explain to me what you were doing at Ivy Cottage that Tuesday night.'

He stopped, as ordered, balancing lightly on the soles of his feet, in his townie's shoes. 'It's perfectly simple ...'

'I'm listening.'

Stuart Peck threw himself forward, making a lunge for the revolver as Adele side stepped and fired at him at point blank range.

The sound was deafening in the cosy room.

19

Barbara stood literally kicking her heels at the edge of the copse a hundred yards from Ivy Cottage, wondering what to do next. Each kick threw up a patch of dead leaves which made a rustling noise as they resettled into a new pattern of red, yellow and brown, like a kaleidoscope.

There was no sign of Peck and Gregory Summers wasn't answering his mobile which probably meant that he was driving and couldn't conveniently stop.

She thought that his fears about Angie were unfounded but how could she be sure?

'What now, Sarge?' Nicolaides asked.

'I wish I knew, Nick. Where else might he be?'

'What's this about, Barbara? Why are we looking for the DCI all of a sudden like he's a wanted man?'

'It may be nothing.'

'What if –' Andy began.

They would never know what Andy was going to suggest since, at that moment, they heard the distant but unmistakable sound of a gun being discharged. They froze in disbelief for perhaps five seconds, trying to convince themselves that it was a car backfiring.

'Was that ... what I think it was?' Andy asked.

'Well, it wasn't fireworks,' Nick said.

'Honeysuckle Cottage!' Barbara yelled. 'Come on.'

The three officers began to run through the dark wood, tripping over tree roots and each other, in the direction the sound had come from.

As they reached the cottage, a short bundle in a red t-shirt came hurtling towards them from the direction of the village, cannoning into Andy who said, 'Woah!'

'I heard a shot.' Madonna Murphy's eager little face looked up at the three police officers in turn. 'From the old witch's cottage ... Well, what are we waiting for? Two murders in Denford in a week.' She beamed at them. 'This is bloody *brilliant*!'

The cottage door opened and Adele Finnegan looked out at them in surprise. She was holding the revolver in one hand and a portable phone in the other. At the sight of the gun, Andy shoved Murphy behind him for protection. She squealed in indignation and tried to break free, darting quick, avid glances round his broad back.

'That was fast,' Adele said. 'I only just finished dialling 999. You'd better come in.' She offered the gun butt-first to Barbara. 'You'll be wanting this, Sergeant Carey.'

Barbara stared at the gun without moving. Nick stepped forward with an evidence bag and slipped it in. She gave him a grateful look.

'Rather a lot of blood,' Adele remarked conversationally, 'though I was careful to avoid the femoral artery. So hard to get out of the soft furnishings.'

'How's DCI Peck?' Sergeant Barnes asked Greg three hours later. 'Keeping his pecker up?'

He laughed at his own joke but Greg didn't join in.

So far the official line was that Peck had been wounded in a shooting accident and none of the junior officers at Newbury police station knew any different. When the man was under arrest then it would no longer be possible to keep it secret; for the moment he was in hospital under police guard, supposedly for his own protection.

It was a little more than a flesh wound but nothing life threatening: he'd taken the revolver bullet deep in his right thigh and gone down like an ox, according to Aunt Adele, bellowing.

'That sort of language doesn't impress me,' she told Greg. 'I grew up where people hunt.'

The doctors at the Kennet hospital had removed the bullet and sedated Peck for the pain. They were adamant that he would not be fit for questioning until the following morning. Meanwhile, Greg and Andy were interviewing Mrs Finnegan, who had scornfully refused the help of a solicitor and signed the form confirming this with a brazen flourish.

She had added a duffel coat to her stylish ensemble and it was hard to believe that she was half French.

'You do know that it's illegal to be in possession of a hand gun?' Greg began. 'An offence which carries a maximum penalty of ten years.'

'It's just a war souvenir.'

'A war souvenir which you've kept carefully in working order,' Greg pointed out.

'Very well. I'm an old woman and I live alone in an isolated place. I have a right to protect myself and your anti-gun laws are absurd, passed as a knee-jerk reaction to a killing spree by a madman. Criminals have no difficulty in getting hold of them – *they* don't worry about their being illegal – while simple householders such as myself are left without protection.'

Greg wasn't going to argue with her. Much as he disliked guns, he thought that she had a point. The legislation outlawing them had been passed at high speed in response to public outrage. It had been two madmen, in fact, one in Scotland and one here, on his own doorstep, in Hungerford.

All he said was, 'I don't make the laws, Mrs Finnegan. I just enforce them.'

He had been there, in Hungerford, that August day in 1987 and it was as fresh in his mind as yesterday. The gunman, Michael Ryan, had turned his weapon on himself at the end, leaving the madness never to be satisfactorily explained.

'You could have killed DCI Peck,' he said, 'and then you'd be facing a murder charge. Life imprisonment.'

'If I'd been shooting to kill,' Adele said icily, 'then he would be lying in the morgue now, not in a hospital bed. I sought only to defend myself by disabling him. I wasn't afraid of him. I've garrotted war criminals.'

'Garrotted!' Andy said, in disbelief.

'Saves valuable bullets. Also quieter. And no, Superintendent, I didn't garrotte Gillian Lestrange. Let's not go back over old ground. I couldn't be sure that your officer hadn't come to silence me and I wasn't going take that risk. Why did he come? Has he said?'

Greg sighed. It was getting late and he was tired. 'What I don't understand, Aunt – Mrs Finnegan – is why you didn't contact me immediately when you recognised DCI Peck as the man you'd seen skulking round Ivy Cottage that Tuesday night. You had my mobile number. And, as I understand it, Sergeant Carey was standing right there at the time, giving you the opportunity to speak to her in private.'

'... I thought you might all be in it together, a conspiracy,' Adele said. Seeing the look on Greg's face, she added, 'Sorry. I keep telling Vinnie she's too untrusting but, when the chips are down, I'm just the same.'

He released her on police bail and got Andy to run her home. He wasn't about to send an eighty-one-year-old woman – and a war hero – to prison for keeping an ancient service revolver in the house to protect herself, whatever the firearms laws said.

He went home. He had unfinished business with Angie.

He rang ahead to gain entry to his own property and heard Piers unlocking, unbolting and unchaining as he got out of the car. It seemed to take forever but at least they had taken his strictures seriously.

Angie was sitting on the sofa, a little flushed, an empty wine bottle on the table in front of her, along with the remains of a fish-and-chip supper which Piers had presumably picked up on his way over. The TV was on but with the sound turned down, moving wallpaper.

Piers followed him into the room. 'Angie has something she wants to tell you,' he said.

'So I gathered.'

'I'll leave you to it.' He picked up his coat from the chair back. 'Don't worry. I'll see myself out.'

'Thanks, mate. I owe you one.'

'Well, you can pop round and give me one some time.' Piers paused and laid a hand on his arm. 'It'll be all right, Gregory. Seriously.'

Neither of them spoke until they heard the front door slam behind the young photographer then Greg took his place on the sofa beside her.

'It was just a flirtation,' she said. 'I meant nothing by it. Stupid showing off, prove I could still pull.'

He put his arm round her and she nestled into his shoulder. He nuzzled her ear and her hooped earring banged against his chin. 'But it got out of hand?'

'He took it too seriously, started badgering me to go out with him, though he knew from the start I had a partner. In the end, I had to tell him straight out to leave me alone. And then the phone calls started.'

'How long ago was this?'

'Ten days, maybe twelve. First it was one every couple

of days, then every day, then twice a day, all hours. It got so I was afraid to answer the phone.'

'He's harassing you,' Greg said, 'stalking, and there are laws against that.'

'I didn't want to involve the police, which is why I didn't say anything to you all this time. He's very young and a bit inadequate and I suppose I did send out the wrong signals.'

He grimaced. It was strange how women blamed themselves in these situations. He heard it so often in the interview room.

'I don't want to see him up in court,' she added. 'Maybe mess up his life.'

'That would be a last resort,' Greg said. 'I'm sure we can deal with it without going in mob handed at dawn and dragging him out in handcuffs, tempting though that is. What's his name?'

'Aaron. Aaron Milner.'

'Do you know where he lives?'

'In student accommodation at the Uni. He's a first year. He's only eighteen, just a kid, first time away from home. I'm old enough to know better and I feel so stupid and embarrassed.'

'Okay. First thing in the morning, I'm going to call a friend of mine at Reading nick, a uniformed inspector. He'll send a couple of his boys round to have a quiet word with Mr Aaron Milner. Nine times out of ten with stalkers that's enough, brings them to their senses.'

'I'm really sorry, Gregory.'

'It's not your fault, Angel.' He turned her face round to his and kissed her gently on the nose, eyelids, cheeks, settling finally on her lips. She tasted so right and good, despite the lingering odour of chippie vinegar, but it brought up the memory of Martha Childs and he shivered slightly. What was he supposed to do about that? Pretend it had never happened and hope she did the same.

What if he'd acquired a stalker of his own? What if he came home one day and found his lovely Bellini simmering in a casserole on top of the stove?

He hoped he was not going to be the one making the embarrassing confessions next time. It would make the grace with which he'd accepted Angie's apologies look feeble and self-serving.

'Let's get this cleared up,' he said briskly, 'and then have an early night.' They would have the house to themselves tonight, for sure.

He gathered up an armful of chip papers, tucked the wine bottle under his arm and headed for the kitchen.

Greg and Barbara arrived at the hospital early the next morning but, in true NHS fashion, the place had been up for hours, waking sleepy patients, feeding them, cleaning the wards, all with a view to having everyone tucked up in bed again by 8.30 that evening.

'Any trouble?' Greg asked PC Chris Clements who was sitting on an upright chair outside the door of the private room allocated to Peck.

'No, sir.'

Clements looked as if he didn't understand what he was doing here and why he'd spent the whole night twiddling his thumbs on this chair, expecting some sort of full-scale assault against the Kent DCI which had not materialised. 'The doctor stopped by half an hour ago and said he was fit for questioning this morning.'

'Good,' Greg said. 'You can wait here.'

He pushed open the door of the room without knocking. Peck was half reclining against a bank of stiff white pillows, the remains of breakfast on a tray on the floor –

muesli, by the look of it, and a pot of tea. His right leg was bare on top of the scratchy white sheet, the thigh heavily bandaged, the calf hairy, the foot pale.

'How are you feeling?' Greg asked.

'Bullet in the thigh hurts like buggery,' Peck grunted. 'Who knew?'

'Never taken a bullet,' Greg said. 'Hope I never do.' He pulled up a chair and sat down by the bed; Barbara remained standing, her back against the door, her arms folded across her chest. Peck looked at them both warily, as if wondering how much they knew.

Greg watched as he decided to bluff.

'Hope you've taken that mad old bat into custody. I mean, I just looked in on her in passing, make sure she was okay, and she pulled a gun on me.'

Greg remembered how solicitous Peck had been for Peter Bateman at the inquest, offering his arm to the man he had helped to imprison. The hypocrisy sickened him. 'Stuart Peck,' he said, 'I am arresting you on suspicion of the murder of Gillian Lester –'

'NO!' Peck yelled. 'No, no, no, no, no!'

He began to bang his head against the bedside cabinet until Greg grabbed him and forced him forward, holding him by the elbows in an iron grip, as he completed the caution.

'I didn't kill her.' He was sobbing now. 'You're mad. The old woman is mad. You're all mad.'

'Then what were you doing in Oaken Copse Tuesday evening of last week, and at Gillian's flat in London later that night?'

'I never went near the copse. I never saw the place in my life till the other day.' Peck spoke quickly, not leaving space for Greg to interrupt. 'You surely don't believe a word the old woman says. I wasn't even in the country –'

'We have your prints, Stuart.'

'What? Rubbish!'

'Oh, I know you wore gloves to search the flat but you left one on the light fitting in the stairwell when you took the bulb out.' Greg paused then flung down his trump card. 'And we know you never went to Malta.'

Peck hesitated, visibly racking his brains as he contemplated the errors he had made. As a police officer, he knew the value of silence, but when you were faced with an accusation of murder, there was a lot to be said for admitting to a lesser crime.

Greg gave him a sardonic grin. 'You might call it a no-brainer.'

'Look, I'll tell you the truth and it's bad enough but I'm not a murderer.'

'I'm listening,' Greg said. He released Peck who sank back on the pillows, defeated. 'Let's start with how well you knew Gillian all those years ago back in Kent, shall we?'

'Yes, all right. I knew her. Better than I let on.'

'You were the "boyfriend" she mentioned to Vinnie Latham years later.'

'... Yes.'

'And when she ran away from home, you gave her shelter.' Peck didn't immediately reply and he went on. 'You helped her change her appearance and acquire a new identity. All the time you were out with the rest of your force searching half of Kent for her, watching her parents go frantic with worry, you knew exactly where she was and that she was perfectly safe.'

'Yes. All right? Yes.'

'And then Ashton arrested Peter Bateman and you let him. You stood by and watched while that poor man was tried for murder and sentenced to life imprisonment, when one word from you ...'

'It was her,' Peck said quickly. 'Gilly. I was ... obsessed with her. Crazy about her. I'd have done anything she asked of me. I begged her to come forward when we arrested Bateman. She laughed. Said a murder trial would do him good, thinking he could come barging into her home, screwing her mother and telling her what she could and couldn't do. It was all her.'

'She was *fifteen*,' Barbara said through gritted teeth. 'You were a grown man and a police officer.'

Peck seemed not to hear her but went on with his story. 'I thought Bateman would be acquitted for lack of evidence. When he wasn't, I thought Gilly would relent and tell the truth then but she wouldn't.'

'Never occurred to you that *you* might tell the truth, I suppose,' Greg said.

'It was too late by then. I was in too deep.'

'You were too scared?'

'Yes. I was too bloody scared.'

'What about the clothes?' Greg said. 'Gillian's school clothes that were found buried in a field.'

'... That was me,' Peck admitted. 'I dumped those.'

'Which didn't exactly help Bateman's case, did it?' Barbara said.

Peck made a helpless gesture.

'It confirmed Ashton's conviction that the girl was dead,' Greg added.

'I suppose.'

'Why was she so anxious to leave home?' Greg asked.

'They were strict, especially him, treated her like a kid, wouldn't even let her go out with boys, which is why she kept me a secret.'

'So there was no abuse?' Greg asked. 'No problems with Peter Bateman pestering her?'

Peck looked puzzled. 'That wimp? You must be joking. Gilly wouldn't have put up with anything like that.'

'She put up with it from you,' Barbara said.

'I was her *boyfriend*. Like I said, Bateman was strict.'

'So what happened then?'

'She left me after a couple of years –'

'You kept her hidden all that time?' Barbara asked incredulously.

'It wasn't so hard. We changed her hair with one of those home colouring kits you get at the chemist. Her clothes were different. I transferred to the Norfolk force to put some distance between her and everyone who'd known her. Mostly she stayed in my flat.'

Greg didn't find it hard to believe. A recent case against a serial killer in Australia had collapsed after one of his supposed victims had been found living with her boyfriend five years after her disappearance. She would hide in a cupboard if anyone came to his house.

'And then she left you,' he said.

'Got bored, I suppose.' For a moment he looked deeply unhappy. 'I came home one day and she was gone, left me a note saying she'd had enough of hiding and enough of me. She was heading off to another part of the country to start a new life.' He laughed hollowly. 'Took any cash I had lying around and everything portable of value as well.'

'So what did you do?'

'What could I do? Call the cops and report her missing? I got over it and moved back home to Kent, which was timely, as it happened, as my mum was getting poorly.'

He shuddered. 'And did you see what she'd become? That fat frump? Jesus. And she made me … Tuesday night.' He took a deep breath, recalling the event, what she had made him do before she let him leave.

'Prefer them young, do you, Stuart?' Greg asked. 'Under the age of consent and skinny like a boy?'

'Oh, that's bloody rich,' Peck said. 'You're a fine one to talk – man your age shacked up with a teenager.'

'Angie?' Greg said in disbelief. 'She's twenty-four.'

'Still young enough to be your daughter, squire.'

'We're getting off the point.' Greg swallowed his anger; Peck was only saying what a lot of people thought and you couldn't spend thirty years as a policeman if you had a thin skin. 'Let's get back to how and why you went to Ivy Cottage that night. Did it have anything to do with Gillian's idea that she would publish her life story?'

'How do you know about that?' Peck asked sullenly.

'She told Vinnie Latham.'

'Bit of a chatterbox, wasn't she. Both of them. Bloody women can never keep their mouths shut.'

'And those threatened memoirs provide you with an excellent motive for murder,' Greg reminded him, 'so let's hear why you didn't kill her, because you're a long way from convincing me yet.'

20

Hello, Pecker.
Remember me? It's been a long time.

'You all right, sir?' The constable had just handed him the letter addressed to him by name and rank at Rochester police station. It was marked 'private and personal' and he was mildly curious.

'Oh, yes. Fine thanks, Degsie. I just ... remembered something I forgot to do.'

Have you been wondering all these years what happened to me? Well, I haven't done too badly, all things considered. While you, I learn from Googling your name on the internet – what a price-less tool that is – are now a detective chief inspector, no less.

Not too badly, as I say, although somehow not quite as well as I hoped when I left Kent all those years ago. I became a writer. Something I'd always fancied and which my mother told me I couldn't do because it 'wasn't for people like us, dear'.

I like the work but it doesn't pay that well, contrary to what people seem to think. I have to do celebrity biographies to make ends meet and, even so, I have a crap flat in a dismal suburb of London and a car that's held together by rust. I did come into a bit of money a few years back but somehow I ran through it, as you do.

Do you read much, Pecker? You never did, I know, preferred to look at the pictures in the porn mags – pubescent girls with implausibly large knockers and absolutely no knickers – but time might have educated you. These days it's memoirs that make the big money. My mummy beat me; my daddy screwed me; I'm a drug addict and it's not my fault.

Boo, hoo.

So what I thought was, how about instead of writing other people's autobiographies, I wrote my own. It's a pretty good story after all, when a fifteen-year-old girl comes back from the dead and names the man she ran off with, a senior and much respected policeman.

Don't you think so? Don't you think people will pay good money to read about that? Don't you think publishers will jump at it?

'Blackmail letter,' Barbara remarked. 'Not exactly subtle.'

'That's obvious to you, is it?' Peck said, 'because in my panic, I assumed she was serious.'

The bright side is that they may ask you to put your side of the story, Pecker, help make up for that nice fat public service pension you'll be losing. Though the money won't really come in useful till after you get out of prison, assuming you make it out in one piece, that is, since I gather policemen do not fare well in jail.

Or maybe we should write it together.

Let me know what you think.

Love, Gilly.

'So she told you her address?' Greg said.

'Email address only, and not a real one – one of those web-based spares you can pay for. I sent her a message at once, of course, asking for a meet. She didn't reply for about a week, letting me stew, then she told me she was staying at a friend's house in the depths of the country while she worked on a book.'

'Ivy Cottage,' Greg said.

'Yeah. We arranged for me to go over there Tuesday of last week. I'd already cancelled my trip to Malta and was lying low in my flat, living off tins of beans and pretending to the neighbours that I was away.'

Watching your career and your freedom disappear before your eyes, Greg thought. He had seldom heard such a convincing motive for murder.

'She wasn't afraid to meet you in a remote place?' Barbara said.

'Apparently not. I told you before, she was always the one who had the whip hand, the one who made the running.'

'I know what you *said*.' Barbara's voice was chilly.

'I'm telling the truth. *She* started the affair. *She* came up with the plan to run away together. She used me and then she dumped me.' He laughed bitterly. 'No, she wasn't afraid of me, not the least bit in the world.'

'So what happened,' Greg asked, 'that Tuesday night?'

The tall, thin man in the dark overcoat approached the cottage uncertainly. He could not see a name plate identifying it as Ivy Cottage but it must be the right place, surely. The white Ford Capri parked in front certainly fit the description of 'held together by rust'.

He made a note of the number plate, force of habit. He knew that he would never dare use it to search the police computer. Such private enquiries were forbidden and what would he say if taxed with it?

I was just checking to find out the current name and address of Gillian Lester. Yes, that's right, the girl we declared dead fifteen years back.

He tapped lightly on the door and heard movement within.

He didn't know her at first. Or rather he couldn't believe it was her. Always, in his memory, was a slender girl child with hollow cheeks; with legs like a gazelle jutting out from under the grey school skirt which she would roll over at the waist the moment she was out of sight of her mother's house, making a mini of it. When he thought of her breasts it was of two tender buds beneath his hands; now her bosom stuck out like a shelf.

She smiled and it was not a nice smile. 'Hello, Pecker. You haven't changed a bit.'

He could not return the compliment, was mute, and she said, 'Cat got your tongue? You better come in.'

He intended to say 'Nice place you have here' but the words wouldn't come out, especially as it was not a nice place. Following his eyes, she said, 'Yeah, it's a dump. It belongs to the woman whose bio I'm writing and she's out of the country most of the time. It's good for working, no distractions. Not even a telly. Coffee? It's instant.'

He found his voice though it sounded alien to his own ears, rasping, as if he had a sore throat. 'Got anything stronger?'

'Supermarket whisky?'

'That'll do nicely.'

He needed strong drink; he needed it badly. All these years he had dreamed of being reunited with Gilly, his first love. Even when he had received the hideous letter, beneath all his anguish, he'd been aware of a leaping in his heart, of a small part of him which thought that these untender words might mean reconciliation.

Seeing her now, under the bleak unshaded bulb of the sitting room, an obese woman who was thirty but looked more like forty, her features heavy and shapeless with spare flesh, dressed in some sort of red woollen sack that fell to her swollen ankles, he wanted to vomit.

Was it for this repulsive creature that he had destroyed his life?

* * *

'Was she really prepared to go public?' Greg asked. 'She'd have been in as much trouble as you were – are. Why didn't you call her bluff – tell her to publish and be damned?'

'I tried,' Peck said. 'She had the whip hand and she knew it.'

'I was fifteen,' Gilly said calmly, as if explaining something to a backward child. 'A minor, a little girl. You were – what? – twenty-three?' He nodded. 'You corrupted me, Pecker.'
You know it wasn't like that,' he muttered.

'It doesn't matter what I know, only what the jury will believe. Do you know what they do to paedophiles in jail?'

He made no reply. He knew.

'Okay, I might do some prison time too.' She shrugged. 'A few months, perhaps, but nobody's going to believe that you weren't the motive force behind the whole thing.'

She was right and he knew it.

'And a short spell in an open prison would be useful material,' she said, 'especially with me being so famous by then. Top up?'

He looked at his empty glass. He didn't remember draining it and he felt no effect from the amber liquid, just a cold, unhappy sobriety that he was suddenly desperate to throw off. He held it up and she refilled it. He sipped; it was cheap blended whisky, bitter on his tongue. He was driving but that was the least of his problems.

'Of course, there may be alternatives.' Gillian sat down on the sofa opposite him and curled her feet under her. He thought she looked like an overfed cat – like the grotesque abomination he had seen once in a suburban restaurant in Paris, swollen by leftovers, slumped on a table by the door, too hefty to move – licking her lips at the prospect of cream. 'What does a DCI earn these days?'

'Here it comes,' Barbara said. 'Blackmail.'

'Yes,' Peck said. 'That was when poor stupid Stuart finally got it. She had no intention of publishing her story if she could possibly avoid it because that would set Bateman free. If she could get me to pay her to keep quiet, then she'd be content with that. I was relieved.'

He looked round the cottage with the eyes of a police officer, looking for evidence. He could see a laptop computer open on the table.

Her eyes followed his. 'Yes, I have the whole story down in there, but I have it backed up at home too.'

'Where's home?' he asked.

She laughed. 'Wouldn't you like to know? Now, if I were to meet with a nasty accident – just in case it was going through your mind that we're alone here in an isolated place where nobody can hear me scream ... Well, I don't have to spell it out for you.'

'You think of everything, don't you?'

'I try.'

He said, 'How much?'

'I'm not greedy; that would be counter-productive. Fifteen years ago you wanted us to get married, play happy families. If I'd gone along with that then you'd be supporting me by now. What's the difference?'

She named a sum. He was surprised by its modesty, the price of freedom. He could afford it, although he'd have to remortgage his flat in Rochester. Unless he sold the place in Malta, and that would be a false economy because everybody said that prices would soar once the island joined the EU next spring.

Or he could sell his beloved BMW.

He realised that these jumbled thoughts were clogging his brain, stopping him from thinking clearly, and he forced himself to concentrate.

'I need two things,' he said, 'if we're to have a deal – all the copies of your life story and your word that this will be your last and only demand.'

'I'm a reasonable woman.' She raised her own glass in toast to him. 'We are agreed.'

'And precisely how much did you think her word was worth?' Greg asked.

'Not much.'

'She'd have milked you dry,' Barbara said. 'She'd have come back to the fountain again and again.'

'I believed her because I wanted to believe her,' Peck said, 'because I had no choice.'

She came and took the glass from his hand, placing it on the floor. As she bent over him, her heavy chest thrust in his face, he looked unwillingly into her eyes. The deep, dark, hypnotic pools that he remembered were squashed by her plump cheeks into black malevolent ponds.

She took his hand and he allowed himself to be pulled to his feet. 'Let's seal our agreement,' she said, 'with a kiss, for old time's sake.'

If only it had stopped at a kiss. She made him go upstairs with her, leading him into the front bedroom where a narrow double was crammed into the corner, spread with a gaudy cotton throw.

She pushed him across it and climbed on to straddle him, her thighs with their stark white stretch marks holding him tight, the woollen material of her robe bunched, scratchy, against his hands. Her breath was loud in his ears, panting not from lust but from the exertion of the stairs. Her fingers fumbled with his trousers and he turned his head into the pillow and closed his eyes, understanding at last what she meant to do ...

He could bear to remember no further, shutting his mind down from the horror of the next few minutes. He knew that she had wanted it no more than he did, that she had done it to humiliate him, the way a man will use sex to cast down a woman and show her who's boss.

In this way, she would drain him of any residue of resistance.

He had been able to perform – to avoid the ultimate humiliation – only by closing his eyes and envisaging the compliant body of WPC Trisha Moran, one of Rochester's newest and youngest recruits.

He pulled the sheet over his head and began to whimper. 'My leg hurts.'

Greg gave a curt nod to Barbara and the two of them left the room to consult in private.

'Go and get a cup of tea,' Greg told PC Clements.

'Sir.'

'Do you believe him?' Barbara asked, when Chris was out of earshot.

'I think I do rather.'

'Me too ... on the whole. What a damn nuisance.'

'In general I prefer it when people I know turn out *not* to be murderers,' Greg said, 'especially policemen, especially policemen who are staying at my house.'

'Yes, but we thought we had the crime cracked,' Barbara pointed out, 'and now we haven't. We're pretty much right back where we started.'

'True, but let's deal with the criminal we have got. I just wish we were back at the station and getting all this down on tape in an interview room.'

'At least he's talking. At least he hasn't clammed up and demanded a lawyer.'

Greg led the way back into the room, sat down and pulled the sheet away from the injured man's face.

'Tell me about the trip to Isleworth, Stuart.'

'I watched her delete the file from her laptop but, like she said, it was backed up at her flat so I insisted on getting rid of that too.'

'She gave you her keys?' Greg asked.

'*Lent* me her keys. She even gave me the password to her PC. I went there that night and I deleted anything I could find that mentioned me.'

'But as long as she was alive, she could always write it up again,' Barbara said. 'She knew that, which was why she was so co-operative.'

'I didn't kill her,' he said sullenly.

'What about the answering machine?' Greg said. 'What was the point of that?'

'Of what?' Peck looked puzzled. 'I don't know anything about any answering machine.'

'Gillian's is missing from her flat.'

'Then the killer must have taken it,' Peck said in triumph. 'Like you say, it'd be of no use to me.'

'Or perhaps it's just away being repaired,' Barbara suggested. 'Has anyone thought of that?'

Greg had to admit that he hadn't; it would be too much of a coincidence.

'Stuart Peck,' he said. 'I'm arresting you for conspiracy to pervert the course of justice. You are not obliged to say anything but it may harm your defence if you fail to mention when questioned something you later rely on in court. Anything you do say may be given in evidence.' He stood up. 'I won't ask if you understood that.'

'Actually,' Peck admitted glumly, 'I've never really understood it. At least it isn't murder.'

But conspiracy to pervert carried a potential life sentence too and Greg privately thought that he'd be lucky to be out of jail in time for his fiftieth birthday.

Peck was whimpering with pain again. The door opened at that moment and a cross-looking woman in a white coat walked in. She was in her mid thirties and wore a badge which informed Greg that she was Dr Masefield. She glanced at Peck and looked, if anything, even crosser, turning her eyes accusingly on the two police officers as her patient moaned 'My leg' again.

Greg decided swiftly that Peck had had enough for the moment. He preferred to leave with dignity rather than be thrown out by a doctor who had not slept for twenty hours.

In the doorway he paused. 'Tell me something, Stuart, all these years, did you ever think about Peter Bateman and what you'd done to him?' Peck turned his face to the wall without replying.

'I'll take that as a no,' Greg said. On his way out he met Clements coming back with his cup of tea.

'DCI Peck is under arrest,' he told the gawping constable. 'Go in and sit with him. Don't speak to him, but he's been cautioned so make a note of anything he says. He's fairly immobilised but keep an eye on him; I don't want to hear he jumped out of the window while you went for a pee. Use a bedpan if you have to. I'll send back-up as soon as possible.

Clements was too stunned to reply.

'He could still be our murderer,' Barbara said, as she turned the car back towards headquarters.

'He could,' Greg agreed.

'Admitting to the lesser crimes while continuing to deny the greater – he wouldn't be the first.'

'I know.'

'He had motive – God, did he have motive – and he had opportunity. What more do we want?'

'The truth,' Greg said. 'Always we want the truth. We have Peck's car so we can check his tyres against the ones Martha took prints of at the crime scene.'

'Here's a riddle for you,' Barbara said. 'Why is Gillian like the Sleeping Beauty?'

'I don't know. Why is Gillian like the Sleeping Beauty?'

'Because her life was ruined by a prick.'

Greg smiled dutifully. But had it been as simple as that, he wondered, the automatic feminist response? Man villain; woman victim. Black and white.

They were blaming Stuart, just as a court would, but he couldn't forget Philip Abernethy's story. Fifteen was old enough to know right from wrong and little Gilly Lester sounded like a wrong'un to him.

21

Greg decided that he needed to break the news about Peck to Ashton as soon as possible and that this was best done in person. Since he was no further forward on the Gillian Lester murder, he would take the opportunity to talk to the Batemans. They would also need to know the truth about that old family friend from Lower Shorne – Sally Peck's little boy – but not yet.

Oh good, another long drive to Kent round the M25.

He took Jonathan Atkins' card out of his wallet and telephoned him. The solicitor immediately repeated what he had said at the inquest: that the Batemans would co-operate in any way possible to help solve their daughter's murder.

'They're back home,' he said. 'If you'd like to collect me at my office, then we can go together. You won't object to my sitting in – mere formality?'

'Not at all, sir,' Greg said.

He arranged to pick Atkins up at four o'clock that afternoon. It was now eleven, so if he set off for Kent right away, he could have his interview with Ashton in good time to deal with the Batemans.

He would also need to arrange to search Peck's flat for evidence, but Alan's people could do that.

He didn't call Ashton in advance. If the head of CID was away then he'd talk to the station Chief Superintendent to explain why Peck must be suspended. His appointment with Atkins and the Batemans would make a good excuse not to linger at Rochester nick for the wailing and gnashing of teeth, the recriminations and the wake.

With luck, he'd be back in Kintbury tonight.

Very late.

* * *

'Mr Milner?'

'Yes.'

'Mr Aaron Milner.'

'Yes.' Milner blinked sleepily at the two constables standing in the corridor outside his student bedsit. He was in his pyjamas and had bed hair, standing on end at one side like a cartoon character. 'What is it?'

'May we come in, sir?' The first constable moved into the room without waiting for an answer, forcing Milner to back away before him. 'I'm PC Baines and this is PC Anderson.'

'Morning,' Anderson said.

Milner took a dressing gown from a hook on the back of the door and wrapped it tightly round him. He groped around on the bedside table for his glasses and put them on, then picked up his watch and looked at it.

'Did we wake you?' Baines asked blandly. 'It's almost ten. Me, I've been on duty since six.'

'Me too,' Anderson said.

'Please tell me what this is about.'

Milner looked very young, a frightened child. The two men did not seem overtly hostile; indeed, they had the air of a double act, yet somehow he doubted they were truly comical. The police had a way of calling you 'sir' which made it sound like an insult.

Baines continued to do the talking. 'We've had a complaint, sir, about nuisance phone calls to a young lady in the Newbury area. We've had them traced to the call box on this landing and found your finger-prints on it.'

'Oh!' Milner sat down abruptly on the bed, not doubting for a moment the veracity of this statement, not wondering in his just-awake state how the police came to have his prints to check them against.

Baines sat down next to him and assumed an expression that was probably meant to be avuncular but which did not reassure. 'Thing is, Aaron – may I call you Aaron?'

'Um.'

'Guess your parents got bored with the "What shall we call our baby?" book real quick,' Anderson said.

Baines snorted. 'Good one, Trev! Thing is, *Aaron*, that sort of thing's illegal. We call it harassment or stalking and they send people to jail for it these days.'

'Then there's the public humiliation,' Anderson added. 'Your parents, friends, future employers, they'll all know you've been behaving like a prat.'

'And when the young lady's partner is a senior police officer,' Baines concluded, '... well, I don't have to spell it out, do I?' When Milner did not immediately reply, he repeated, 'Do I?'

The boy whimpered, 'No.'

'Good.' Baines clapped a heavy hand on his shoulder. 'So it stops now, okay?'

'I swear it won't happen again. I swear. I swear. Oh, Jesus. I swear.'

Anderson made a tutting noise and Baines said, 'My colleague is a born-again Christian and he doesn't like people taking the Lord's name in vain, *Aaron*.'

'Upsets me something chronic,' Anderson said.

'Sorry.'

'We'll leave it at that then.' Baines rose to go. 'If you know what's good for you.'

As they left the building, Anderson started to laugh. 'Born-again Christian. That was a good one, Ron.'

'I think we've carried out Inspector Merton's

instructions to the letter,' Baines said with satisfaction. 'Problem solved. Time for a nice cup of tea.'

'Good looking boy, though,' said Anderson who, at forty-two, was gay but in the closet.

Baines snorted. 'What are you – queer?'

Anderson nailed the closet door more firmly shut.

'Still,' Baines added. 'I bet there's more to it than the inspector's letting on.'

'No smoke without fire,' Anderson agreed, tapping the side of his nose.

The desk staff at Rochester police station greeted Greg like an old friend.

'Couldn't stay away then, sir?' the desk sergeant said.

'Rushing back to the Garden of England, Sergeant. Is Superintendent Ashton in?'

'He's in his office,' the man replied, reaching for the phone. 'I'll tell him you're here.'

'Blimey,' said a passing constable, 'are all the golf courses in Kent closed today, or what?'

The sergeant frowned. 'That'll do, Paderevski. Sir, Mr Summers from Newbury is here to see you ... Okay.' He hung up. 'He'll be right down. How's the Pecker doing in the wilds of Berkshire?'

The constable, who was clearly the office wag, added, 'Is he a) having a whale of a time, b) bored titless, c) –'

'Haven't you got a beat to pound?' the sergeant asked very loudly and Paderevski made himself scarce as Greg stifled a smile.

It was fortunate that the sergeant's original question appeared to have been rhetorical, since Greg found himself quite unable to answer it. *He's in hospital with a nasty bullet wound in the thigh. Oh, and he's under arrest for conspiracy to pervert the course of justice.*

He passed the time reading the notices until Ashton appeared. Greg thought he looked older, more world-weary, asking himself how long it had been since he'd last seen him and realising with a shock that it was exactly a week.

'Gregory,' he said, shaking hands. 'What brings you back so soon?'

'I needed to speak to you in person, Alan. It's important. Can we go somewhere quiet?'

Ashton took the news blankly at first. Greg had made him sit down, under protest; now he sat leaning forward, staring at the unforgiving floor of the interview room, trying to take in what he had heard. Greg waited for him to speak, wondering what he would say.

Finally, he lifted his head and surprised his colleague by saying, 'That explains a lot.'

'It does?'

'I mean, if she had help to run away from home, a bloke, a boyfriend, older, knew the ropes.' His calm demeanour collapsed and he gnawed at the knuckles of his right hand. 'Knew every step the bloody investigation was taking!'

'You didn't ask about that at the time – a boyfriend?'

'Of course we did! It's one of the first questions you ask when a teenage girl goes missing – did she have a boyfriend? – but nobody thought she did, not her parents, not even her schoolfriends ... And they weren't lying, her friends, they were scared, worried for her.'

Greg said neutrally, 'He was careful.'

Ashton rubbed his face. 'Jesus Christ!' The news was sinking in. 'Stuart. He's always liked the women and he likes them young, in that he's got older and they've stayed eighteen, but never anything under age ... obviously.'

'Obviously,' Greg said.

'Ten minutes ago he was my best friend and now I fucking hate him. How could he?' Ashton got up and kicked the table which shuddered but, being bolted to the floor, did not budge. 'How could you do this to me, Stuart, you little shit?'

Greg said, 'I'm so sorry, Alan.'

Ashton continued kicking the table. Greg made no move to stop him, thinking it best to let him play out his rage.

'Thirty-eight years unblemished record and now I'll be remembered as the man who sent Peter Bateman down. I'll spend the first couple of years of my retirement in front of a series of tribunals while they decide whether to take my pension away or not.'

'Steady, Alan.'

Greg placed a hand on his arm but Ashton broke away, bellowing, 'They'll say I was corrupt and I wasn't. I AM NOT!' He was screaming now. 'I HATE corrupt coppers.' He kicked the table again.

A uniformed constable poked his head round the door to see what the noise was about but, spotting not one but two superintendents apparently engaged in vandalising police property, hastily withdrew and went to tell all his friends.

Finally running out of fury, Ashton asked, 'Have you ruled him out for the murder?'

'Not entirely, not yet.'

Although the tyre prints did not match those of Peck's BMW, which gave his story some credibility. The car that had been at Ivy Cottage on the night of the murder had been smaller, less well-maintained.

Ashton's shoulders sagged. If he had looked tired before, now he was exhausted. His concern was only for himself and his own reputation, but Greg couldn't be certain that he wouldn't have felt the same in the circumstances.

'I arranged with the Chief that I'd clear my desk and be out by the end of next week, with Stuart acting head of CID until they could confirm his promotion. But now ...'

'That's not going to happen,' Greg agreed.

'Looks like I'm stuck here, even beyond my official retirement date, until I can find a new DCI.'

'Good luck with that,' Greg said.

When he'd calmed down sufficiently to function normally, Ashton agreed to send a SOC team to search Peck's flat. Greg wanted Peck's home computer so he could go through the emails the two ex-lovers had exchanged.

He also asked if he could take a look at the original case files from Gillian's disappearance. Alan took him to the archives and left him to it. Police paperwork fifteen years ago had not been as overwhelming as it was today; even so, there were a dozen boxes of statements and reports.

Greg settled down at a spare desk and began to rummage through them with no order or method.

He soon lighted on some family photographs which must have been borrowed for release to the media and, in the frenzy of the murder enquiry, never returned. They were amateur efforts, often blurry or badly composed, so it was no wonder that the press office had gone with the school portrait in the end.

He saw Peter Bateman as a fresh-faced boy, looking about twenty years old, although he must have been over thirty. He looked happy here, playful, giving Gillian a piggy-back, a child of about ten who clung to his shoulders and laughed for the camera.

Apparently things had been all right between them at

that point; so when did they start to go wrong? There came a point when teenagers, especially girls, turned, for the space of a few years, into monsters. Most families weathered that storm; the good ship Bateman had sunk with all hands.

Glancing at his watch, he saw that he was overdue for his next appointment and hastily stuffed the pictures and papers back in the boxes. He would have them taken to Newbury. It was unlikely that they would help with his investigation but he couldn't overlook any avenue.

By running out to his car and stepping on the gas, the superintendent found himself pulling up outside the offices of Atkins & Sons, solicitors, on Castle Hill no more than fifteen minutes after the promised time.

Jonathan Atkins emerged before he could get out of the car, pulling the door to behind him with a click. He was wearing what looked like the same blue suit, topped by a scarlet anorak.

'Only me in the office this afternoon,' he explained, as he took his seat and strapped himself in, the belt a little tight across his bulging frame. 'Small family firm. Mum comes in to do the paperwork but she's gone to see the quack about her HRT today.'

Solicitors who did Legal Aid work for people like the Batemans were at the poorer end of the spectrum of lawyers, Greg knew. Often, the money they got from the state, sometimes months after the event, barely covered their expenses.

Somebody had to do it – somebody had to provide justice to those who couldn't afford to pay for it – and Greg admired the men like Atkins who volunteered. He gave him a warm smile and thanked him for his help, apologising mentally for having misjudged him at first.

'Do you know this area?' the lawyer asked.

'A bit. I was here in connection with the Emerson murder cases a week or so back.'

'Oh, that was a nasty business. Mum was frightened to be alone in the house. I'm just thankful I wasn't duty solicitor the night he was arrested. The firm who represent him got doggy poo pushed through their letter box last weekend. Just follow the signs to Chatham.'

Greg knew that Rochester and Chatham were, in effect, one town, the boundary distinguishable only by the natives.

'And what do you make of us?' Atkins asked. 'Don't tell me – a picturesque town stuck in the past?'

'That was my first impression,' Greg admitted, 'until I saw the syringe-disposal boxes in the public lavs.'

They had crossed the imaginary boundary now and Greg was driving along streets lined with boarded-up units and shops where everything cost a pound.

'Chatham has got very run down,' Atkins explained, his voice sad, 'since the dockyards closed. We were great once. We held our heads up. An Able Seaman Atkins served with Nelson at Trafalgar – my seven-times-great grandfather.'

'Wow!' Greg wished he could make such claims on history; maybe his umpteen-times-great grandfather had fought at one of the battles of Newbury, but who knew? Or, if so, what side he'd have been on.

The lawyer abruptly changed the subject. 'Have there been developments at your end?'

'I'm no nearer an arrest for Gillian's murder, if that's what you mean,' Greg said.

He was in a difficult position; he couldn't tell Atkins or the Batemans about the part Peck had played in Gillian's original disappearance since he hadn't yet charged the man with anything. He had a lot more questions to ask him first, when he'd recovered from the initial shock of his bullet wound.

'How are they doing,' he asked. 'The Batemans?'

'... Frankly, not good, either of them. People imagine that they're living it up with champagne, celebrating, but ... Peter especially. What should be a dream come true looks more like a nightmare from where I'm standing. It breaks my heart, Mr Summers.'

'Mine too, Mr Atkins.'

The two men exchanged a glance of sympathy and Greg hoped that he had made a new friend, even if they had not yet got round to calling each other by their Christian names.

They drew up in a small council estate on the outskirts of Chatham. They weren't called that any more: Social Housing; that was the politically correct term. Greg saw a cluster of tower blocks, ten storeys high, circling a green where the grass was untended, open ground where ball games were forbidden by notice.

People complained that children spent all their time indoors, hunched over Playstations, yet no one wanted their windows broken or would tolerate the noise of youngsters enjoying themselves.

There was nothing intrinsically wrong with tower blocks. Rich people lived in them in the centre of London, Paris or Rome, paying a premium price for the views. So why did these concrete blocks make his heart heavy?

'Which one?' he asked, though he had the address in his pocket.

'Henderson Tower.'

Atkins pointed and Greg could make out the remnants of the press pack – the local reporters and the ones who had nothing better to do – walking up and down on the tarmac, talking into mobile phones, smoking, eating food

240

from polystyrene cartons which they dropped without shame on the ground.

Peter Bateman was already yesterday's news to most of the media.

'They were named after the local councillors at the time,' Atkins went on. 'Seventh floor. Far corner.' With no change of inflection he added, 'Bloody hell.'

Greg followed his finger. Each flat had a tiny concrete balcony jutting over the apartment beneath, barely room for two people. As he squinted into the dull autumn light, he thought he could see someone on the Bateman's balcony, unless it was an illusion, a washing line.

Some instinct for trouble told him it was not washing. He threw off his seatbelt and flung the door open, setting off across the car park at a run.

Atkins followed him, not accustomed to running, but realising the need. Slowly, the reporters were understanding that something was happening in the sky above them. They fell back to get a better angle of vision, gawping up, reaching for their phones anew.

He was right; that was no washing line. Craning his neck from the ground, Greg could see Peter Bateman climbing with painful slowness on to the narrow parapet. Atkins made a strangled noise in his gullet, then rushed through the front door of the block. Greg reached for his mobile phone and dialled 999.

'Fire brigade,' he snapped.

Atkins was still in the foyer when Greg entered Henderson Tower, waiting for the lift. He decided to use the stairs and arrived on the seventh floor three minutes later to find a much less breathless solicitor stepping out of the lift.

He hammered on the door of 7b. Maureen Bateman opened it as if she'd been standing waiting for his knock.

Greg thought that he had never seen a face so white with misery.

'Mr Atkins,' she said. 'Mr Summers. Thank God.'

Greg pushed past her, still too breathless to speak, and moved swiftly to the end of the hall, stopping at the doorway to the sitting room. The French door onto the balcony was open and Bateman was sitting on the parapet, his feet dangling outside, swaying gently back and forth. He didn't have to jump; he need only let himself fall forward to tumble the seven storeys into oblivion.

Greg could envisage the reporters down below. They would do nothing to help him, nothing to break his fall, only stand and watch, photograph if they could. There were certainly some who were hoping he would jump.

Bateman seemed to be trying to make up his mind, ignoring – perhaps not aware of – Greg, who clung panting to the door frame, wondering what to do next, listening for the roar of sirens.

'Peter ...' he stammered.

The man glanced round and recognised him. 'Oh, you're here, the copper from Newbury, the one who's trying to solve Gilly's murder.'

His tone was indifferent. As Greg took a step forward, he added conversationally, 'I shouldn't come any closer, if I were you. You see, I don't care at all any more. Either way. But you, you strike me as a man who couldn't live with himself if he pushed me to it.'

There was no possibility of rushing him; he'd be off the balcony in an instant. Even the noise of the fire engines arriving might make up his mind for him and Greg began to hope that they would not be too efficient.

'Pete!' Mrs Bateman sobbed. 'Please. Let us help you in.'

Atkins stood mute, momentarily out of his depth.

Greg's eyes automatically took in the room, its meagre contents: the old fawn carpet; the flowery three piece suite with wooden legs; the teak veneer coffee table, a pile of yellow-jacketed magazines on its lower level; the scratched oak sideboard.

It did not take long.

His gaze flickered back to the magazines since they looked familiar, recently seen, and something – an idea – seemed to hover on the edge of his mind without quite making it into his consciousness.

He had to do something. His heart beat had slowed to normal now and he'd got his breath back from the exertions of the staircase.

He said, 'Why, Peter?'

'Ask her.'

'Your wife?'

He nodded, swayed forward again, almost over-balanced, then righted himself as the three watchers took sharp intakes of breath. From below, Greg thought that he heard a collective sigh.

'Pete!' she said.

'Tell them, Maureen.'

'NO!'

'Tell them or I'll do it. I'll jump.'

'Tell me, Mrs Bateman,' Greg said. 'Tell me how you killed Gillian in Berkshire a week ago.'

22

'I'll tell you,' she said.

She raised her voice, projecting it towards the balcony. 'I'll tell him, Pete. You can come in now.'

'Not till you've told him everything.'

Greg cautioned her, the words coming automatically. He bent and picked up the topmost magazine from the coffee table. As he'd thought, a copy of *Today's Author*. He remembered how Maureen had turned to writing as therapy during the empty years of her husband's imprisonment.

'You recognised her,' he said, a statement not a question, 'from the picture in this magazine.'

'Yes.' She was barely audible. 'I knew her at once, despite the weight, despite the hair. I recognised Frank's face and his eyes. I didn't want to believe it for a long time. I told myself I was mistaken but I knew that I wasn't. And the name – it was as if she was taunting me.'

Atkins found his voice and it was steel. 'Be quiet, Maureen. Peter, you've got what you wanted so either jump or stop being so bloody stupid and get back in here.'

Bateman looked as if he were considering these alternatives for a moment, then swung his legs over the parapet and walked into the sitting room to join them.

'Superintendent,' Atkins went on. 'I want Mrs Bateman arrested and taken to the police station before she says another word.'

The little man was full of surprises. Greg said, 'You've got it.' He took out his mobile and called Ashton. He would have to use Rochester's facilities for the time being.

Below, there were sirens. Atkins said, 'I'll go and deal with the firemen. Maureen, I mean it. Not a word.'

Twenty minutes later a marked police car pulled up in the car park below and two constables emerged, putting their hats on and turning their heads away as camera lenses zoomed in on them. Greg took Maureen's arm. 'Come on,' he said. 'Mr Bateman, you'd better come with us too.'

'Am I under arrest?' the man asked, not moving.

'No.'

'Then I'll stay here thanks very much.'

He walked into the kitchen, picked up the kettle and filled it with water. He was clearly aware that Greg couldn't force him to come with them and, if he wasn't, then Atkins would soon tell him.

He shrugged and led Maureen downstairs, guiding her into the back of the police car while ignoring the reporters' questions. British police did not handcuff suspects unless they were dangerous but it was obvious enough that the woman was under arrest. Atkins got in with her and Greg followed in his own vehicle.

As he went to start the engine his mobile phone rang, a series of staccato bleeps. He sighed and examined the screen which told him that Andy Whittaker was calling. He pressed a button. 'What is it, Andy?'

'Sir!' The young man sounded excited. 'Got the gen back from the mobile phone company and you'll never guess who the victim rang a couple of days before she died.'

'Her mother?' Greg suggested.

'Oh!'

'Good job, Andy.' He disconnected and started his engine, hastening to catch up with the police car. So they would have got to the truth in any case, without Peter's

246

histrionics. This was how police work was today, in this age of gadgets and electronic communications. No phone call could be made, no email sent, without leaving a trace.

He'd read in *The Times* three months ago that clothes manufacturers were starting to include 'smart' fibres in their garments. In theory, these helped shops with stock-taking; in practice, it meant that a sweater, skirt or coat could be tracked for the rest of its life and the movements of its wearer recorded.

Sergeant Clifton, whose wife was Polish, had recently told him how she logged onto the internet and found a satellite picture of the town square at home in Legnica. She would arrange with her mum and dad to stand there at a particular time and wave to her. And people thought they could go about their business unobserved.

It was a good thing he had only a few years to go to retirement as science was making him redundant.

Less than an hour later he was back in the same interview room where he had talked to Ashton. Beside him was Sergeant Dave Boxer, co-opted to act as second interviewing officer. Boxer had been a voice of sanity during the Emerson enquiry and Greg liked and respected him. Opposite them were Maureen Bateman and Jonathan Atkins.

Boxer set the tapes rolling in the machine and the four introduced themselves.

'It's eighteen-twenty-seven,' Greg began. 'Interview room two at Rochester police station. I'm Superintendent Gregory Summers of the Thames Valley Police.'

'Detective Sergeant David Boxer from Rochester.'

'Jon Atkins, solicitor, representing Mrs Maureen Bateman.'

The three men of the law looked at the suspect and Atkins said, 'Introduce yourself for the tape, Maureen.'

247

'Mrs Peter Bateman,' she said defiantly. 'I know what everyone thought – that I married Pete because it was easier than being a widow and a single mother – but that's not right. I love him. Everything I've done I did for him. I've stuck by him all these years even when ... although there were times when I wondered myself if ...'

Greg broke in. 'Mrs Bateman. Did you kill Gillian Frances Lester, also known as Lestrange, in Hungerford on the night of the sixth to seventh November last?'

Atkins said, 'You don't have to answer that.'

'... Mrs Bateman is nodding,' Greg continued. 'Can you answer verbally for the tapes please?'

'Yes,' she whispered. Then more loudly. 'Yes.'

Both policemen relaxed visibly. They had an admission and they had it on tape. Greg ran her through her story of seeing Gillian's photograph in the magazine and recognising her.

'How did you make contact?' he asked. 'How did you know where to find her?'

'One of the offices where I clean – MedwayTec – there's a young man there who's always been very nice to me. Sheldon, his name is. I don't think he has many friends or maybe I remind him of his mum.'

Computer geek, Greg thought.

'That's my evening cleaning job and he's usually at his desk till all hours and sometimes we'd chat. I asked him if it was possible to find out where somebody lived and he laughed and said it was the easiest thing in the world and he showed me this internet site.'

'192.com?' Boxer said. 'People Finder?'

'I dunno. I'd never had anything to do with it, the internet, and I was a bit nervous because you hear all sorts of stories about the stuff they got on there – pornography and viruses you can catch – but it was simple enough.

You enter the person's name and town and it said in the article that she lived in London. Then, if they're on the electoral register, it comes up – address, phone number. You can even get a little map if you want.'

Greg had heard this story a number of times in recent years. He'd filled in his own annual form for the register about a month ago. There was now a box you could tick if you wanted your details restricted and he had ticked it, seeing no reason not to. He was in the phone book if any-one needed him. Presumably this new feature would make life harder for stalkers, but he suspected that a lot of people would scribble down their names and post the form back without reading the small print.

One of the prices of representation.

'So you found Gillian,' he said.

'It was easy, such an unusual name. There was only one Gillian Lestrange.'

'Did this Sheldon see you make the search?'

She shook her head. 'I waited till he'd gone back to his desk to find what I was really looking for. I thought he might have heard about Gilly – though he'd have been just a kid at the time – know who I was and suspect.'

'So you were already trying to cover your tracks,' Boxer put in.

'Don't answer that,' Atkins said.

'I don't know what you mean. I waited a long time, wondering what to do, and then one night I couldn't stand it any more so I just put my coat on and went to see her.'

'When was this?' Greg asked.

'Three weeks ago.'

'How did you get to Isleworth?'

'I drove, of course.'

'I didn't think you had a car.' He remembered her saying that she had caught the train back from the Isle of Wight.

She sighed. 'A old banger, for local driving. Some of my cleaning jobs start before the bus service begins. People are at their desks by seven now so they want us out of the way.'

Greg had a mental image of her all these years – throughout her adult life, probably – rising at five to clean offices, then going out again in the evening to mop and dust and hoover at yet another set of soulless glass and concrete buildings where the staff – with the odd honourable exception like Sheldon – looked straight through her, embarrassed by the drudge who emptied their bins and cleaned their toilets, longing for the day when an automaton could perform these tasks. Here was a woman who had left school at fifteen and had none of the skills that modern society demanded if it was to pay a living wage. What a life.

'Where is your car?' he asked.

'At the flats. Where else?'

He took a note of the registration number and announced a short adjournment while Boxer arranged to have the car brought in, to check its tyre marks against those SOCO had found at Ivy Cottage.

'I don't understand,' Maureen said. 'I'm telling you everything, aren't I? Why do you need my car?'

'It's hard evidence, Maureen.' Atkins placed his hand over hers. 'Proof that you were there.'

'But I'm not denying it!'

Confessions were all very well, but juries liked evidence. An admission might be retracted but not a tyre mark in the mud and a SOC officer in a smart suit confirming the match in court. When they resumed, Greg asked Mrs Bateman to go on with her story.

'It took me ages to find the place,' Maureen said, ''cause I don't know London and it was right over the other side and I kept getting lost, so it was late when I got there. The street door was unlocked, though, and I went straight up to the first floor and knocked at the door. There wasn't a spy hole or anything.'

He said, 'She must have got a hell of a shock when she saw you standing there.'

Maureen shook her head. 'She was always good at hiding her feelings. You'd never have known she wasn't expecting me. She laughed when she saw me, told me that time hadn't been kind to me.'

'What a charmer!' Boxer muttered.

'I could have said the same about her. She invited me in, made me coffee, all black and bitter so you could hardly drink it, in a cup like a thimble, showing off, like always.'

'What exactly had you planned to say to her?' Greg asked.

'I'd made no plans. I'd come to make sure that it was her by seeing her in the flesh. I suppose there was part of me that still didn't quite believe it but there she was, large as life and twice as spiteful. I was struck practically dumb. She did the talking.'

'And what did she say?'

'That it was good timing, me turning up like that. She said she'd been planning to make her fortune by writing up her life story and if we all collaborated on it, me and her and Pete, then it'd be that much more saleable.'

'That's pretty cold-blooded,' Greg said.

'After a while she more or less turned me out, told me we'd need to work on the book together and that I should come and see her again at this cottage she was using in Berkshire. She gave me the address and told me to come that Thursday night.'

'You could have gone to the police at that point,' Greg said. 'Wouldn't that have been the logical thing to do?'

251

'I suppose. I was stunned. She told me not to tell anyone and it didn't occur to me that I might disobey her.'

Boxer leaned forward across the table. 'And, besides, you'd made up your mind to kill her –'

'Don't answer that!' Atkins said again, but more emphatically this time.

Again, she took little notice. 'No.' She looked genuinely puzzled. 'I don't believe I had, not then.'

'So when did you decide?'

'Maureen –' Atkins said, but she talked on.

'... Not ever. I didn't make up my mind to do it. Until I felt the ends of the scarf in my hands, I didn't know I was going to do it. I wanted her alive, you see.' She turned to Greg in appeal and, getting no response, to Boxer. 'That way she could come forward and Pete would be set free. Once she was dead, there was a danger that her body would never be identified.'

'That's logical,' Atkins said. 'Is it not, Mr Summers?'

Greg had to agree, silently, that it was, but pressed on. 'If you didn't go there with the intent to kill, Mrs Bateman, then how come you left no fingerprints at the scene?'

She shrugged. 'It was a cold night. I was wearing gloves and, as the cottage wasn't very well heated, I never got round to taking them off.'

'How convenient,' Dave Boxer said with a smirk.

It was convenient, Greg agreed silently, to the point of being suspicious. He would probably have to reconcile himself to the fact that he would never know for sure if Maureen had gone to Oaken Copse that night with the express intention of killing Gillian.

It would not be a logical act, as she had pointed out, but when was hatred ever logical?

In court, it would make little difference, or only to the tariff the judge recommended for her life sentence. Only he, Gregory, would be left with a dissatisfaction, a wondering. In future years, if he happened to be wakeful at three o'clock in the morning, he would lie there, asking himself, among other things, 'Did she go there to kill Gillian, or was it the way she said?'

He thought that he believed her, but he'd believed her act when confronted by her daughter's body in the morgue.

Maureen went on. 'I can't tell you what a relief it was when I got back from Parkhurst on Sunday morning and found those constables waiting for me, telling me I had to come to Newbury. I knew then that she'd been identified somehow. It was all I could do to contain myself.'

She had contained herself astonishingly well, Greg thought: so puzzled as to why she was there; initially denying that the body could be Gillian, which was a neat trick. He had been completely taken in by her.

So much for his belief that he would know instinctively, by her reactions, whether she recognised the corpse or not.

'So Thursday night,' he said. 'The sixth. What happened?'

'I drove out there as arranged. It was a long way, further than I thought. I'm not used to driving long distances and I don't like the motorway. I was afraid the car wouldn't make it. And it was so dark. I hate November, worst month of the year. And the cottage was hard to find so it was gone eleven by the time I got there, and she was annoyed because she'd been kept waiting. She never had any patience.'

'So what happened?'

'I mentioned Pete, right away, because I'd been thinking about that, about how we must get him out of prison as soon as possible but she laughed and said there was no rush, that it'd be better publicity for the book if he was released at the time of publication, that he must have got used to it by now.' Maureen closed her eyes, concentrating. '"He's probably institutionalised". That's what she said. "You won't be doing him any favours." That was what did it.'

'Drove you to kill her?'

'Yes. She'd been drinking heavily before I got there – whisky, the bottle was nearly empty. She asked me if I wanted any and I didn't. She turned away from me to refill her glass ...'

'We were all right,' Gilly said, *'after Dad died, just me and you, till* he *turned up and spoiled things.' She held the whisky bottle up to the light and looked critically at it, perhaps wondering why it was almost empty.*

'It wasn't as if he brought anything to the family – a decent wage, say. We were better off without him. He was a worthless piece of ...'

'She was wearing a red and white scarf round her neck, falling down her back. Before I knew what I was doing, my hands just reached out to seize the ends of it.'

She held her hands out in demonstration to the three men. They were the strong, knotty hands of a woman who had done hard, physical work all her life.

'She was much bigger than me, of course, much heavier, but she was drunk and I caught her off balance. She fell awkwardly and couldn't get up.'

It was the first principle of unarmed combat, as Greg well knew: use your opponents size and weight against him. Somehow, over the years, when he'd got into scraps with bigger and stronger blokes, what had seemed so simple in the police college gym had never quite worked out that way.

'I hardly know what happened –' Maureen went on,

'it's as if I've blanked it out – but the next thing I knew she was dead. I'd strangled her. I was horrified. I thought I'd ruined everything – Pete's last chance at freedom.'

'She could maybe have been revived, if you'd tried the kiss of life,' Greg said, 'at least rung for an ambulance.'

'I didn't know ... I thought dead was dead. I wouldn't know how to do that kiss of life thing. I didn't mean to kill her so that means it wasn't murder. Doesn't it?' She looked eagerly at the three men in turn. 'You have to mean to kill someone for it to be murder.'

'It doesn't work quite like that,' Greg said.

Maureen looked mute appeal at Atkins who said, 'I'm afraid the Superintendent is right, Maureen.'

She sighed and went on with her story. 'I was in a panic. All I could think of was covering my tracks, so I took her bag and her laptop and drove back to the flat in London and cleared anything that might be incriminating out of there.'

'Including the telephone?'

'She phoned me once, a couple of days before I went to Newbury, to make sure I was still coming. I didn't know where from, so I took that phone as well as her mobile. I took everything back to Kent with me and dumped it at the bottom of the Medway.'

'You thought very fast,' Greg commented. 'If I'd just killed someone without meaning to, I reckon I'd be in a right panic. I wouldn't be thinking straight.'

'Me neither,' Boxer said.

She flushed. 'You're as bad as she was, Gilly. You think because I'm poor and never had any education that I'm stupid. Well, I'm not ...'

He had indeed made that assumption, Greg realised, or one very like it, which was why she had fooled him so easily.

'... The only stupid thing I did was to tell Pete what I'd done because I thought he'd understand. I thought he'd be *grateful*.'

There was a silence as the three men avoided each other's eyes. Finally, Greg said sadly, 'Your own daughter.'

Her face was white as the memories of what she'd done that night were vivid in her mind. She spoke slowly, pricking out the words.

'My Gillian died fifteen years ago. It took a long time, but I finally accepted that she was dead and she wasn't coming back. So it cost me nothing that she should die again, that she should be punished for her appalling cruelty.'

When they had run out of questions to ask Maureen, Greg and Boxer adjourned to the corridor to confer.

The sergeant puffed out his cheeks. 'I feel drained,' he said, 'and I've only sat in on the interview. I can just imagine how you must be feeling, sir.'

'I've had better weeks,' Greg admitted. 'You can see why she hated the girl.'

'She was a piece of work all right, but it sounds to me like she always hated her,' Boxer commented, 'even before she did her runner. Do you want her charged here or extradited to Newbury?'

'Better go ahead and charge her, I suppose, then I'll take her back to Newbury.' It was Thames Valley's case and would best be dealt with at home. 'I can't take her in my car – not secure enough.'

He looked hopefully at Boxer but the local man said, 'Don't think we can spare the manpower, sir. Sorry, but we're short staffed.'

'Who isn't?' But Greg, accepting that the problem was

his, reached for his phone and in a few minutes had arranged for some uniformed constables to come down in a police van and collect his prisoner.

'On the bright side,' Boxer added sarcastically, 'I daresay we can have our Mr Peck back now. Lock up your daughters, Rochester.' Greg managed a wan smile. It was not his job to explain to Ashton's staff that the daughters of the Medway towns would be safe for many years to come.

The sergeant said, 'So, you off home now?'

Greg glanced at his watch; it was twenty to nine. He really wanted to get home to Kintbury and make love with Angie, maybe in the sitting room. 'I think I'll just drop in at Henderson Towers and see how Mr Bateman is getting on.'

Bateman answered the door to Greg's knock and brandished a sheaf of papers at him.

'*Outlook* had this biked round half an hour ago,' he explained. '"Our fifteen years of hell by Gilly Lester's parents." Don't reckon they'll be printing it now.'

'I reckon not,' Greg agreed.

The news that Maureen Bateman had been charged with the murder of her daughter would make the television bulletins tomorrow, Saturday, and a cursing *Outlook* staff would be working overtime to change their pages.

'They paid half the money up front,' Bateman said. 'It's only sitting in the bank. They can have it back. I'll not fight them for it.'

He went into the kitchen and Greg followed him, thinking that there was a new vigour in the older man's step, as if Atlas had just taken the weight of the world back from him.

Peter filled the kettle once more. 'You wanna cup of tea?'

'Why not?' Greg sat down at the table.

'Know what the best thing about being out of prison is?'

The open sky above you, Greg thought, the woods, the rain on your face, the indefinable thing that was freedom.

'You can have a cup of tea whenever you want one,' Bateman answered himself. ''Stead of being shut up in your cell overnight for fifteen hours with nothing but water from the sink what's only meant for washing.'

They did say it was the small things that made all the difference, Greg thought. He said, 'We've charged your wife with Gillian's murder.'

'Oh, yes.' His voice was indifferent.

'So now your positions are reversed. You'll be visiting her in jail.'

'I won't be going to see her,' he said.

'When did she tell you?' Greg asked.

'When did I get out? Was it Monday?' Greg nodded. 'Yes. That's right. One minute I was sitting in my cell reading the paper with another five years of that to look forward to. Next minute the screw's saying I'm wanted in the Governor's office. And not the way they usually say it – "Hey, Bateman, get your arse to the Governor's office NOW!" – all polite.'

He busied himself with a heavy brown teapot. 'And there's Tubby Atkins with the Governor and some stiff from the Home Office in a suit that must have cost a month's wages.'

'Xavier Browne?' Greg suggested.

'Didn't catch his name, but he was with you at that inquest. And they're calling me *Mister* Bateman and nobody's called me *Mister* in fifteen years and Tubby says they're letting me go because they know I'm innocent and I said, "You've found Gilly. She's alive" and just for a

258

minute everything was all right again, but they looked at each other and Suit-man says, "We've found her, all right, only she's dead". Here.' He handed Greg his tea. 'And that was the worst moment of my life. Sugar?'

'No thanks.' Greg had let him ramble on, telling his story in his own way, but now he repeated, 'When did Maureen tell you what she had done, Mr Bateman?'

Peter sat down and drank tea while he thought about it. 'The *Outlook* took us to some swish hotel in Hampshire. In a helicopter. You been in one of them?'

'Once or twice.'

'Made me feel sick, all the time we were in the air, even though it couldn't have been more than fifteen minutes.'

'Mr Bateman –'

'I suppose it was the next morning. I was awake early, like you are in prison, and she told me, like she was proud of it.'

He winced. 'She said she done it for me, to set me free. There was a swimming pool in that hotel and a gym and a restaurant with a – whatchamacallit? – a Michelin star, but it felt like just another prison cell after that.'

'So that's why you've looked so ill these last few days?' Greg said.

'Don't you think I'd have spent the rest of my life in jail rather than know Gilly was dead? And dead like that? When she killed Gilly she killed any feeling I'd ever had for her. All these years, I wanted only to be released, to be at home with her the way we used to be, but now ... it was unbearable.'

'Why didn't you come to me?' Greg asked.

'She had to tell you herself. She had to understand that what she did was wrong.'

The two men sat drinking tea in silence for some minutes.

'I held her in my arms when she was six hours old,' Bateman said. 'Frank was called away from work to the hospital because she was two weeks early and born real quick. I went round there soon as I'd finished my shift and there she was, Frank and Maureen's baby girl, the most perfect thing you ever saw.

'They let me hold her and I'd never held a baby before and I was that nervous. Her eyes were closed and there was a little bubble of drool on her mouth and she was beautiful. I'd have done anything for her.'

She hated you, Greg wanted to tell him. *She must have done. With a hatred I'm relieved to say I cannot understand.*

He said nothing; he didn't think it would help.

Bateman said, 'Have you any more idea where she's been all these years?'

'She was married briefly,' Greg said, 'to a man named Walter Abernethy, in Lincolnshire.'

'Married? A husband? Can I meet him? Are there children?'

Greg held up a hand to stop him. 'It wasn't an ordinary sort of marriage. He was an old man and died within months of the wedding, leaving Gillian his money.'

'Yes.' Bateman subsided. 'Walter. It's an old man's name. I see. I'm glad she had some money. When can I have her body to bury?'

Would he be expected to go to the funeral, Greg wondered, as he drove home along the slick wet surface of the M25, his windscreen wipers battling against steady rain? It was a courtesy generally accorded to murder victims but it would mean another trip to Kent.

Did he owe that much to the woman whose personality and motivation remained as big a mystery to him as when he'd first set foot in Ivy Cottage just seven days ago?

* * *

'Gillian clearly meant to double cross Stuart,' Greg remarked to Barbara the following morning, after they had watched Maureen Bateman remanded in custody by the Newbury magistrates. 'She was going to take his money, then go public with her story anyway.'

'I wonder,' Barbara said. 'Maybe it was her mother she meant to double cross.'

'How so?'

'Think about it. Her mother turns up on her doorstep without warning but Gillian's obviously a quick thinker. She decides to string her along while she waits for Stuart to come up with the money, torment her some more by letting her think she'll help her get Peter out of jail. Then she'd have disappeared with the cash, leaving her mother high and dry. Who would believe her story? Would you?'

'I suppose not.'

'It would look like just another desperate ploy to win an appeal.' A thought struck her. 'I wonder who'll inherit Gillian's estate now. Assuming we get a conviction, her mother can't profit from her crime.'

'It may end up going to the Crown,' Greg said. 'Shame we can't return it to the Abernethy family to whom it rightfully belongs.'

23

When Greg's mobile rang one morning a few days later – a cricket rubbing its back legs together by the sound of it – he had no difficulty in recognising the seductive tones of Lavinia Latham.

'Can we have a meet?' she asked.

'When and where?'

'Same place as before in five minutes.'

He laughed and hung up. She'd been very sure that he would come. He made his way down to the car park and watched as she appeared from one of the underpasses, striding to meet him.

An Amazon, he thought.

'So you made an arrest,' she said once she was in earshot. 'Gilly's mother? I can hardly believe it.'

'Yes, as it turned out it was nothing to do with you.' It might be hard for her, he thought, to accept that, in the end, it had not been about her.

But she grinned. 'Quite a kerfuffle in the media about this DCI from Kent.'

The *Outlook on Sunday* had filled some of its redundant pages with the scandal of Stuart Peck. Greg said, 'Let's say that being shot by Aunt Adele is the least of his problems.'

'That's why I'm here really.'

'I thought it might be. Don't worry. He's decided he doesn't want to take the case any further and the CPS accept that there's not a jury in England would convict her. She's been released with a caution although I have, naturally, confiscated the revolver.'

'She'll be annoyed about that. It was one of her most

precious possessions – that, her *Croix de Guerre* and the famous cyanide pill.'

'Oh, dear God!'

Vinnie laughed. 'Calm down. She doesn't know that I replaced it years ago, with a Tic Tac. If she ever tries to use it the worse she can expect is a fierce bout of breath freshening.'

'Those Tic Tacs stand in for anything,' he said.

'Sorry?'

'Nothing important.'

'Aunt Adele is being uncharacteristically vague about the circumstances of the shooting. It's amazing how convenient her little-old-lady's lapses of memory can be.'

'She'd seen Peck in Oaken Copse two days before the murder and recognised him when she met him again.'

Vinnie considered this. 'So do we know why he went to Honeysuckle Cottage that evening?'

'He claims he just wanted to explain but she pulled the gun on him and he panicked.'

'Sounds like you don't believe him.' Greg shrugged. 'Might he have been a danger to her?'

'When I think of Stuart Peck the words *stupid* and *cowardly* spring to mind quicker than *dangerous*. Whatever his reason for going there, he found he'd bitten off more than he could chew.' He held out his hand. 'Its been a pleasure, Miss Latham.'

'Vinnie.' She gave him a firm handshake. 'Likewise, Mr Summers.'

'Gregory.'

'I've been thinking,' she said, 'how nobody will miss Gilly. That's rather sad.'

'Peter Bateman misses her,' he said.

'Now, are you going to arrest me, Gregory?'

'How fast can you run, Vinnie?'

'Pretty fast. I was offered a try-out for the Olympic team when I was at school.'

'Of course you were! Then how about I glance away for a minute while you make yourself scarce?'

She laughed. 'Deal!'

He examined the hedge with great interest while counting to sixty. When he turned round she was still there.

'If you check your computers, you'll find that my arrest warrant has been rescinded,' she said, 'but thank you for the thought.'

'How come?'

'I've shelved my memoirs and I'm going back into the service.'

'You're kidding.'

She shook her head. 'The western world has been fighting a war since September 11th and they need all the experienced soldiers they can get.'

'You speak Arabic,' he remembered.

'My favourite language. It's the job I was born to do: "What God writes on your forehead, you will become."'

'The Koran?' he guessed.

'Very good. I've been talking to my old partner, Martin Palmer – we call him Harry, after the Len Deighton character. The fatted calf is being killed as we speak.'

'Harry' Palmer, who had called her a psychopathic mercenary a few days ago, but maybe psychopathic mercenaries were okay, so long as they were on your side. Perhaps he should warn her not to turn her back on him.

'Well, good luck,' he said.

'And you. *Au revoir.*'

She walked away at a dignified pace, tall and slender and very, very sure of herself. He hoped that it was indeed *au revoir* and not goodbye, but he feared that she would not make old bones, not like Aunt Adele.

'"And how can man die better,"' he quoted aloud, '"than facing fearful odds, for the ... *something* of his fathers and the temples of his Gods?"'

'"*Ashes*. The ashes of his fathers." Quoting Macauley before lunch, Gregory, never a good sign.'

'Jim.' He turned and smiled at Chief Superintendent Barkiss who was staring after the departing Vinnie.

'Who was that striking woman?'

'That was Lavinia Latham.'

'Oh? Aren't we supposed to be arresting her?'

'Apparently not.'

'... Okay. I've just had the DCC on the phone, told me to tell you how pleased he is with the way the Lestrange case was handled.'

'Thanks.'

'Nasty business.'

'Yes.' Greg began to walk back towards the station, the CS falling into step beside him. 'In a way I feel sorry for the woman. We both know how hard it can be with teenagers but that girl set out deliberately to destroy her stepfather's life, and her mother's with it.'

'Adolescents can be horribly cruel,' Barkiss agreed, 'and they don't forgive anything, but that girl wins first prize. Still, she didn't deserve the death penalty. Anyway, good result for us; not so much for Kent.'

Greg stopped at the back door of the police station and sniffed the cold autumn air, the tang of woodsmoke. 'Ah! I love the smell of *schadenfreude* in the morning.'

'Well ...' Barkiss laughed. 'Better them than us.'

Maybe, Greg thought, but when police officers got it so horribly wrong like Ashton, or went bad like Peck, it reflected badly on all of them.

'And another DCI bites the dust,' Barkiss remarked, as they walked into the fuggy heat of the station.

'Peck wasn't actually *my* DCI,' Greg objected.

'I know. That's what worries me.' Barkiss stood with his hands in his trouser pockets, shaking his head sadly, and his closest friend wouldn't know if he was serious or not. 'The curse of Newbury CID no longer confines itself to members of the Thames Valley force.'

He'd had a brief telephone call from Xavier Browne the previous day, also pleased with the result.

'The Home Secretary asked me to pass on his thanks for a job well done,' he said.

'Oh, yes?'

'Now the press can't paint the Bateman family as innocent victims of an incompetent and oppressive regime.'

No, Greg thought, as he hung up. Maureen had killed her daughter and Peter was guilty by association. Public sympathy had evaporated and the why-oh-why articles had disappeared. What worried him was that the Home Secretary seemed to think that the right result had been concocted to suit him, but then politicians were like that.

Greg's mobile played the EU Anthem at him after lunch and the display told him it was Alan Ashton. He sometimes thought that he could throttle the bloke who invented the telephone. What were you thinking, Alexander Graham Bell?

He pressed the requisite button and said, 'Hello, Alan.'

Ashton began without salutation. 'Simon Emerson hanged himself at the remand centre last night.'

'How did they let that happen?' Greg asked. 'I thought he was on suicide watch.'

'He was, but they're short handed – load of people out with this flu virus. Besides, if a prisoner's really determined ... He was going to spend the rest of his life in jail. What would you have done?'

'I have absolutely no idea,' Greg said.

Ashton lowered his voice. 'Don't quote me on this but ... good riddance. Eh?'

'Goodbye, Alan.'

'... Bye, Greg.'

They hung up. Greg deleted Ashton's number from his address book. Then he pressed a few buttons and restored the original boring ring tone. Life was exciting enough.

Nadia Polycarpou walked slowly out of the hospital grounds. It had been a long shift and she was bone tired, wanting only to put her feet in a bowl of warm, soapy water.

She spotted Nicolaides before he saw her, leaning against a lamp post with his arms folded, a supermarket carrier bag dangling from one wrist. She got the impression that he'd been waiting a long time and grinned to herself, suddenly reinvigorated.

He saw her and straightened up. He could do with being an inch or two taller, she thought, and he'd probably run to fat in middle age like her dad, but he was nicely made and she'd bet he was good and hairy, the way she liked them.

'Hi, Nick,' she said neutrally.

'Nadger.'

He fell into step with her as she crossed the road at the zebra crossing, the carrier bag banging rhythmically against his knee. She felt in her bag for her keys. The street door to the flats was locked – in a belated surge of security – and he waited while she opened it and followed her in. She made a mental note to do something about that aftershave of his, soonest, even if it meant buying him a new one.

'Somebody put a light bulb in,' she said, as she started up the stairs.

'Actually, that was me.'

'Proper little Sir Galahad, ain't yer?' She glanced at the door on the first floor at they passed, closed and still sealed with incident tape, and gave a little shiver. 'You not finished your work here then?'

'Yeah. We have, actually. Takes a while to wind down.'

'Who dunnit then?'

'Her mum. Don't you read the papers?'

She shrugged. 'Not much. I prefer *Hello*.'

Now they were standing outside her front door. He said, 'I give in.'

'Huh?'

'I wanna see the tattoo.'

'All in good time, my friend. I know what blokes think about nurses but I'm a good Greek girl, I am. I have to be wined and dined.'

'Deal,' he said. 'As it happens, I have a bottle of Demestica and some humous and olives in this bag.'

She laughed, standing aside to let him in to her domain. 'You know what they say – beware of Greeks bearing gifts.'

Greg and Angie sat enjoying the peace and silence of their house in Kintbury that evening.

'No more phone calls,' Angie said with satisfaction. 'Phone hasn't rung all day.'

'I got a call from Tommy Merton at Reading. He sent two of his goons round to put the fear of God into Mr Milner.' Greg imagined that a certain amount of bullying had taken place but he could live with that. What had Milner's phone calls to Angie been but bullying?

'Guess this means we won't be getting a loan of Stuart's flat in Malta,' Angie remarked.

'Oh, I don't know. It's not as if he'll be using it for the next fifteen to twenty years,' Greg said.

'As long as that?' Angie stared at him. 'All those politicians who get done for perverting the course of justice get out in a couple of years.'

'They didn't send an innocent man to prison, my love. If I were the judge, I'd make sure Peck serves at least as long as Peter Bateman did.'

And if prison was purgatory for ordinary people, for an ex-policeman it was hell.

He seemed to see the unhappy-but-determined features of Peter Bateman, whose sentence hadn't ended merely because he'd been released, who had come home to face the worst thing of all.

Greg could think of few punishments too harsh for the people who'd done that to him.

All of them.